OUT OF TIME

Out of Time

by

Abigail Dobbs

PORTLAND•OREGON
INKWATERPRESS.COM

Publisher: Inkwater Press | www.inkwaterpress.com

Paperback   ISBN-13 978-1-62901-654-2 | ISBN-10 1-62901-654-3
Kindle   ISBN-13 978-1-62901-655-9 | ISBN-10 1-62901-655-1

1 3 5 7 9 10 8 6 4 2

To my Dad, who was the first to hear about *Out of Time* and has somehow dealt with me talking about it every day since.

ACKNOWLEDGEMENTS

I want to thank my Dad, Mom, younger sister Liz for their love and help through every stage of the process and cat Hulio (the H is a long story) for truly being the one to write this novel.

Thank you, Grandma Marilyn for thinking of the title and Grandpa Richard for his insights on history that I never would have thought of otherwise. Grandma Barbara and Grandpa Bob also offered enormous support and gave valuable opinions on the draft.

To MADDY.

And last but not least, Jeanne for her editorial eye and assistance finalizing the manuscript.

"Nine hundred years of time and space, and I've never met anyone who wasn't important."
—The 11th Doctor

On one end of the ballroom, electronic beats pulse in my ears but classical chords replace them as I pass through the dance floor. Women in ancient Greek chitons dance around me with men in metallic suits. In the towering jeweled window, I see speeding levitators filled with fashionably late guests. As the levitators pass by, their gleaming lights illuminate the sleeping of the city—the West School, *Dolce's*, even the Alloys. But to my side I see something brighter and more powerful, the Golden Grandfather Clock. No matter where you go in the Palace, you can hear its ticking.

My life wasn't this nice a few months ago.

CHAPTER 1

"SOMETIMES I WONDER WHY THAT clock means so much to all of you," Ms. Gutierrez sighed, her hand waving towards the wall. The clock's hands were slowly crawling across its white face. "No matter what I'm teaching, each of you keeps at least one eye glued to that object like your life depends on it. What, are you worried that if you miss the changing of a minute, it's a minute lost? I'll tell you all. You lose a whole lot more of a minute if you spend it waiting for the next. And I know some of you will come to me after class and ask, 'Ms. Gutierrez, what did your speech have to do with the American Revolution?' Well, I'll save you all the effort and just give the answer right now. The birth of a country is a timeless event, as it happened millennia ago and will definitely happen again. The hands of a clock might make revolutions, but *you* could never start one by just staring at them."

Twenty pairs of eyes found somewhere else to gaze, anywhere besides the clock. Walls, desks, posters, and cardboard boxes all became objects of fascination. The clock's black-and- white frame haunted us, its slow ticking burning in our ears. I'll admit, even if our class rarely left a lasting feeling, Ms. Gutierrez knew how to be heard.

Once the bell finally rang, the students shuffled out onto the next period of clock- watching, with me buried in the center. I could hear a couple of whispers about our teacher's rant. Some were interested, some were confused, and some said they wanted to punch her in the face. But as I walked out, I felt Ms. Gutierrez's words place a weight on my shoulders, a weight I could not totally understand. All the time spent with the few friends I had was about one thing: not being alone. I had no use for the minutes on clocks except to finish my homework and clean my room. Wasting a few always seemed like a solution, not a problem.

I ARRIVED AT math next and took a seat with Harper, one of my three friends. I glanced at her black t-shirt and compared it to my own. They looked alike. I thought that was almost too perfect. Together, we added to the constantly-growing population of simple black t-shirts in this school. It was safer to be invisible than conspicuous.

"Did she give any homework in social studies, Keira?" Harper asked, writing the date *May 11th, 2018,* in her notebook.

"No."

She nodded and began to organize her notes. We never talked about much.

I decided to try a level of conversation we hadn't reached in a while. It required listening.

"Ms. Gutierrez went *off* on our class today, and like, not her usual rants about some kids not doing homework or anything. She was talking about clocks for some reason, and that they had something to do with colonial America. Weird, right?"

Harper zipped her zebra-print pencil case. "Sure."

I ducked my head to my own notebook, accepting her response because I knew I had to. We didn't talk, we chatted. I occasionally forgot that they are two different things.

"Homework out, everyone! The test is Monday, so I hope you all were able to complete this assignment without too much trouble," said our math teacher, Ms. Summers.

With the awkward silence broken, I began shuffling through my notebook to find the problems. I felt Ms. Summers peering over my shoulder from a distance. She was tapping her foot on the floor impatiently. Finally, I came across a set of problems that I had completed last night. Ms. Summers walked over and, exasperated, reached toward the page sticking out of my notebook.

"You had several minutes before I came over, Keira. Try to be as prepared as possible," Ms. Summers poked, clasping the thin paper between her glossy fingernails.

She grunted. "Study tonight, alright? I'm sure your big sister would love to help."

She handed me back the page and quickly stepped over to a grinning Harper. I looked down at my homework, staring at the invisible red X's.

Study, I thought. *Willow will help, she always does.* As I lost myself in a hopeful tomorrow, I felt Harper nudge my shoulder.

"I'm gonna ace this test," she asserted. "I'll probably just skip studying and chill this weekend."

I snapped a new pencil under my desk, pushing my frustrations into the writing tool.

Ms. Summers went to the front of the room and lit up the smartboard. She handed out cards for those unlucky kids who had to go up and complete last night's problems.

"Hey, could you tell me what you got for #4, Harper? I think that was the one I was most stuck on," I pleaded, hoping that for once our five years of friendship would pay off after I saw the blue card on my desk.

"It wasn't that hard. Just guess if you really couldn't find the answer 'cause I already put my book away and I don't feel like looking at it again," Harper answered, lazily twisting her braids.

I grimaced and walked up to the board, unsteady and nervous, as if I were being forced onto some kind of guillotine. As I looked behind me, I knew nobody was watching, but I couldn't shake the feeling. I carried the marker to the board and let the digital ink touch the surface. I closed my eyes and wrote $x=9$. I heard a couple snickers behind me. Harper had a hand covering her face, embarrassed either for me or for being my friend. Ms. Summers was shaking her head as well.

"This is the easiest part of the test, Keira. The answer is 17, alright? Other than her mistake, though, everybody looks a-okay! Before class is over, please finish the review sheet I gave out yesterday," Ms. Summers demanded. Slowly her eyes set on me. "Make sure you're getting them right."

My spine tightened as I hurried back to my desk, my notebook clasped in my fists. I saw Harper staring at the white on my knuckles, making me shove my notebook into my backpack before it got any worse.

After what felt like decades, the bell finally rung. As I left the class, I felt a rough hand push my shoulder. It was Max with his greasy blond hair and chipped tooth.

"Hey Keira, I thought Chinese people were supposed to be smart," he sneered, his obnoxious friends snickering.

Usually, I stayed quiet when people said this kind of thing to me. In fact, I always stayed quiet. Nobody could use anything against you when you were quiet. But first it was my teacher, now these boys. I could only handle so much.

"I am smart! One question doesn't say anything, and you're the idiot for making fun of me. I know that I'm—I'm special or different, but you're just plain old normal. I bet you didn't even know the answers either and you just want to embarrass me to hide that," I announced confidently.

The kids around me looked astonished. A couple of them grinned, empowered by my lack of silence. Others were not as nice. They laughed and continued to shove me as they mimicked my words.

"Guys look, I'm-I'm-I'm special, blah blah blah," a kid named Jared mocked, getting a pat on the back from Max.

I managed to wedge out of the mob, sneaking between rioters. In the hallway, I found Harper heading towards her next class, which meant she didn't even care about waiting for me after I had just been attacked by bullies. I ran to catch up to her and latched my hand onto her shoulder.

"Hey, Harper!" I exclaimed, making her jolt. "You

were just going to leave without me? After Max and Jared and them?" I forced a pout.

Harper hesitantly turned back to me with her eyes obviously post-roll. "Do you know how embarrassing you were? I couldn't be seen there. I'm like your only friend."

I cocked an eyebrow. "I stood up for myself. They were being mean... and racist! Do you not care about that?"

Harper crossed her arms and sighed. "Keira, they didn't hurt you, they were just being annoying. Please get over it so you don't make another scene. Now, do you want to go to lunch or not?"

I COULD HAVE stayed on the lunch line forever, just letting Harper, Taylor, and Sadie have fun with each other at the table, leaving me out. I didn't even want to talk to Harper after she ignored what happened to me in math. Knowing Taylor and Sadie, they would probably just stick by her. I still don't really know why I was friends with them anyway—all they ever did was leave me out of stuff or make fun of me if I was there. Our moms made us have playdates years ago. I guess none of us knew what the group would be without all four of us in it. I also needed somewhere to sit at lunch.

"Hey, could you tell me what's for lunch?" a voice asked, pulling me away from my thoughts.

I turned and saw it was Isaac, *the* Isaac, the only boy I had had a crush on since third grade. He had always been the only boy in the whole school that was nice to me, like actually giving back a pencil when I lent him one. But also, that was just not being a jerk. Maybe it was his curly hair I liked, that's definitely a contender.

"Uh...uh..." I stumbled. "Burritos."

Isaac nodded and stretched to look over me. "Just beef or..."

I shook my head violently, *too* violently. "No, no, there's chicken and vegetables, too."

"Ok, good, thanks," he said before heading to the back of the line. I was about to let him step in front of me, but I think it was good that he left before I could say that. I could see no non-awkward way of suggesting it.

I bought my burrito and dreadfully headed over to the lunch table, letting my feet lag behind me. Taylor and Sadie would be laughing at my "overreaction" from earlier, or at best, Harper had just forgotten to tell them. At the table, they were all talking about something, but as I stepped closer I could pick up on their conversation.

"The movie was so good last night," Sadie chirped.

Harper grinned as she reached for her soup. "Yeah, and everyone had already seen it so I'm happy we finally went."

"And thank *God* it was just the three of us," Taylor finished, rolling her eyes.

And that was it. I wasn't surprised, I just hated knowing what I worried about was actually true. I wanted to be ignorant and I just couldn't at that moment. Between Ms. Summers and Max and just *them* here, it was all obvious that I wasn't meant to be here. The best I could do was just go home early. I wanted to bawl my eyes out, but honestly, I didn't think crying would get me anywhere.

I MANAGED TO get the nurse to believe my "cold" and was called down to the main office. Leaning against the secretary's desk was my big sister Willow, her circular glasses resting on her nose. She still had her internship clothes on, the way-too-ironed pants she hated so much. I knew I had pulled her from something important.

Willow sent me a smirk and then shook her head. "I already signed you out, weirdo. Let's get you home."

We walked out of the school and into my Dad's old Ford. Willow soon reclined in the driver's seat. She had just one hand on the wheel and was holding it there lazily while she drove, something I knew my Mom would have yelled about.

"Mom's house tonight, right?" I asked her, trying to start up a conversation.

Willow exhaled. "Dude, it's been the same schedule for years. You know we only stay at Dad's house now and then. Are you trying to distract me from something?" She paused for a second. "Keira! Are you not even sick? I had a meeting at my internship today, girl."

I sulked further into my seat. "It was a bad day at school."

She softened her expression and patted my arm. "Oh, I'm sorry. Do you want to talk about it? Was it teachers, bullies, or friends?"

"All three, actually," I moaned.

Willow laughed. "Then you got the trifecta! I'm proud of your accomplishment."

"Shut up. People were being mean. Do you have no compassion?"

Willow ruffled her bob-cut hair. "You know I have

compassion. Just give me the details so I know whose addresses I need to visit. I've got a few words to say to them."

"Well, Ms. Summers kept pointing out that I couldn't do math and then this kid Max said something racist about me being Chinese. Oh, and the worst part was that Harper didn't care and told me I was overreacting! And *then* I found out they all went to a movie without me and were joking about it," I spilled.

Willow frowned. "Harper's trash, and so are those other two. I've known that since you guys started hanging out. Also, wanna know a secret about Ms. Summers? She graded two of my tests wrong back in the day and refused to change them because she was embarrassed. I don't know this Max person but I'm sure he's an idiot. Don't listen to anyone who's just jealous of how great you are, Keira."

I tried to hold back a smile, but I could tell that Willow saw it in the corner of her eye. She started spinning the radio controller through music channels, not stopping on a single note. A couple times I actually wanted to listen to a song, but Willow didn't work that way.

"Hey, Willow, why are you even interning with a therapist anyway?" I pushed, starting up a new subject.

"Oh ok, little liar. Just because I supported you with your bullying situation doesn't mean you can still forget the elephant in the room," Willow stated.

"Oh, come on. We're done with my thing. I want to know what you see in psychology and all that office stuff. Don't you want to like travel the world and have an adventure or something?" I reasoned.

Willow laughed. "And when Mom or Dad wants to write me a check for that, please let me know. Therapy's pretty cool, though. Talking to different people is an adventure in itself. I know right now human beings seem like the worst possible options to speak with, but soon, you're going to know that I'm right."

BACK AT MY small yellow house on Eastview Lane, I was stuck solving equations that my teacher didn't even give an answer key for. It was awful doing work when I had no way to find out if I was doing it right. I felt useless. It seemed like nothing I could do would help, but I had to keep studying. I was repeatedly told tests, especially 8th grade tests, did not matter at all. I knew that was true in the long run, but the thing is, we're never in the long run. We only run as far as our feet can take us at that very second, so yeah, this average 8th grade math test mattered.

I decided to let myself relax in the kitchen with my beloved salt-and-vinegar potato chips, far away from my responsibilities. It would be so easy to just sit here the whole night without my demon math sheets.

I heard steps coming downstairs and looked out of the kitchen to see Willow, already changed into her pajamas. She walked inside the kitchen and grabbed an apple before coming over to me. "Taking a break from studying?" she questioned, tucking a lock of hair behind my ear.

I hopped off the counter and ran to get question sheet. "I was... but can you check these?"

Willow picked up the paper and began working. After a couple minutes, she handed the materials back to me with a smile.

"Considering it was twenty problems, you did pretty well, dude. Just check numbers 2, 8, 17 and 19 again. I'll write down the answers for you on a post-it to check. I believe in you," Willow reassured me.

Life was awful but at least my big sister wasn't.

I BROUGHT THE rest of my chips to the dining-room table and redid the questions Willow had listed. Luckily, I got two more right on my first try. After a few more attempts, I had fixed the others.

I heard the click of a key and the front door swung open with my Mom, struggling with a pile of essays to grade. She wore her usual stern "after-work" face that reminded me that while neither of us was at a school anymore, everything was still *no nonsense*.

Mei Sun was professor of Greek philosophical texts at Cornell University, meaning her entire life was Greek philosophical texts and Cornell University. Each night she was poring over essays and books and everything I wasn't interested in. She never had any time to talk about what I cared about. Once I asked her to look at a watercolor painting I had worked on in art class and she told me she wasn't an art critic so I was wasting my time.

Why do parents always think you need critiquing?

"Hey Mom!" I called as she dropped her papers on the dining table.

"I got an email from Ms. Summers. You talk to Willow?" Mom pointed.

"Yeah, she helped. I've been doing well, I promise." I sunk into my chair a bit further after finishing my sentence.

Mom nodded and looked over to me, apparently sizing me up. "Keira, I told you not to wear those loose jeans again. They make you look disheveled."

Of course, she would ridicule me with words I barely understood.

"And stop with those pure black shirts, they... "

"Wash my hair out," I completed for her. "I know, Mom, I'll stop."

With that, Mom strutted out of the dining room to her office, leaving me alone in this inner suburbia wasteland. I pulled at my black shirt and rubbed it against my ebony locks of hair. I thought they harmonized nicely together, but Mom was always right.

Hearing my Mom groaning from her office, I crawled in so I could check on her. Her mahogany desk was buried in essays, many with angrily scribbled red marks on them. Mom was reclined in her swivel chair, her knuckles set firmly in her lap. I noticed her laptop screen was open on Facebook, her keyboard hidden by a schedule book.

"What's wrong, Mom?" I asked gently.

She turned to me sharply, her brown eyes piercing mine. "Everything, actually, Keira. I teach in the Ivy League and my students still can't manage to develop their essays. I know it's all about improvement and working on yourself, but there are *certain guidelines* of work that a few of them just can't meet."

Though I didn't really care about analyses of Aristotle, I heaved a sigh of relief that she wasn't mad at me anymore. Maybe if I kept sympathizing with her she would be even nicer to me. I had to give it a try.

"Mom, you can talk more to me about it. I like to hear about your job," I cooed.

With a sudden change of emotion, my Mom's eyes lowered. She crossed her arms but slowly let them loose. "Keira, just please go. All I need from you, Keira, is to not talk to me when I'm working. Otherwise, when Willow leaves for college, you're going to have to live with your Dad and his deadbeat fiancé more of the time, ok? And I know I can't do that because I don't trust a twenty-two-year-old woman named Clarke to raise you, but just... You know what I mean," Mom spoke sternly.

I nodded. "Yes, Mom. I'll get going." But as I turned, I heard her flat voice again.

"Oh, Keira, I forgot to ask. I saw yesterday on Harper's Mom's Facebook that she took her daughter and your friends Sadie and Taylor to see a movie. Were you not invited?"

A gust of air seemed to punch my stomach, sending me curling over. I was trying to forget about it, why did Mom *have* to bring it up?

"No, I wasn't," I stammered.

"Talk to them," she commanded. "You must have said something wrong."

I clenched my teeth. "No Mom, I actually didn't. They're just not good friends. I heard them talking today about how happy they were that I wasn't there."

Mom shook her head. "Well, you still need to resolve it. You need friends, it's healthy, you should be there next time."

And with that, I stomped out of her office, making sure to kick the rug as I left. I grabbed the rest of the salt-and-vinegar chips and dragged them up to my room. Here I would definitely be able to leave her alone. She would love it if I just stayed here because she never cared about any of my problems. I could look at the pale, yellow walls or my sweet-pea green sheets all day and she wouldn't know. Also, I hated yellow and green. Maybe years ago, before my parents' divorce, when I was three or four, they were my favorite colors. But now I saw them in my worst nightmares.

As I was getting lost in my frustrations with my mother and bright colors, I heard crying from Willow's room. I rushed to her door. Willow *never* cried.

"Willow, hey, what's wrong?" I asked.

Willow extended her arms and I moved closer to give her a hug. "Keira, Dad eloped last night. He and Clarke got married several months early without even telling us, his family! I know I shouldn't take it as a big deal, but Clarke is not the right woman for him. She's only four years older than *me*, Keira! She's just 22, and Dad is not the kind of man who can handle a marriage to a woman 27 years younger than him. Plus, they've been together for less than a year. I don't think Dad will be able to survive a third divorce, Keira. I know he's awful in so many ways, but Peter Sun is our Dad and I can't bear to see him hurt," Willow croaked.

I had promised myself earlier today I would not cry anymore, and, for Willow's sake, I was standing by that right now. I barely knew Dad, because he divorced Mom when I was four and he was never around when we stayed at his house. But I knew three divorces could not be healthy for anyone, and I suddenly wished something I never did before. I hoped he really did love Clarke more than Mom. I hoped they'd make it.

And I think I knew why I wanted this so badly. If a man with as messed-up a life as his could make things work, then maybe I could too.

I soon knew that on this dreadful Friday, sleep was the only release I was going to get. Maybe I would wake up in a different world in the morning.

CHAPTER 2

AT 3:30 IN THE MORNING, I WOKE UP to walk downstairs and get a glass of water. The glow-in-the-dark lights in my room seemed brighter than they had been the night before, but it was probably just the sleep still residing in my eyes. I tiptoed down the steps silently, careful to not wake Willow or Mom. After I had poured myself a cup of ice water, I sat at the dining room table and stared at my Mom's glass jewelry display, which held only an emerald amulet that my great-grandmother had in China. I had always wanted to wear it but I was too scared to get even a slight scratch on the jewel.

I felt my eyes burning again as the amulet started shining brightly just as the glow-in-the-dark lights had before. I rubbed my face, hoping to stabilize my vision. I was rarely awake at this hour of the morning, yet something had pulled me out of bed. I could feel the effects the odd hour was having on my vision. But the amulet only shone brighter. Overcome with curiosity, I reached my hand toward the case and felt a sudden hotspot in the air. Recoiling, I peered down at my hand and then at the amulet, now nearly blinding me.

I held in a scream, bewildered by the necklace. I calmed down enough to try and touch it again. Finally, I slid open the lock of the case and pointed a finger to the amulet once more. White light pierced the room, highlighting both the rugs and ceiling. After looking around again, I finally allowed my palms to grace the now-burning green emerald. I soon felt myself becoming surrounded in an extreme glow.

As though in a dream, I was absorbed into the sun. The lights were too bright for me to see a single thing, but as energy raced up my body, sending occasional shock waves through my nerves, I realized I was moving.

When the electric sensation didn't stop, I *knew* I must have been stuck in some sort of crazy dream. But no matter how much I jerked, I couldn't wake up. Suddenly, the light dimmed and the shocks halted. I blinked several times, hoping I was awake and back in my bed, only to see what appeared to be an office lobby.

The walls were a faint cream color, with simple dotted paintings scattered about. On either side of me were two sets of standard brown cushioned chairs, just comfortable enough to sit in for a few minutes. The floor beneath me was a freshly polished wood, and I let my sock- covered foot graze over the varnish, trying to feel something, anything, in this dream I could not begin to understand. Peering around the cookie-cutter room one last time, as if I was trying to decide my next stop on a "choose your own adventure," I saw the strangest thing yet.

Standing just two feet away from me was a boy with the bright blue eyes, the irises speckled with cobalt against the aqua surface. His chin-length hair was a soft brown and more carefully combed than any other guy I had met before. He wore boring clothes though, almost too boring, a plain grey shirt and black pants. They were so boxy that it looked as though they had been ironed so heavily as to encase him. But the unflattering apparel did not distract from his handsome face, especially the faint smile that he was expressing.

"Beautiful boy, what are you doing in my dream?" I exclaimed, knowing that nobody can see unknown faces while asleep. I must have met him somewhere, long ago.

The boy cleared his throat, but I noticed a red blush run to his cheeks. "Uh, uh, Keira this is... this is not a dream."

I stepped back a moment. "Of course, it is. How else could I have seen a necklace glowing and been transported into some generic lobby?" I reasoned.

"Keira, read this for me," the boy said, pulling a piece of paper out of his pants pocket. He handed me a folded-up sheet with a few words written on it. I peered into his eyes again before reading and then started to focus on the words.

"With great power comes great responsibility," I read to him. "That's Spider-Man."

"And... from others. But just please read it again." the boy responded.

"With great power comes great responsibility," I recited once more, getting sort of bored of the dream at this point. "That's it?"

"Yes, but do you see the problem here, why this means you're not in a dream?"

I shook my head, still dazed about the fact that I could sense everything happening.

"People cannot read in their dreams, and even if they can make out the sounds, it's impossible to understand. Also, the text cannot remain the same the second time you read it in a dream, and I think you just proved that it's stable. And for you to be able to analyze the quotation and sense that it is from, as you said, 'Spider-Man,' you would need to be awake," the boy told me.

A sudden sense of panic arose in me as my heart started beating fast. I had to be dreaming. That was the only thing that could have possibly happened. Out of nowhere, almost on instinct, I began pinching my arm in hope of waking myself up.

"This is weird!" I cried. "Wake up, wake up!"

"Stop, Keira!" The boy screamed, though I didn't listen. I had never had a dream where I was repeatedly told this was all real and I'd read enough creepy stories to know this was a bad sign.

Then, I felt the boy pull my hands from my forearms and grab them, not letting me pinch myself anymore. "Keira, you're going to hurt yourself. Please stop and just listen to me." Slowly, he released my hands and let them fall by my side.

"My name is Alden Fischer, and while this is going to seem insane and not make any sense, you are fully awake and everything you can see right now is real," Alden conveyed, his gaze kinder than before.

I was having none of his nonchalant attitude. "Have I

been kidnapped? How could you kidnap me? You look my age. Take me back home!"

"Yes, I am your age. But, actually, we have brought you home." Alden's voice was shaky and tense, as if he was unsure of what his next move had to be.

"That sounds like the exact kind of thing a kidnapper would say."

Alden let out an exasperated laugh. "I promise, you are meant to be here. I think you would have sensed something other than light if you were being kidnapped. You said you saw a necklace glowing, right?"

I nodded. "Yeah, this amulet my great-grandmother used to wear." I was unsure of why I was suddenly answering this *Alden* as if everything was perfectly normal, but I knew that conversation was the only way I was going to learn about where I was.

"Good, that's what's supposed to happen." Alden paused. "Keira, I'm about to explain this all to you. Please don't faint, and if you do, try to give me a warning."

"Is warning you even possible?" I pointed out.

Alden sighed. "You know, the first thing you called me was a 'beautiful boy,' so let's not pretend I'm the only awkward one here." As he said it again, I noticed his cheeks redden once more. Also, realizing that *I* had said that and that it was all real, I was not feeling great.

"Keira, you have never belonged, but in the best way. You were meant to be born in another year, far from whenever and wherever you have been. In fact, you have powers so great that being out of your true time is possible."

"Are you calling me a superhero?" I near fantasized.

"Keira, I'm calling you a time traveler."

I choked on my breath. A time traveler? That made

about as much sense as everything else that was happening right now, which I suppose was fitting. "Well, then where's my time machine?"

Alden's eyes widened, as if he had never really thought about this before. "Oh, Keira, that's what makes us so amazing! *We* are the time machines. We can control everything with our heads!"

"No!" I screamed, my jaw dropping. "You can't tell me something like that and still expect me to believe I'm not dreaming! Can you just kill me so I'll wake up?"

"I'm not going to kill you, oh my gosh! This is real! We are in a city named Lana Ilu that exists in another dimension. Everyone who lives here is just like you, a natural born time traveler. I swear on the Golden Grandfather Clock that I am telling you the truth."

"And what even is that?"

"Soon after you come with me, you'll find out." At that, he began walking towards a door at the opposite side of the room. I remained standing, fearing what I would see next. I had promised myself the day before that I would stop crying from then on out, but I had never been this terrified. Yet again, I felt the familiar heat of tears on my cheeks.

"Come on, we have—" Alden cut himself off. "Oh."

At least he understood that crying was a human thing, as he forced a smile towards me.

"Am I ever going to see my sister again?" I pleaded.

Alden set his hand on my shoulder. "Of course, you're not trapped here. It's all going to be alright, Keira."

But I didn't dry my eyes. How was I supposed to trust this random boy or this crazy city or anything else? I grew up having one person I could rely on and a pair of pretty blue eyes was not going to change that.

Out of nowhere, the most surprising thing of the entire event happened. The boy, Alden, wrapped me in a hug, a gesture I had never gotten from anyone other than Willow or occasionally my grandparents. He remained there for a second, and at one point, I probably hugged him back.

"You good?" Alden asked, pulling away.

"Yep."

CHAPTER 3

AFTER WE LEFT WHAT I SAW AS THE
waiting room, Alden led me into a metal-walled
office. Inside was a large steel chair standing in front of
what looked like two cylindrical lasers. The floor was a
glimmering silver, which distracted me for a moment from
the brace encasing the lasers. Aside from who appeared to
be two doctors sitting across from me, there was only one
seat which I knew would be mine. What worried me most
about the iron chair were the two heavy bars attached to
the arm rests, ending in cuffs fit for my wrists. To bring
a calming atmosphere to the room, there was a brightly
painted exit door to the right, which I guess suggested
that better times were coming. But I was still pretty sure
this is where all alien abduction victims were tested.

"Quite a sudden change," I mumbled to Alden.

"Yeah, I think they should have some sort of carpeted connecting hallway," he answered, "with smooth jazz."

I let out a quick laugh before the male doctor came to shake my hand. Like in movies, he wore a stereotypical lab coat and had some sort of stethoscope, which only made me feel more like I was in some carefully fabricated place. "Hello, Miss Keira Sun. I'm Dr. Sharma. Behind me is my student, Dr. Hughes." The redheaded lady waved at me. "Now, I know all of this seems incredibly sudden and overwhelming to the point where it may appear to be fake, but this is all true and we do have more information for you," Dr. Sharma said.

"Could you please take a seat here, Miss Sun?" Dr. Hughes asked, pointing to the metal contraption I had eyed before.

Hesitantly, I trudged over to the chair and rested my hand on the cold metal back. The giant handcuffs from before were still not reassuring and I had no interest in having them trap me. Just a second before I let myself recline, I asked, "What are those bars for?"

"Oh, just to make sure you don't pinch or hit yourself anymore to try to wake up. No matter how much we talk to newcomers, believing that you are asleep takes a while to fade. Don't worry, they won't hurt," Dr. Sharma informed me. "And anyway, we're going to talk a bit before you put them on."

I slowly sat down, the metal grazing against the thick Donnie's Diner tee shirt I had gotten two years before. From that, I realized I was still wearing my bright purple donut pajama pants, making every conversation I had so far that much weirder. My only nice article of clothing was my double-infinity necklace. But I still knew that there were stranger things to focus on.

"Keira, before we start the test, which you will feel no pain from and will take only a few seconds, I want to talk to you a bit more about where we are and how we got here. You see, you are one of the Dianimous people of this planet, and we often go by the name 'Gradiens' instead. The people from the outside world are Sianimous, but we usually call them 'Idums.' But I'll start from the beginning to clarify more." Dr. Sharma took a deep breath. He walked around the chair a few times, leaning down to inspect that everything was in place.

"Time is not a line, but a circle. Instead of the past happening before the future, everything that happens in one second in our year is also happening in that exact second in every other year. Time is always affecting itself. That's why the past is reshaped based on studies in the present and the future always changes because of our different views of the past and on and on and on. It's complicated, but so is everything in life," Dr. Sharma told me.

"And what does this have to do with my existence?" I questioned, nervous already about the answer.

"Keira, as I believe Alden told you, you never really belonged."

I felt a punch to the gut at that.

"But don't worry. There's actually a wonderfully amazing scientific reason for that. When I talked about circular time, there is an energy vortex that exists in it, allowing time to exist at all. Now, as you may know, every human does have natural electric energy to them, which is where we connect with this time vortex. Still, the average human, a Sianimous one, never will have their energy pass through time. But you and I, Dianimous people, were born at the exact same microscopic fraction of a nano-second as someone else in a different year."

Seeing me trying to follow, he paused. "By being born at the same time, our energy touches the time vortex at the same time, meaning one person's energy touches another's, and in a flash, they swap. So, your energy inside of you, your soul if you believe in that, technically comes from a different year. Biologically, you are you and related to your family, but your energy is incredibly unique. And if you want to know about our time-travel abilities, well, that swap picked up the energy from the vortex, giving you plenty to go back in. Get all that?"

I stared, dumbfounded. Everything and nothing made sense. Now I could see why I had never fit in, why I acted so differently from my parents or Willow, but I never felt *that* strange. Maybe I needed to hear that, though, to explain the horrible, awkward life I had led. But I was still secretly hoping I just had not found the right people yet, not that I was missing a whole era.

"No," I admitted, "that was a lot."

Dr. Sharma scratched his chin. "It always is, but you'll catch on soon. Now, the test we're going to run is to find exactly where your energy is from. It's just a simple eye scan. We'll have the results back to you by tomorrow." He turned to Dr. Hughes. "Please set up the program, Katherine."

She quickly walked to a perfectly round computing device and started a program that looked like it was planned out a thousand years into the future. Or *would be* planned out? I didn't know.

Softly, Dr. Sharma brought the bars I'd seen before near my arms and secured them around my wrists. I felt the clasps encase my hands but, surprisingly, they were neither cold nor tight. They did restrict me from moving, which I wasn't much of a fan of. I had to admit, with my time travel education, pinching myself to wake up did seem appetizing.

"It will just be a little bright," Dr. Sharma instructed me.

Suddenly, a white light like that from the amulet pierced my eyes. He was right that it wouldn't hurt, but he had clearly downplayed the brightness. For what seemed like a minute, as the laser scanned my eyes, I was completely blind.

Finally, the light turned off and my hands were released from the clasps. I peered over to the computing device and saw a long string of numbers and figures, almost like a mythological pi.

"What's that?" I asked.

"Your energy code," Dr. Hughes responded. "We can only find it through your eyes."

"Is that why people always say that the eyes are the windows to the soul?" I asked.

Dr. Hughes let out a chuckle. "I guess, but Keira, you'll quickly learn here in Lana Ilu that every metaphor that you learned as a little kid back in Ithaca is based on complete rational scientific theory. See, the eyes are connected by the optic nerve to the brain, which doesn't truly have your soul, but it does contain your source of energy, thus powering hormones, personality, etc."

Dr. Sharma shook his head. "It takes a lot to be creative around here."

I nodded, realizing that Dr. Hughes had mentioned Ithaca, my hometown. They also knew my name. Had I been watched my entire life, even though I always lived thinking I was ignored? Honestly, that wouldn't surprise me at this point.

Afterwards, I followed Alden, who'd been standing in the corner quietly, out the exit.

"How did it feel?" he asked. "The test?"

"I just felt blind, I guess. It was like the sun was right in front of me." I paused. "You never had it done?"

"No, I did, but immediately after I was born. That's how all babies actually from Lana Ilu do it. The doctors determine their correct time and if they even are a Gradien, because if their energy code is the same as the time they were born, well, the family decides what to do," Alden said.

I squinted my eyes at him. "Are normal people, I mean, Idums, not allowed to live in Lana Ilu? And are they even common?"

"No, they're not common at all if both parents are Gradiens as all are here. I'd say 99.9% of the time it is a Gradien baby. The other 0.1% can be difficult, and most of the time the parents just leave *it* with the closest Idum family member. It's just too dangerous and unstable to have any *others* here. But like I said, it's rare, especially when you're descended from a lot of other Gradiens."

I noticed the tension he put on *it* and *others*, like he thought Idum people, people unlike us, were lesser beings. But he probably just grew up not knowing any different, so I tried not to see anything offensive.

"And when are you from?" I asked. My voice caught as I finished saying the words. I had seen people take DNA ancestry tests, trying to find out if they were Italian or

Jewish or Senegalese or from a million other places. I had never imagined trying to find out the time of one's history.

"From the good old American Revolution," Alden grinned. "My energy partner was born on December 16th, 1772, meaning he is alive right now in 1786. Cool, right?"

"Yeah," I said. "Can't wait to find out mine."

Alden agreed and continued walking through the hallway, finally connecting and carpeted like Alden had recommended. When we arrived at the door leading to a new room, he sent me one more flash of his incredible eyes. He smiled at me. "This is where I let you off. I hope you can really make Lana Ilu your home."

Just as he was about to leave, I did something Ithaca Keira would have never done. I grabbed his arm and gestured that I needed to ask him something.

"Will I see you again, Alden?" I questioned, hoping deep down that I would. I wasn't sure how easy making friends here would be, knowing that it definitely was not a talent I held.

Alden smirked, but I noticed he was blushing. Wow, did this kid turn red. "Probably. We're all a pretty tight community here. But if not, meeting people is really easy."

I shrugged my shoulders, hoping for a more confident reply. "Bye, and thanks," I said.

"Bye." And with that, I was alone as we went through different doors, he back to his home, and me to the one I would hopefully soon call my own.

When I finally walked into the new room, I came to the conclusion that I was in some sort of funhouse. I had transferred from a waiting lobby, to an experimenting lab, to now a grand hall. Bustling with people, having a gorgeously tiled ceiling, and floors painted with some sort of zig-zagging maze, the place was absolutely incredible. There were around a hundred people inside, some chatting, others racing across the expanse, and still others hunched over desks, filing paperwork and holographic messages. It became clear to me that it was the middle of the workday here. With the buzzing of a million languages being spoken and the constant clatter of footsteps, I was amazed I didn't hear anything on the other side of the door. I guess they used some sort of futuristic noise-cancelling technology here in, er, *Lana Ilu*?

Just a second after I was inside, and still bewildered by all around me, a lady in dark bell- bottom pants and a red striped top came up to me, her coily curls styled in an Afro. "And we have number five!" she called. "Miss Sun, hello, I'm Alessandra. If you could just come with me to that desk over there. Oh, and please watch your step, there's a coffee spill that should be cleaned up soon if *Carlos* would just check that my report was sent!" Alessandra yelled in no particular direction.

"Turn around now, Alessandra. It's gone," a voice a few feet away, which I assumed belonged to this *Carlos*, alerted.

I looked behind me and saw that the coffee had indeed disappeared. I let my jaw drop until Alessandra, keen to my confusion, said, "there's heated steam that comes out of the floor when we report the location. It's not as cool as it seems."

I nodded aggressively. "It's still really cool."

Alessandra grinned, her bushy brows rising. "I love to see the expressions on newcomers' faces, all the wide eyes. My dad's an Idum-born and he tells me tons of stories about getting adjusted to Lana Ilu. Speaking of that, did your welcoming and time diagnostic tests go smoothly?"

"I guess," I shrugged. "It's all very weird."

"I bet! But let me tell you, in a matter of weeks, this place will feel like every other city you've been to, with just an extra little twist. I mean, yeah, I was born in 1985 and my energy stems from 1970 which can confuse a lot of people, but trust me, I'm still working my day job like everyone else in the Idum-world," Alessandra said.

"Trust me, it's still *really cool*." It was incredibly refreshing to repeat that again. Since the coffee spill, one of the most mundane human things, had been shown to me, I realized that nothing was being made up. Even dreams have their limits. Now I just had to wait until I found out more.

"As you may see, there are four other people waiting by our dormitory administration desks. They have also arrived at Lana Ilu just like you, the earliest less than an hour ago. I will get you acquainted with them and then we will continue with your little check-in to your new home!" Alessandra paused. "Carlos, we're about to head out, so come with me!" she called.

I looked up to her quickly, leaving Alessandra to shake her head. "He's our new clueless intern, but as head of Idum Introductions, he's my responsibility. But those high school seniors..."

At that, I was suddenly jolted back to Ithaca. Somewhere, in another world, Willow was sleeping in, since as a high school senior she didn't have to go to her internship today. I started to wonder if she had woken up and checked on me, only to find that I was missing. Was she freaking out? Was she going to report me missing? Was I hurting her?

"Hey?" I called, realizing our walk over was almost done. "Am I going to seem like I'm missing back home? My sister might freak out!"

"No, once we've taught you a bit about time travel and how to control it, we'll send you back to right when you left to talk things out with your family. Don't worry, you're like the 500th Idum-born I've helped bring in. It's all under control."

I nodded, feeling comforted by that statistic she gave me. *It's all under control*, I thought.

At last, we arrived at the other group of newcomers, or as Alessandra called them, Idum-borns. Amongst them were three boys and one girl, all dressed in pajamas like myself. The oldest was a blonde boy who looked about 17, wearing the grimmest of frowns upon his face. Though he was obviously still a teenager, his skin was etched with worry lines. On the other hand, the youngest of the group was a little girl in brunette pigtails. I was surprised that she looked so excited and joyful considering she appeared to be only eight or nine. At that age, I would have been terrified to be away from home. One of the other boys looked about a year older than me, and he wore an oversized embarrassing t-shirt with a diner on it just as I did. He was fiddling with his thumbs and constantly looking over his shoulder, his black eyes seemingly trying to explore the next thing he missed. Finally, there was a boy who I thought to be fourteen, like me. He had dark brown hair that stuck up in places from his previous sleeping. It went well with his matching navy-blue pajamas. He smiled at me and sent a wave that urged me to do the same back. He definitely looked to be the most inviting to talk to.

Before Alessandra began to talk, I noticed that a man working at a heavily covered desk had handed the smiling boy a tablet. Then I realized that when Alessandra clicked a small gadget into her ear, it made a big screen light up with words.

It's a translator, I thought.

"Hello! I just came back with our last inductee, so before we go, I want to do one last run-through of who we are and where we are from. My name is Alessandra Okar and I live in the 1970's sector of Lana Ilu. Once we leave, if you have a question for me, just mention my name to anyone in the building and I will get it. We have Mark Highsmith from Camden, Maine," Alessandra said, gesturing towards the older blonde teen. "Also, our youngest here is Rosie MacGregor from Toronto, Ontario, Canada." The little girl jumped up at hearing her name. "This is Aaron Williams from Atlanta, Georgia," Alessandra added, smiling at the boy with curious eyes. "And from Carolina, Puerto Rico is Lucas Acosta." The friendly kid smiled once again, settling into the situation. "Oh, and of course, here with me now is Keira Sun, who is from Ithaca, New York! Now that we are all acquainted, let's get moving. Right now, we are on the second floor of the Idum-Born Relations Department. Above us is the 1850's to 1900's Department and also the 1900's to 1950's one. You can visit those with tours later on if you ever want to, but we should move on."

Alessandra turned quickly, her heeled boots clicking behind her. "If you haven't gotten a chance already, our grand window here has a terrific view of the northwest side of the city and I would love for you to get a look before we get settled." The group soon assembled behind her, with that boy Lucas on my arm. "And in the meantime, Carlos…" Alessandra said, and the young man in a metallic-button down shirt and a color-changing shaved head, suddenly materialized next to her. "Please go fetch their dormitory assignments for me." Carlos ran to the side, allowing our tour to begin.

Once I saw the window, the *grand window*, I felt my eyes bug out of my head. It was framed with spectacular gold tiles, which appeared to move their jeweled specks across the structure. The window took up nearly an entire wall, with not a single desk hiding it. Even the people who worked in this very room everyday still crowded around the glass, peering down at the world below them. At last, I got up to the window and blinked, preparing my eyes. I could still feel the brightness from before, but I had a feeling that would never go away.

As I opened my eyes, a place out of movies—no, not even movies could do this—a place born from pure imagination appeared. A glimmering pyramid, so sharp and fresh like I was in ancient Egypt itself, was the first thing that caught my attention. Next my eyes quickly moved to a glimpse of a figure far behind it, a great coliseum like in Rome, yet without the rubble I had seen in pictures. The streets were decorated with everything from clothing shops to multi-cultural restaurants to robot-building carts. But the most amazing were the people. Couples wearing poodle skirts and classical Chinese styles roamed the sidewalks, trailed by kids racing mini hot-air balloons and toy cars more realistic than I had ever seen before. Horse-drawn carriages and motorcycles crowded the roads of the obviously ancient-themed place, yet it all seemed to harmonize perfectly together. It was a song I couldn't wait to sing.

Soon, I felt a hand tug at my pajama shirt. Behind me was Rosie, the young girl from before. She was grinning at me, her smile taking up half her face while her puppy dog eyes grabbed the other.

"It's so amazing!" Rosie exclaimed, twirling as she said it. "I can't wait to go down and find out when I'm from and make new friends and live here forever!"

"You're not scared?" I asked. "To be so far away from home when you're so young?"

Rosie shook her head wildly. "No, I'm not scared! Yeah, I was at first, but being scared gets boring. Sometimes you see that the scary things are just fun things you haven't tried yet."

I smiled at her. "I guess you're right. We just have to see it."

Rosie laughed at me once more and then ran to the other end of the window, hoping to catch another peak of something new. The waving boy from before, Lucas, filled her place.

"You like?" he questioned suddenly, his voice woven with a heavy accent.

"Sure! The city is the most incredible thing I have seen. Like, who wouldn't want to go to a realistic pyramid and control a mini sports car at the same time?"

Lucas cocked his head, but nodded. "Sorry, less words please?"

I wanted to hit myself at that. I forgot he needed the translator, and I just threw a confusing line of phrases at him, expecting an answer. "I just said there's lots of things to do."

Lucas smiled. "Yeah, so much. Exciting!"

There was a moment of silence before I piped up. "We could walk around later, see the city," I suggested.

Lucas turned to me. "Yeah, that is good. So much to do, good to have more than one person."

Just as I was about to respond to that, Alessandra started heading back to the exit door. "That was great, right? Well, soon enough you'll actually get to be down there. But for now, we have some logistical things to get done, which we can carry out in the quieter hallway."

I noticed Lucas with his tablet, half of the time looking at it for words, half of the time facing Alessandra. He looked like a curious kind of person, ready to experience things he didn't know. In Rosie's words, he wasn't one to see different things as scary.

When we got into the hallway, the noise from within the grand room cancelled out like before.

"Here are your room cards," Alessandra said, passing us all keys like I had seen at fancy hotels. "You are all on Floor 1 of the Dormitory Building. The girls will be in Rooms D and E, Rosie in the first, Keira in the next. For you boys, Lucas in Room H, Aaron in Room I, and Mark in Room J. You can make your way there right now with Marie, who should be coming in any second to help you on your way. She will aid you in the next step of the process. Remember, any questions, come find me here. And please, enjoy your new home."

CHAPTER 4

To MY DISAPPOINTMENT, THE SMALL space between the Introductions building and the Dormitory building was pretty plain, with just an ordinary grass yard, sidewalk, and some simple office buildings lining the path. But I was excited for the opportunity to have a place to stay again, even if just for a night. The Dormitory building looked like one I would expect to see at a classic college, like Ithaca's Cornell back in the 1870's. Indoors, it was incredibly quiet, vacant in fact.

"People usually only stay here for no more than two nights, so you guys will be alone in here except for me and another guide. I can guarantee that by tomorrow you will all find out your correct energy times," our guide Marie said, explaining the silence.

We made our way to the dorms, each of us finding our own room. It was a simple layout, but beautifully comforting as well. The bed was better cushioned than any dorm at Cornell, with an oak nightstand carefully carved with flowers next to it. On the stand was a small metal contraption that piqued my interest, leading me to push the large button on top. Soon, it opened.

"Welcome to Lana Ilu! I hope you find your first day here comfortable. I am your personal map explorer, Lana (like the city, get it?), and I would love to help you on your way today! Would you like to keep me opened?" asked the holographic pop-up woman.

I grinned down at the machine. "Yes, but not to see the city."

The hologram smiled, displaying her pearly white teeth. "Sure thing! I can give you another walk through of concepts here. You can choose from the menu below."

Just as I was about to pick the "where are you?" option, I heard a knock at the door. I closed the object, letting the small lady disappear into the air. When I opened the door, I saw Marie again, dressed in the same odd flowing top from before, almost like the shirt was a jellyfish.

"Hello, Keira! Have you gotten a chance to meet Lana, our welcoming device? We call it a multi since it covers almost everything you need!" she asked.

"Yes," I answered, unable to stop smiling as I remembered my holographic encounter.

"Wonderful. If you ever need quick explanations for anything, please just open that up. She is yours to keep. Later on, you can change her name, appearance, gender, voice, clothing, and more, but for right now, I have some things to ask you before I let you out into the city." Marie stopped talking to pull out a small scanning bar. "We can't have you walking around in pajamas, so I would like to find out what clothes you would like our department to get for you for the next few days until you go back home. Oh, and don't worry, your family will not think you've been missing for that long, it's all handled."

Marie waved the bar up and down me, the red light marking my body. *They really liked lights here.*

"Alright, your size is in. And what kind of clothes would you like us to get you? There's basically no limit, so just choose whatever you please."

I imagined everything my mom would never buy me and asked for all of it- ripped jeans and overalls and black tank tops and stripes and everything else that crossed my mind. Marie nodded and left, leaving me excited to see my new clothes soon. It felt like my first moment of freedom.

While I waited, I went over to customize my multi as Marie had told me about. I ended up trying to make the ideal, older version of myself. I changed her skin tone from the very pale one in the original to my tanner complexion. Afterwards, I added flowing black hair on her head, longer than I was ever able to grow mine. Then, after reshaping her face with the makeup I always hoped to wear when I got to high school, I chose her outfit. I found a small black dress that completely absorbed the shade of her tresses, just as my Mom always scolded me for doing.

Perfect, I thought. Now I just need to name her. The first name that crossed my mind was that of my class's bunny back in first grade—*Daisy*. I honestly did not feel like thinking much more about it and it wasn't like the holograph was an actual person. She could have the same name as a bunny.

Though I was in a state I never imagined, I felt myself

drifting off to sleep again. In my defense, not even a wondrous time-travel city could change the fact that I had been woken up at three in the morning.

After about an hour though, there was a knock at my door.

"I have your new clothes, Keira, and some other stuff before you get going," Marie told me through the wall.

I rubbed my eyes and stepped out of the bed, both to wake myself up and get the new clothes.

After dressing and grabbing *Daisy*, my personal technological helper, I left the dorm room. Running through my mind, I tried to remember which slot Lucas had been given, and I recalled that it was Room H.

I wandered down the short hallway until I reached Lucas's dorm and knocked on the door. A few seconds later, in a long sleeve shirt and rolled up jeans not too different from my own (though he didn't have embroidered flowers), he appeared. *Good taste in style*, I thought.

"Have your multi?" I asked.

Lucas paused for a moment and made a clicking sound with his tongue, but then grinned. "Yes, I do! Good to go?"

I smiled, walking towards the exit until I remembered Rosie. When I suggested we take her too, Lucas grinned and shook his head.

"I saw her leave before, she was too excited," Lucas told me, stopping a bit after each word.

"Well then, I think we're free."

After checking out where instructed, we finally stepped out into the city for real. Directly behind the dorms was a beautiful clay building I identified as an "ancient cosmetics shop" from its magnificent pottered sign. Amazingly, in an instant, the language of the sign changed and then altered again a moment later. This city, *Lana Ilu*, seemed to be everything, ever, in the universe.

We continued walking past the cosmetics store onto one of the main streets of what was called the *2500-2400 BCE* Sector. The streets were made of carefully cut stone and lined with uniform clay buildings, some detailed with well-known paintings and hieroglyphics. Outside of what looked like an extravagant apartment complex stood a vendor holding a container of mini pyramids. I noticed Lucas pick one up and find a lock on the outside, sliding it open. Inside was a small bag of toys and candies. He smiled at the vendor and bought one, sharing a piece of chocolate with me.

"This!" Lucas exclaimed. "Is it really true?"

Then, all of a sudden, I froze. Lucas had a point to his question, though I knew he was saying it hypothetically. Though all the people here had just spent hours convincing me that Lana Ilu was real, was a home, was *my home*, I still caught myself questioning it. Why was I just going along with all of this? Why was I wearing my dream clothes, that by the way were free, clothes some strange futuristic lady had given me? Why was I walking down streets that looked like they belonged in Ancient Egypt without slipping for second? Why was I here eating chocolate from a mini pyramid with a random guy that I had known for less than a day? Why was I not home? Why did I not think I was crazy?

I peered down at the stones beneath my feet, feet clad in shoes I never owned before, and wondered how I was not falling. The ground could not be stable; it wasn't real. I mean, with how everything felt, I should be able to fly off the street, onto a building or into the air. I should be able to read Lucas's mind or move a table across the road.

But that was all wrong. Like Alden had said, I was not a superhero, but a time traveler, and I was not even close to figuring out what abilities I had with that. Really, why was I even considering possibilities?

Abruptly, I felt Lucas's hand shake my shoulder. "You are good," he told me, not in question, but in fact.

I unclasped my hands, realizing they were stuck in fists and agreed. *I am good.* I just had to enjoy myself.

After my little mental breakdown, we continued walking, passing through gates into different sectors, such as the *400-500* Sector, which we took a shortcut to get to. Inspired by what I guessed was older India stood a towering temple-like building with a large lawn in front. The carved boulders shaped into delicate windows on the outside of the structure. Some of the rooms inside were illuminated, electric, which I was pretty sure was inaccurate to the era of the building. There was a sign on the entrance to the place that read *Lana Ilu West School: Era-Gupta Age, India.* On the grass, some kids were playing field hockey and holding picnics, just like I had seen at home in Ithaca.

In front of me on the sidewalk was a couple that looked distinctly familiar. Suddenly, I recalled seeing the young woman's outfit, that exact poodle skirt from the grand window in the Idum-Born Relations room. And that must be her boyfriend, I thought, in traditional ancient Chinese clothing. The pair looked strikingly odd, yet their steps were perfectly in unison. Anywhere else, I would have thought they were wearing a failed couple's costume, but with their linked hands, no difference in style could keep them apart.

Coming up the street was a half-packed trolley car with an elderly man as the driver. Considering all the innovations of the city, I was surprised that the trolley even needed to be manned. Even cars back in the outside world were being built to drive themselves. As the trolley came to a halt and a couple of people got off, Lucas walked up to the driver.

"Where?" he asked shakily, referring to destination.

The driver, in a heavily ironed, button-down shirt grinned. "Doing a beeline to 1300-1400's Sector, the Italian part. There's an opera this afternoon, is that where you're going?"

Lucas, clearly confused by the man's quick speaking, stood quietly, leaving me to hop in. "No sir, but we would love to head that way. How much is a ticket?"

"Five points each! Just hand me your multis and I'll get those scanned."

I motioned to Lucas for his multi and gave mine in as well. In a second, two tickets showed up on a screen and I noticed a glow come from my multi.

"You're all set," said the driver. "Take any seat you want."

After we mounted the steps of the trolley and located a pair of seats near the back, Lucas pulled out his multi, and opened it. The hologram was of a woman with her long dark brown hair in a ponytail and wireframe glasses resting upon her nose. I noticed, especially in her bright smile, that she had a strong resemblance to Lucas. Hovering above her was the name *Cameron*.

"She looks like mamá, but her name is Cameron, no

Camille," Lucas whispered, noticing me staring. "I want to see her."

I stopped for a moment to take in his words, more distracting than the passing of time, quite literally, outside of the trolley. I would have loved to miss my Mom, to want her here with me on this new adventure. But right now, one of my favorite things about Lana Ilu was being free of her restrictions. In fact, the only person I longed to see was Willow. I wanted nothing more than to share this world with my sister. So, I guess I could understand Lucas's distress.

"You'll see her soon. This city doesn't seem like a prison to me," I coaxed.

Lucas narrowed his brows and then mumbled the word "prison" into his multi. After a second, he peered at me, now understanding my claim.

I looked out the window of the trolley, examining time as it literally passed by my eyes. There were medieval castles and fantastic African palaces like I had never seen before. But amongst these world wonders that could easily beat out the seven we know, hundreds of people walked by as if they were just going about their normal days. Actually, they *were* just living their regular lives. Some people were heading to work or going on dates or simply buying that outfit for a party next weekend. That was the most amazing thing.

After about a ten-minute ride, the driver finally called out, "This is our final stop! I hope to see you all again!"

The trolley filtered out, people ranging from those who were older heading to the opera and younger like us, just trying to explore. Lucas and I hopped off the steps of the trolley and began scaling the ascending sidewalk. In and out of the domed columns of old Italy and walking across the gated barriers of red-domed roofs were people in possibly the most fabulous arrangement of clothing I had ever seen. Dozens were dressed in the traditional garb of the era: wide-sleeved multi-colored gowns, midnight gothic cloaks, and dazzling tights that I was surprised anyone could pull off. But that was not where the hubbub of style ended. Color-changing pants and reflective blouses walked the roads, partnered by Aztec shawls, flapper dresses, and somehow-casual armor. I had heard Willow go on and on about Fashion Weeks going on in the world's most glamorous cities, like New York, Paris, Milan, and Tokyo. Part of this experience made me believe Lana Ilu was having its own period of catwalks.

We walked through the streets and passed by delicate brick architecture and an amphitheater that we figured must be holding today's opera. Lucas, his dark hair falling into his face, tugged on my arm. "Rich people here?" he joked, noticing the clothing of the pedestrians around, many of them carrying what looked like designer accessories.

I rolled my eyes at him but laughed. "Definitely, every city has its part. Want more food?"

Lucas read his multi to make sure he got what I said and then started pulling me towards what looked like a cute neighborhood cafe. In careful script lettering, a board above the crafted entrance door read *Dolce Dente del Tempo*, which I guessed was Italian. But unlike the cosmetics store I had seen earlier, the name did not change languages for translation. I guessed that was all part of its aesthetic.

People walked out of the restaurant holding sweets, hot drinks, and sandwiches, all of which made my mouth water. I saw a young girl, her purple hair done in a high ponytail on top of her head, munching down on a muffin nearly the size of her face. Her parents were watching her with wide eyes as the child shoved the baked delicacy into her mouth. *Food*, I thought. *It transcends the barriers of time.*

A young man whistled a flute against the entrance, playing a sweet, soft melody. An older couple was dancing to the music while teens around our age occupied the outside tables, laughing, arms around each other. Above the restaurant was a delicate balcony, gated by metal bars twisted into hearts and roses. Part of me imagined famous authors and poets finding their way into this city, however possible, just to sit in this exact cafe and write.

Inside the cafe, a long line waited against the counter, people placing their orders in various languages. When I got up to the stand, a woman in traditional clothing for the era, a pressed apron around her waist, stood patiently across from me.

The woman presented a board in front of me to pick my language and I located English on the screen. Once I pressed the button, the woman, who I saw from a name card was named *Giovanna*, lit up.

"Perfect, English is one of my twelve tongues! What would you like?" she chirped.

I jumped back for a moment, impressed with her many languages, but turned my attention to the menu. The first thing that piqued my attention was a spiced cheese and bread dish, which apparently was derived from an actual menu that existed centuries ago. Along with that, I ordered a water because I still felt heavily dehydrated, and what was called the *Clock Cookie*, which was "Voted Best in

Lana Ilu 234 years in a row!" I mean, anything with that long of a legacy had to be good.

I passed Lucas in line as I went to the side to pick up my order. "Clock Cookie," I mumbled to him as he smiled in response. He met me at the front entrance of the cafe, his hands filled with a sandwich, hot chocolate and like I had suggested, the famous Clock Cookie. At last, finally ready to fill our stomachs, we found a table inside and finished off our lunches, both of us relieved to be full at last after all the mayhem.

"Good," I grinned. "This is good."

Lucas gave a thumbs up, and grinned with his mouth full, an act I would usually find gross, but considering everything, I couldn't help but laugh back at him. For a second, I saw Lucas turn away from me and peer around the restaurant, almost as if someone was behind me. He then turned again, frowning, and rubbed his dark eyes. Like I had been before, he looked stuck, like he thought he was asleep, too. He stared down at his sandwich, half eaten, and placed his hand on the part of the plate the sandwich did not make up, like he was wondering why it wasn't there. Now I knew I had to do the same thing for Lucas that he had done for me.

I patted his arm and made sure to get him to look at me. "Lucas, remember, you are good. We are good, this is real, and this is amazing."

Lucas blushed for a moment and rolled his eyes. "Keira, you use my words."

"Yeah, I guess I'm not original," I said, smirking. Then, I held up the Clock Cookie I had bought before, a cinnamon sweet carved with doughy numbers and actual moving hands dipped in milk chocolate. "Now we should eat these."

Lucas picked up his cookie and knocked it against mine, a ceremonial toast of some sort and we bit down on desserts at the same time. To say this was the best thing I had ever eaten would be an understatement. I felt particles of sugar race through my taste buds, running to beat the spice the cookie also held. It was chewy and crunchy and what I imagined 234 years of baking would taste like. The one bad thing was that I could never eat another cookie again. Even the best in the Idum-world would pale in comparison.

Lucas stared at me, his mouth gaping open. He moved as if he was trying to talk, but was left speechless just as I was. Out of nowhere, we both broke out into laughter, not knowing another way to express our newfound love for the Clock Cookies. I knew now for sure that Lana Ilu was the best city in existence.

"See more? Go buy stuff?" Lucas questioned, leading me out of the restaurant.

Just as I was about to answer him and suggest we go explore some of the homes around here (sort of like an alternate-dimension Beverly Hills tour), I collided with someone standing by a table.

"Oh, I'm so sorry—" I yelled a bit too loud, until I saw a familiar pair of blue eyes. "Alden, hey! Lana Ilu is great, and look at that, I did see you again."

Alden, now dressed in a green shirt and cuffed pants, jumped back suddenly. "Keira, I gotta go. I'm glad that you like it here," he muttered, barely even looking at me.

"You ok?" I exclaimed, still trying to get his attention.

Alden was so kind and open when I met him, and now he looked like he wanted nothing to do with me.

Without even speaking another word, Alden ran off, grabbing a tall blonde girl by the arm. I wondered who she was and why she so quickly went with him. I felt a knot in my stomach grow tighter from that quick instance. Back at home, people used to find any way possible to ignore me. I was hoping Lana Ilu was different.

Lucas, wiping cinnamon off his chin, came up behind me. "Who?"

"My welcomer." I bit my lip and crossed my arms over my chest. "Not so welcoming now, though."

CHAPTER 5

I WAS WATCHING A MOVIE THAT WOULD come out in 2033, eating authentic 1880's popcorn with a boy I'd known less than a day who was still probably the closest friend I had ever had. My life seemed pretty amazing. Yet, I could not focus on a single good thing happening to me. Why had Alden just run away like that? What had I done wrong? Did that blonde girl put him up to it? Why did I even care?

I tried to readjust my eyes again to the screen, which by the way was showing a horror film based on true events the Idum-world was yet to learn about. The glide of the bloodied knife on walls would have piqued my interest during any other scary movie, but considering the earlier parts of my day in Lana Ilu, it was just too mundane.

I peered over my shoulder to Lucas, who was lazily watching hovering translated subtitles of the script. He looked to be dozing off, his head falling back as his eyes occasionally blinked shut.

"You tired?" I whispered.

Lucas shook his head to wake up. "Yes. I am sad, but yes."

"We can go now, back to our rooms," I suggested.

"Yeah," Lucas answered, rubbing his full stomach.

We crept out of the theater, earning *shhhh*'s from several people sitting behind us. Lucas, embarrassed, apologized to each person we walked by, while I kept shuffling on. I was not one for heavy eye contact. Lucas obviously needed to check the color of each person's irises in order to offer an apology!

Outside, we saw a trolley car stop, and though I was curious about taking a ride in some levitation devices or robotic cars, I was too exhausted to appreciate the new experiences.

"Trolley alright?" I asked Lucas, rubbing my eyes.

"Yes, and I can sleep in the car," he added.

We hopped on, got our tickets, and just as Lucas foreshadowed, he was asleep in seconds. Although I wanted to drift off too, I knew I had to be on the lookout to keep from missing our dorm, so I stayed focused on the lights of Lana Ilu instead. Neon illuminated the apartment buildings while everyday houses shone with their own unique glow. Almost like a domino effect, the lights of workplaces seemed to fade continuously behind me. But booming nightclubs and spinning restaurants, and even electric shows that filled sidewalks, replaced the lights of the day. It was a flicker, from one life to another. It was a flicker I could understand.

THE NEXT MORNING when I awoke, part of me expected to be back in my Ithaca bedroom again, seeing the yellow walls and green sheets I despised. I blinked enough to check for my star-shaped glow-in-the-dark lights on the ceiling and my chipped wooden lamp. I strained my ear to hear Willow singing in the shower or Mom shuffling her papers for work. But there was not a chirp, nor a spot of light-gold tile or a glittering above me. Everything yesterday—it was real. I was wrapped in carefully quilted blankets that my Mom had never bought and surrounded by a pale, welcoming lavender. I only knew this room from my arrival here yesterday. I was truly in Lana Ilu.

Feeling my stomach grumbling, I quickly dressed so that I could get Lucas and buy breakfast. I found the overalls Marie had brought me, a thinly striped shirt, and a pair of sneakers similar to those from before. Before I opened the door, I swiftly tugged my dark hair into a ponytail, hoping it would make me look slightly presentable. Just as I stepped outside, I remembered my multi, now named *Daisy*, and stuck it into my pocket. And with that, I was ready to try to figure out my second day here.

When I left the dorm room, I was surprised by a group of all the other Idum-borns from yesterday sitting in the lobby, chatting with Marie and a young man. As soon as I stepped into the room, each person turned to me.

"Keira, you have a trend for being the last one, don't you?" Marie joked. "But don't worry, now we're ready to get moving. You can grab a muffin from here before we leave."

Lucas walked up to me and rested his cheek on his hands, mocking someone sleeping. I stuck out my tongue at him before grabbing my breakfast, earning a similar gesture back.

"Good sleep?" Lucas asked me, taking a bite of toast.

I shrugged. "Yeah, but the new room is still weird. Thought I would still be home when I woke up."

Lucas stared at me blankly for a moment, but nodded once he got the gist of what I was saying. He was dressed similarly to yesterday, though his jeans had been replaced by pink shorts. I respected any boy who was proud to wear pink. In fact, from the little I knew of him, I respected a whole lot about Lucas. It would mean the world if he thought the same way about me.

"Where are we going?" I asked.

Lucas stopped to think for nearly a minute, leaving me on edge in this strange otherworldly morning, before he widened his mouth in eagerness. Then, all of a sudden, he muttered, "No sé."

I translated that to a simple *I don't know* and shoved his shoulder for stressing me out. "You're mean, Lucas Acosta," I jeered.

Lucas held his arm and whined dramatically. "No, you are the, uh…, mean person. Bad friend, very," he laughed, wrapping an arm around my shoulders as we walked out of the building with the rest of the people.

My heart warmed a bit at not only the half-hug, but just what Lucas said to me. I was used to being called *mean* or a *bad friend*, but never before in the midst of giggles I was invited to be a part of. I had never heard those words spoken to me when, in truth, the person meant the opposite.

I turned my attention back to the walk, the same

buildings from yesterday still lining the path. But then a sharp turn changed our course, and I noticed a structure I had somehow missed the day before. Standing a few blocks away was a castle that I was sure Buckingham Palace wished it could be. Definitely over a thousand feet tall, with spinning towers carved from marble, a glittering aqua moat, domes painted with the world's finest jewels, and a soft eerie glow, I was sure this was the center of Lana Ilu. Crowds circled the Palace, some people walking inside and others posing for photographs.

"What is that place?" I heard Aaron gawk.

Marie spun to us, her dress sparkling with electricity, almost like in a pattern. "Our destination, home to our own Royal Family, the Imamus. It is the spectacular Palace of Time."

Whoas echoed around me as kids grabbed the arms of others, jaws agape with excitement. I smiled at all of them, Lucas's jittering shoulders mostly, when I looked upon the blonde guy from yesterday, Mark. He stood much stiller than all the others, his arms tense and expression dark. He looked more resentful of the Palace than amazed by it. I tried not to let his negativity bother me as we finally arrived at the castle. Even the crisp, fresh smell was wondrous, with flowers and spices filling the air.

"We will be conducting today's event in the Royal Gardens. I'll be happy to give you a short tour. Here, every flower that did, does, and will exist prospers. We have everything from roses to Cry violets of the past and Homilias of the future," Marie explained.

We skipped further into the dazzling plants, passing through blossoms I'm sure my father, the professor of Plant Sciences at Cornell, would give anything to visit.

Marie stopped at a collection of simple white flowers, some that I thought I might have seen on an outdoor walk with my grandparents.

"These here are Queen Prima's sacred flowers, the Gardenia," Marie whistled, softly caressing a single ivory petal. "If you visit the Gardens, you may see our Majesty sitting here if you are lucky." Marie stood softly, perusing the flowers as if she was waiting for them to speak to her. But what I found much more shocking than any plant here was that a city as progressive and futurist as Lana Ilu would be ruled by a monarch, not through a democracy like millions had revolted for. I guess that was just another question of this place.

Marie began in another direction, bringing us to a set of shining purple flowers none of us had seen before.

"What are these?" the small girl, Rosie, squeaked.

"These are the flowers I mentioned before, Homilias, which will sprout dozens of thousands of years into the future, after the next ice age. And their shine is not just for beauty, but a sign of immense healing power. These Homilias have nearly magical connections to cells of all animals, putting them back on track when diseased. Nearly any modern sickness can be healed with a medicine from its petals."

I noticed Lucas's eyes glimmer at the fact, and his hand quickly shot into the air. "No person is sick in Lana Ilu?" he asked.

Marie shook her head. "Unfortunately, like any place, with new cures come new problems that we are yet to solve. Diseases and deformities come about all the time, but we are working hard to find a solution."

"But cancer...? Lucas inquired, his hands nearly reaching out.

"Most forms that exist today, yes, Homilias are the fix."

Lucas bit away a smile, but this was easily the happiest I had seen him. I wanted to ask him about this later.

Marie took a seat on a nearby bench and pulled out a thick metallic folder. "I feel now is the best time of any to explain to you all why Maddox here and I have brought you all to the Royal Gardens," Marie breathed, letting us curl onto our toes in anticipation. "Although the results did arrive sooner than I had expected, all of your assignments relating to your energies are in! I'll announce them in the order you woke up, so Rosie, could you come here please?"

Rosie, clad in a corduroy dress, hopped over to the bench where she sat next to Marie. My heart was racing both for the young girl and mostly, myself. "Now Rosie, dear, nobody here knows your rightful year yet. Not me, not Maddox, not a single person except the scientists who deduced it. Are you excited?"

Rosie nearly fell off the bench. "So much! I thought about it all day!"

Marie carefully slid a sheet of paper out of the envelope, holding it up to her face and nodding. "Well no need to wonder anymore. Rosie Macgregor, you are from the year 1590, location—southern Italy!"

Rosie shrugged her shoulders, but clapped her hands. "I don't know anything about that time, but cool!" She then scampered over to the back of the group, quickly opening her multi to deduce anything she could about southern Italy in 1590 as possible. I gave her a little high-five, as well.

"That's fantastic!" I told Rosie.

"Thanks, Keira! I can't wait for you!"

"Siguiente, Lucas, ven por favor," Marie called out in Spanish. Lucas sprinted from my side, eager to hear his assignment.

"Lucas, tu año es 2418, el futuro, en el norte de Canadá."

Lucas nodded and clasped his hands together tightly. He had a grin tugging at the side of his mouth, yet his eyes were focused everywhere, like he was trying to find a sign of 2418 in Northern Canada wherever he could look. He ambled over to me, clenching his pockets.

"That's cool! You're from the future!" I proclaimed.

Lucas cocked his eyebrows. "Yeah, it is! I don't know what happens in uh... dos mil... two thou... you know, year."

Next up was Aaron Williams, who discovered he was from the year 207 and Mark, from 5992. Finally, it was my turn. Shakily, I sauntered over to Marie. Despite the fact that everyone else looked pretty content with their eras, overjoyed in fact for learning their true identities, I was scared. This was one of the most, if the not *the* most, important moments of my life, and I was just sitting there waiting for it to happen.

When Marie slid the last sheet out of the envelope, I noticed her hands begin to tremble. She shook her head slightly, but kept her eyes glued to the paper. Marie waved her arm towards Maddox, who quickly rushed over to get a read. Then he too fell into shock, covering his mouth.

"Keira Sun," Marie quivered, "you are the only one of your kind here." She stopped, letting the entire folder collapse onto the ground. "You are from 200,000 years into the future, one of the last people on Earth."

CHAPTER 6

BACK AT THE IDUM-BORN RELATIONS Department, the strangest thing was not discovering my time period (though I admit, it was pretty jarring) but the tension and anxiety vibrating off of both Marie and Maddox. Neither of them would make direct eye contact with me, yet I could feel them staring every time I turned my back. Marie and Maddox were quick to talk with the rest of the group, congratulating them on truly becoming citizens of Lana Ilu, but I did not receive so much as a nod. To be honest, I finally realized just how close this place still was to Ithaca, leaving me an outsider in the place that was supposed to be my home.

The worst part was that I felt guilty about when I was from. Last people on Earth? 200,000 years into the future? That seemed amazing to me. Every possible reason I never fit in now made sense. There were endless

possibilities for things I could learn, and though I was
sad to be the only one, there had to be some people close
to me. I knew that they could become my closest friends
in the world. I wanted to run home to Willow and tell
her every detail about my energy's time and create stories about the adventures I would have then. And oh,
the questions! What are people going to be like 200,000
years from now? How do humans even survive until then?
Did global warming ever get fixed for them or are they
just living in fire? Do all the continents fuse together
again like in Pangea? But Marie and Maddox stole those
chances of wonder for me. They made me look like some
unwanted villain.

The first floor of the building was just as busy, crowded
by people in business clothing from many eras, just as the
second floor had been. One by one, each member of our
group was brought over to a desk for housing assignments,
finding out the places we would live until adulthood.
Pretty important. Of course, like before, Marie and Maddox
acknowledged me last. When Marie did tap my shoulder
to alert me that it was finally my turn, I jumped at the
contact. From how mortified she looked before, I was surprised she had the nerve to touch me.

At the desk, Marie looked into the eyes of the elderly
man in charge solemnly. "Mr. Roberts, Keira Sun is from
the year 204,020, so she will have to be in the Final Era
Complex. What apartment is her assignment, please?"
Marie inquired, shaking softly.

The man, *Mr. Roberts* of all titles, bit his lip and
adjusted his glasses at hearing my time. As he typed the
year into his programming, I noticed he was half-holding
his breath. Why was he just as edgy?

"Hello, Ms. Sun," Mr. Roberts mumbled. "You will be living with those from the 150,000 to 200,000 Sector, not your own from the 200,000 and up because we have no adult occupants to supervise you there. Well, actually, there is no sector for your era because of the rarity. I believe you understand. The years are longer in the sector you will live in just because the population is so much smaller for that area. Apartment number three, on Katali Road. I will call your supervisor, Omar Handal, right now, to alert him of your induction. Also, can you please give me your palm for a scan?" I hesitantly put my hand forward as he used a beam to draw light on the lines of my palm. "That will be used for your key. I... I hope you enjoy your new home."

"Thank you, I'm very excited," I told him gently, even though I knew I was faking most of what I said. People were so terrified of me that they didn't even *have* the correct place for me? What, was it destroyed?

Mr. Roberts nodded and then quickly went back to his work.

"Come on, Keira. I'm going to be taking you to your apartment, and please be quick because we have a levitator to catch. We'll have the rest of your clothing shipped to you right away," Marie said, leading me out of the floor.

"Have you been to the sector I will be living in?" I asked, hoping for a lighter conversation.

Marie forced a smile. "Of course, I've been everywhere in the city. My husband loves the mineral restaurant there."

I wanted to ask about what the heck a *mineral restaurant* was or why anybody would want to eat there, yet with everything in Lana Ilu, I figured that was pretty low on the strange scale. We finally got back outside where a contraption straight out of an 80's futuristic alien movie hovered, yes, *hovered*. Just like in comic book drawings, the flying saucer had a glass hood and several seats inside. But it was shaped in something closer to a sphere, with a defined floor cutting through the center. The metal part of the machine was like none I had ever seen, a white light that somehow shimmered and dulled at the same time.

"So that's a levitator," I gasped.

Marie nodded at me and then walked over to scan what looked like some post-modern cell phone against the side of the levitator. The hood propped open to clarify to me that there was no driver, yet Marie continued moving in like no problem. She took a seat in front and beckoned for me to sit next to her.

"Why isn't there a driver?" I queried. "Is this yours?"

"Oh no, I wish I had my own levitator. This is rented by the Idum-Born Relations Department for these trips. And they're automated, so once you put in the location, no driver is needed," said Marie matter-of-factly. With that, she leaned forward and typed into the screen *150,000 to 200,000 Sector, Katali Road*. Almost immediately, the levitator began buzzing and rose dozens of feet above the ground. As if it were an amusement park ride, the levitator whisked through the air, fast enough that the outside became a blur. But inside, it was calm and steady, not a single shake for the entire ride. Now *that* was a technological innovation.

Marie fixed her hair and peaked into the mirror of the levitator. "We're here, Keira. I'll lead you there and then if you need me anymore, you'll need to stop by the department."

We left the levitator and even though I thought I

couldn't be more shocked by Lana Ilu, I was finally close to passing out. A line of small apartments, each slightly separated from the next, hovered floors above the ground. They resembled bubbles, reflective glass spheres of the ocean. Levitators zipped through the streets, and pedestrians skipped to similar glass shops. To my right was a glistening street sign, shimmering like the water on a summer day. It read a name I had heard earlier today, *Katali Road*. Even though I knew this sector was a little off for me, there was something I knew for sure. This was my road, much more than Eastview Lane ever was.

"Mr. Handal notified me that he is waiting at the front door of his home. Once you're with him, he will handle everything from here on out," Marie said.

We continued walking and I tried not to let my eyes bug out of my head. One of these, Number 3, the one I was looking for, would be all mine for years here! Independence was never something I was awarded in my place back in Ithaca, and now, I would experience it from the second I woke up.

After a few more steps, we came up to a large rounded glass house, figured like a wide *S*. I didn't fully understand how anyone was able to live in there and not bump into a wall at every turn, but there was probably some Mary Poppins' kind of technology going on in there. Leaning against the front door was a man who looked like he was about sixty, with light grey hair and a dark beard. I expected him to be in some sort of crazy merman costume considering the layout of the street, but he was dressed in business clothing similar to what I had seen my own father wearing. The man put out a hand to me as I came closer, and I reached to shake it.

"Keira, I'm Mr. Handal, the supervisor of the neighborhood. We are so excited to have you as an addition to our little family here."

"Hi!" I exclaimed, not able to quiet myself. "I'm so happy to be here."

"That's terrific, I can escort you to your apartment now if you would like."

I nodded, probably a little too enthusiastically. Quickly, I turned back to Marie, who waved goodbye as she headed into the levitator. "Yes, I would love that so much!"

As we trekked down the block again, Mr. Handal took interest in talking to me. "Where I was standing is my family's home, where my wife and I live. We hold dinners there for you kids all the time, so you're always welcome."

"Kids?" I poked, interested by its plurality.

"Oh yes, we have two other minors living in apartments here right now. Their names are Theo Chevalier and Holly Hawkridge, and they're just a bit older than you—they are both 16. I'll message them so they know you're here and then they can greet you at your apartment later. They're wonderful people, and sometimes... I do feel like a father to them," Mr. Handal said warmly.

I grinned. "They sound great. Do they live in the apartments next to me?"

Mr. Handal laughed, nodding his head. "Yes, Holly is in Apartment 2 and Theo in Apartment 1. Hopefully you'll be a bit more responsible than they are about getting back to your own place every day. They're inseparable. Now, even though we do provide you with more independence here in Lana Ilu than you would receive back at home, we do need to supervise you a bit. There is a curfew each night, 9:30 on school nights and 11:00 on weekends. We have cars or levitators each morning at 8:00 to go to school, and if you're late, getting there is your responsibility. Breakfast is also held at our house every week morning at 7:30 sharp, and weekends you can stop by whenever or handle your own food. Got that?"

"That sounds amazing, Mr. Handal. Thank you so much for welcoming me into your home!" I exclaimed, trying to remember every manner rulebook from pre-school.

"Of course, Keira. I began volunteering as supervisor three years ago after my younger child, my daughter, went to college. With my son all grown up and my daughter out at university in the Idum-world, my wife Farida and I were really suffering from empty-nest syndrome. Trust me, having you kids around is our pleasure."

Even though what he said was incredibly kind, I mainly held onto the surprising fact about his daughter. "Your daughter's in the Idum-world? Is there not a college in Lana Ilu?"

"Oh no, we definitely have one, it is perhaps the best in the world. But Malak, always the curious one, wanted to have some experiences outside and get to know a whole different people. She's studying at Stanford in California right now, which she enjoys but sometimes complains about not challenging her enough."

I couldn't help but scoff at that. I knew enough Cornell students to see that regardless of which school, classes are *always* difficult. Willow often liked to make fun of people like Mr. Handal's daughter, those who went to the hardest schools and acted like they weren't experiencing any troubles whatsoever. I remember one time when Willow came home from a study group ranting about some guy named

Michael, who kept saying that the teacher was learning more from him than he was from her. Willow said that she didn't care that he thought he was so much smarter than his classmates, learning is learning, no matter how you are taking it in.

Finally, we came up to an apartment which I realized I had passed just before. On the ground before us was a large metallic rectangle embedded in the turf of some sort of seagrass hybrid. It looked like it could fit about six people, which I verified when Mr. Handal brought me to stand on it, leaving tons of room for others.

"There's a button to move up and down to the apartment door, since these housings float exactly ten feet above ground." Mr. Handal tapped on a small red button with the sole of his shoe. Slowly, the rectangle elevated towards the apartment entrance and took a gradual stop so we could get off. The door was the same reflective glass as the rest of the sphere. It had a deceiving glimmer, like you were sure it was a window, until you squinted enough to settle that it was opaque.

Mr. Handal gestured to a square to the right of the door. "Put your palm there, Keira, so that you can enter."

As I did, I recalled the quick scan I had done back at Idum-Born Relations. I couldn't believe they had sent this information so quickly, but then again, I did come here in a flying-saucer's cousin. The door abruptly slid open and I hesitantly stepped inside, gawking at every little detail of the residence. I turned, waiting for Mr. Handal to meet me inside, yet he stayed on the rectangle.

"Please, make yourself at home... because this is your home!" he laughed. "If you have any questions, please just message or call me using your multi. I already sent you my information."

I smiled at him, my hands clasped together. "Thank you so much for bringing me here. I really am so grateful to get to be neighbors with such kind people."

Mr. Handal shook his head. "We always have the best of the best here."

A second later, the door slid shut and I was alone. But, I was alone in my home, *my home.*

I was home.

CHAPTER 7

THE FIRST THING I NOTICED ABOUT my apartment was the fact that not only was *every room* furnished, it was all stuff that I would like. I couldn't find a speck of green or yellow, but rather crisp blues and blacks. The living room had a small dark couch accessorized with striped pillows. There was a hovering table in front of it, topped with remotes for what looked like a holographic television. In the next room, the kitchen, glass cupboards lined the wall along with a flat refrigerator. Confused, I opened the door of the device and discovered the levels of food (which were filled) caved into the wall. Attached to the kitchen was a small bathroom, holding a crystal sink, toilet and strange shower with neon tiles and no nozzle for water, which honestly made me nervous. Finally, and probably the most important, was my bedroom. A queen-sized bed topped with fluffed silver sheets took the center of the room, paired with a floating bean bag chair and pearly nightstand. Eager to get accustomed to my bed, I raced to the mattress and jumped on. To my surprise, the mattress shaped under me, perfectly fitting my body. I hoped this smart-sleeping technology would help with my case of insomnia.

A second later, I heard a ring at my doorbell. Knowing it was probably those people—Holly Hawkridge and Theo Chevalier—Mr. Handal had told me about, I raced to the front door and saw that I had to press a button to slide it open.

Before me stood a tall redheaded boy with freckles. At his side was a girl who looked to be his age, with long jet-black hair and mismatched eyes, one dark brown and another hazel. She smiled at me and reached out a hand. "Hi, I'm Holly Hawkridge and this is my friend Theo Chevalier. You must be Keira!"

I nodded, a little surprised by her maturity. She definitely seemed a lot more than "a bit older" than myself. Even Holly's clothes looked beyond sixteen years old, with a glamorous red skirt and heeled boots. I was also surprised that her parents, or I guess Mr. and Mrs. Handal, let her wear the maroon lipstick she had on.

Theo, on the other hand, looked more like a teenage boy I might see back at home. He was wearing ripped jeans and a button-down shirt, paired with what looked like purposely uncombed red locks.

The two stepped into my apartment, each looking around before again making eye contact with me. Theo put his hands into his pockets and nodded towards me. "Nice place, I like the furniture," he noted in a light French accent.

Holly rolled her eyes. "Theo, your apartment looks

almost exactly like this. But it's true, Keira. Lana Ilu *detected* your good taste."

They moved over to my couch and took a seat next to one another. I tried not to feel like a third wheel in my own house, but it was hard to ignore the fact that Theo had his arm around Holly's shoulders.

"So, where are you from?" Theo asked, actually appearing interested in the question.

"Oh, Ithaca... in New York. It's kind of boring there," I admitted.

"Oh, tell me about it. I'm from Annecy in France. You know, I used to think it was the greatest place in the world but then I got here five years ago and I could never imagine going back. There's nothing to do back there!" Theo exclaimed.

"Annecy is beautiful and Theo should be happy to be from there," Holly reasoned.

Realizing the conversation shifting between them again, I coughed to get attention. "So, Holly, what about you?"

Holly brushed a lock of ebony hair behind her ear, revealing a delicate ruby earring. "Oh, from Lana Ilu actually, born and raised. I grew up with my family in the 2400 to 2500 Sector, but after seeing what a spectacular era I was from and the fact that I'm quite independent, as Theo can verify, I asked to move to my own place last year."

"So, you've just known each other for the past year then?" I asked, confused considering how close they seemed.

"No, I met her my first week here at school. We both tried to check out the same book in the library and our friendship just sort of took off from there. Guess it was a crazy coincidence that we were from the same era. So yeah, we've been best friends for five years now," Theo reminisced. I noticed him stroke Holly's hand, which convinced me they were at least a little more than *best friends*.

Holly's pale cheeks were filled with blush before she began speaking again. "We're so happy to have someone else here, to make our little family bigger. I mean, there's people besides us three and the Handals in this Sector but no other minors without families. And even then, there's just a few other houses occupied. Down the road is Sean Rockford and his husband, Steven. They just moved here a few months ago, but Sean lived here for years before. In the other direction are the Medicis, but none of them are actually from this era, they just liked the architecture. But other than that, it's just us."

"Not that we really mind being close together here, but hey, from everyone in the Idum-world, we are the farthest in this city. I guess we're meant to be the outsiders, right?" Theo coaxed.

I realized after what he said, it was best a time of any to reveal that I was even more of an outsider than Theo and Holly imagined. Hopefully, they wouldn't freak like everyone else at the news. "You know... I should really tell you guys something about me before we talk more."

Holly leaned in and put a hand on my shoulder, something that an older sister would do. "Of course, Keira, you're one of us. Whatever you need to say, we're all ears."

I nearly choked on my words at that. "Um... well I'm, I'm not really one of you. I'm from the Final Era actually, the year 204,020. Not that far from you guys all things considered, but definitely a whole different world."

Theo's jaw dropped, but he closed it as soon as I looked his way. Holly was not nearly as calm. She sat rigid in her seat, eyes wide. Her fists clenched together, and I could tell her nails were digging into her skin. Her blush from hearing Theo's story faded into stark white. Holly's head even shook, with what seemed to be denial. "Y-y-you," she tried to mumble out.

A tear budded in my eye. Why was this happening to me, especially from a girl that welcomed me like family?

"Is there... is there something wrong?" I croaked.

Theo jutted in before Holly could speak anymore. "No, not in *any way*, Keira. It just caught us a bit by surprise and you know, *that far* can shock anyone. But don't get me wrong, you are a Gradien and pretty close to us. Don't worry for a second."

Holly nodded, wiping her eyes but not smearing a lash of mascara. "Yeah, I'm sorry. It's a really long story why I... you know." She stopped and looked at the ground for a second. "Hey Keira, we've got a lot of homework this weekend, but we'll see you at dinner tonight."

Theo hooted in agreement. "Yeah, we need you there! It's at 7:00, the Handals' house. Mrs. Handal makes the best food of anyone in Lana Ilu."

I smiled, grateful for the invite. "Won't miss it."

Even though all I really wanted to do right now was rest and maybe catch up with Lucas later, the doorbell rang once again. Begrudgingly, I rose from the couch and sauntered over to the glittering door. Cracking my knuckles before allowing it to slide open, I grumbled to myself about how I just wanted time alone. But I still remembered a little bit about manners from my childhood.

I'll admit it, deep down, I *really* wanted to see the person I found at the other side of the door even though I hated him yesterday. With those blue eyes and more importantly, cocky grin, I couldn't quite forget Alden Fischer.

"Hi," he said, lifting his brows.

I crossed my arms over my chest. "What are you doing here? And how did you know where I was living?"

"The final thing all welcomers find out about the people they bring in are their eras. Also, since you're the only Final Era living up here, the department said you would be in this sector. I got your apartment just by, you know... process of elimination," Alden directed.

"Alright," I pushed. "That answers my second question. What about the first? "

Alden looked down, like he was embarrassed to confront the topic. Considering how rude he had been to me yesterday, it didn't surprise me that he liked to ignore things.

"Keira, I... I'm here to apologize for how I acted before. Even though in Lana Ilu, welcomers all sort of decide to forget about the people they helped, just 'cause it's such an awkward first interaction, it doesn't make it right for me to do it. So, I want to reverse as much of what I said as possible by trying to be the exact opposite. You up for a tour of the city?" Alden stuttered.

I forced away a smile. "Someone else put you up to this? Your Mom, maybe?"

"No. Listen, Keira Sun, you might be surprised, but I'm kind of a good person," Alden asserted.

"Oh, I definitely saw that yesterday. And when you lied to me before about seeing me again," I said sarcastically.

Alden combed his hands through his hair. "To be fair, I just said we would see each other again, that could mean anything..."

"Are you really trying to make this *worse*?" I nearly yelled.

"You're right, you're right, I'm sorry. I was trying to

just sound nice because that's what welcomers do and I didn't actually act that way. But you do seem really cool Keira, and I just want *one* more chance." Alden was almost pleading at this point. I found it kind of funny.

But I still wasn't satisfied, he had been a jerk. I mean, this whole apology seemed out of character. "Alden, I've made friends in this sector who actually have treated me nicely and they're older, so I think I can trust them for a tour."

Just as I was about to slide the door closed, he held up his hands, stopping it.

Ugh, he's relentless.

"If you won't go on the tour for me, that's fine, I deserve that. But I brought my friend along because she thought you sounded really cool and I don't want to have wasted her time. So, you can hate me this entire day and never see me again, but can I at least give you the opportunity to become friends with someone else?" Alden offered, smiling.

I crossed my arms, considering his proposal. Making new friends was definitely important to me here, especially making friends with other girls. I couldn't turn this down.

"Fine, for whoever she is. *But,* if she ends up being the same entitled trash you are, I'm never talking to either of you again. Got it?"

Alden nodded quickly. "Yes, definitely. And trust me, she is as far from entitled trash as a person can get."

Carefully, since I had not yet used the object going down, I stepped onto the elevator to my apartment. Right away, I moved my foot to the recognizable red button and tapped on it with my shoe. The rectangle descended, moving Alden and me to ground level in less than a minute. Before us was the girl I had seen with Alden yesterday. She had honey blonde hair, dressed in leggings and a green sweatshirt.

"Hey Keira!" the girl proclaimed. "It's great to meet you."

Not knowing what to say in response, especially since I didn't even know her name, I stood there waiting for Alden to jut in. To my luck, he did just that.

"Keira, this is my friend Pandora Dailey. She's been living in Lana Ilu for the past year and a half," Alden said.

"I'm sorry, did you say her name was Panda?" I sputtered, sure I had heard Alden wrong.

The girl laughed and shook her head. "No, it's Pan-*dora*. You know, like if the cartoon character got attached to a skillet. Or you know... the Greek myth."

"Oh..." I murmured. "Well now I just feel stupid."

"Don't worry, I'm glad you said it. Now we have something to always laugh about during awkward silences. By the way, I *love* your overalls and they go with your shirt perfectly."

I laughed, grateful that she liked my outfit and didn't mock me for being confused by her name. In my defense, who calls their kid *Pandora*? But the way she flashed her sparkling green eyes at me did suggest she was the kind of person who *had* to stand out.

"So, Keira, is there anyone else you'd like to bring along? Then we can get this tour all done in one trip," Alden inquired.

I practically lit up at the suggestion. "My friend Lucas! He lives in the 2400-2500 Sector."

"What year exactly just so we can tell the quarter?" Pandora gestured.

"Um..." I began, searching in my mind. I stretched to remember the exact time, hoping to impress them. "It's 2418, I believe."

"Well, then let's head that way. I'll call us a taxi," Pandora offered.

"Oh, you use rides other than levitators?" I asked, shocked that anyone in their right mind would. Levitators were awesome!

"Yeah, sometimes I need variation. Also, we can't use a levitator without a rider with a license and anyway, taxis are cheaper..."

Soon enough, a familiar yellow cab like I had seen roaming the streets of New York City came down the road. Pandora opened the door for us, Alden filing in behind her and then me on the left. "Hey, can you get us to the 2425 Quarter please?" Pandora asked.

"Sure thing," the driver answered, allowing the cab to move forward. Though I wanted to keep with my tradition of attempting to scan every inch of Lana Ilu, I was more wrapped up in the topic of my company. I knew I would ask later how Pandora and Alden met, and more importantly, *how they became friends*, but that was something for Lucas to join in with, too. They seemed to be close, quietly chatting with each other at the moment, but not like how Theo and Holly were. Though I hated to admit it, that comforted me, because I knew I wasn't exactly over my *beautiful boy* comment about Alden back when I was welcomed.

A minute later, the taxi stopped at the gate of a magnificent concrete house with a shuttered roof. It looked somewhat like places I would see in Florida, fit for hot weather. It had a Spanish style, coated in careful mosaics and oil paints. The mansion appeared to go on for miles, but that was likely just an illusion caused by Lana Ilu's technology. Pandora paid and let us get out of the cab.

The neighborhood was bustling with people of all different backgrounds and wardrobes, suggesting a variety of eras. Unlike my own, this sector obviously had a booming population.

"Do you know how many people live here?" I asked Alden.

He scratched his chin in thought. "The whole sector? I would guess around fifteen hundred. It's a pretty large one."

"Definitely bigger than mine, both the real one and my apartment's," I answered.

Pandora, not really in on our discussion, led the way to front door of the mansion. "I think the Supervisor of Minors lives here. They should be able to tell us which place belongs to Lucas."

We followed her up the tiled pathway, passing an odd mixture of palm trees and evergreens covering the lawn. I had seen tons of places in Lana Ilu where cultures had been blended, some from opposites ends of time, yet this was the first instance of geography mixing. It was as if the winters of Canada had moved on to summer vacation in the Bahamas, all in the yard of one family.

Swinging open the front door was a short lady, definitely a couple decades younger than Mr. Handal. She had brown hair down in waves and a gown on, like she had been hosting a fancy luncheon. I noticed she had hazel eyes, each a distinct tone from the other. Holly shared the exact same heterochromia.

"Hello dear, what may I do for you?" the lady said in a breathy voice.

Pandora gestured for me to come forward, even pulling my arm when I looked hesitant. Surprised, I jumped at her touch up to the door of the very rich looking lady. She looked down towards me, too much, considering I stood only an inch below her.

"Um, may I find out the address of Lucas Acosta? He just moved into the quarter earlier today," I blurted.

"Oh, he's our newcomer! Such a sweet boy. Please just wait a moment." The lady turned from the door and looked around in her expensively decorated home. "Bernadette, supervisor business!"

Within a second, a very shaken-up young woman raced to the front door. Her hair was a mess of fly-aways and her dress was wrinkled, giving her a stark contrast to the lady who opened the door. I noticed a pair of glasses shaking upon Bernadette's nose. She hastily pushed the glasses back up to her eyes. The woman from before pulled Bernadette aside and whispered something in her ear, leading the younger lady to nod impatiently. Bernadette stepped up to the door and the other quickly returned to her party.

"Lucas Acosta, was it?" she inquired, opening up a holographic chart.

"Yes."

"Alright, he is in Building A, apartment 3D. You will find it just two blocks down and I will alert him of your visit," Bernadette instructed. "Oh, and before the three of you go on your way, could you please just do some quick eye scans? They will only take a second."

The three of us agreed, each stepping closer to the entrance. Bernadette pulled a pen-like object from behind her ear and flicked on a mellow red light. In a flash, she wiped it past our eyes and looked at a data point that popped up on her screen. She grinned and told us we were good for passing on. But just as Pandora, Alden, and I were beginning to leave, my curiosity got the best of me. I turned back to Bernadette and tried my best to make eye contact with the shakily nervous woman.

"Um, what were those scans for? Just wondering..." I mumbled.

Bernadette stood sharply, her back straight. "Oh... um... just Gradien verification. We just like to assure that everyone in this city is supposed to be in this city."

I tried to nod, but I couldn't brush off how grossly *supremacist* sounding that statement was. And even beyond that, the reason sure was questionable.

I returned back to Alden and Pandora who were, to my surprise, actually waiting for me. They stood next to each other, but weren't talking and were rather looking to start conversation once I could be included. Trust me, that *never* happened, *even once*, when I was in Ithaca. As soon as I was between them, Pandora nudged my shoulder and raised her eyebrows, facing back at the estate.

"Why the heck do they need 'Gradien verification?' I haven't seen a single other place in this city that does that," I imposed, rubbing the back of my neck.

Pandora grunted. "Because that family is nuts."

Alden laughed. "That's for sure. And don't get me started on their ego. They just took up the supervisor job to appear to be good citizens and be respected by the community and all, but they don't do a thing for that job. They pay that lady Bernadette and a whole crew of other people to handle every little responsibility for them, and even though they do nothing to hide their laziness, the family still gets credit. That mansion isn't the Palace of Time, but they've always tried to make it one," he grumbled.

I tried to catch on to what he said, but what I mostly heard was the thick resentment in his voice. Alden spoke like he hated that family with all his being, like he wanted them to fail and lose all their status. I wondered where that came from.

After we continued along the road, a six-story building constructed from delicately carved clay appeared to us. Similar to the yard of the mansion, plants from cold and warm climates peppered the grounds, pansies sprouting next to hibiscus. Sitting on the front steps was Lucas, who looked like he ran down from his apartment just a moment ago. At seeing us, he ran towards me and immediately jumped into conversation.

"Keira, who?" he asked, pointing to the two other members of our group.

"Their names are Pandora Dailey and Alden Fischer. Pandora has been here about a year and Alden was born in Lana Ilu. On that note, Pandora and Alden, meet Lucas Acosta."

The three of them greeted each other, becoming acquainted, just as I had done less than an hour ago with Pandora. It was quite strange, being in the same position Alden had just been in. A girl who just got to this city doing the job of someone else who had always lived here.

"Where are we going?" Lucas asked. I noticed him trying to cover up his accent, which he had not attempted for a second with me. Was he more nervous around Pandora and Alden because they had lived in Lana Ilu longer? Was he trying to impress them?

"The whole city!" Alden answered. "Pandora and I offered to show you two around."

"And I suggest we start with lunch. I know you guys went to *Dolce Dente del Tempo*, so let's pick somewhere else." Pandora clicked her tongue in thought. "Alden, are you up for tacos?"

He grinned and put a hand on Pandora's shoulder. "When am I not? Lucas and Keira, that sound good?"

We both nodded and followed Pandora out of the Sector. We took a sharp turn into the adjourning quarter, which led us to a side road. Paved with gravel and barred off with metal stakes, it looked like the closed down space your parents warned you to stay far away from. But Pandora ducked onto the ground, almost like she was reading a hidden message and hopped back up.

"Yep, this is the passage to the Modern Era Sector. File behind!" she commanded.

Though I kept quiet about my fears of the hidden road, Lucas definitely did not. He stood behind me, rigid and waiting for some kind of verification from Pandora or Alden. "Uh..." Lucas managed to croak out.

"Is this safe?" Alden said, guessing Lucas's question. "Sort of, according to Pandora. But don't worry, we've taken it many times."

Lucas still looked confused, definitely from the quick way Alden was speaking in his second language, but seemed a bit more comfortable with the situation. We all ducked under the bars, which gave me a thrill of rebellion I had never had before. I had no idea what this road was about, but I could tell we were definitely not supposed to be using it as a bee line. After crawling through the rubble of a path, a bright sun ray became visible again. We brushed off the dirt that had caught on our clothes and looked around. To my surprise, this sector closely resembled a thousand neighborhoods I had walked through back in trips to New York City. There were graffitied walls, draped shops, bike stands leaning on sidewalks, and the ever-popular food trucks. A block away was parked a truck bearing a sign saying *Antonio's Tacos*. A line of a dozen people was cued at the window.

"So, they're pretty popular," I said, still a little unsure of how to carry a conversation with everyone.

"Yeah, 'cause nobody makes tacos like Antonio. I mean, I'm from California and even I have to give him the top prize. Is it by a *very* thin margin? Yes. But still, delicious tacos should never go unappreciated," Pandora explained. After her little reminiscing, we joined the lengthy taco line. But the people moved quickly, exiting the line every thirty seconds with their meals. Back in Ithaca, seeing a line like this could mean standing for over twenty minutes, but here, we got our food in less than five. I have to say, I'm *really* starting to like these Lana Ilu methods.

On the line, I got to the question I had been meaning to ask Pandora and Alden about their friendship. "So, how'd you two meet?"

"Just were assigned to sit together in school. It's not that exciting but it's good to be friends," Alden answer.

I grinned. "Hey, you're time travelers. I still think it's exciting."

Once we located a picnic table to have lunch at, the four of us immediately began to talk.

"So, Lucas and Keira, we all know your eras. Do you know ours?" Pandora asked, taking a bite from a tortilla.

"I mean, I know Alden's from the American Revolution but *you* are a mystery," I charmed.

Pandora smirked. "2900 BC, and location being Ancient Egypt."

"But you don't dress like that era at all," I argued.

"Well, I'm not Egyptian at all. Just because it is where

my year is, it's not my culture. I mean, is Alden dressed like he's ready to go kill some Redcoats?" Pandora snarked.

I leaned back from the table, defeated. But I still couldn't wait to speak with them more. "So, I need to ask you guys—well, Pandora and Alden—something." I turned to Lucas. "Sorry, not trying to exclude you."

Lucas pointed to his mouth filled with beef and cheese. "No problema," he muffled out.

I grinned at him and then moved to clear my throat. I prayed that these two would give me a better answer than Theo and Holly bothered to supply. "I was just... I was... ugh. Why does everyone get so scared when they hear what my true year is? Why is it any different than any other era?"

Alden and Pandora simultaneously looked down, peeking at each other before facing me again. "It's a long, *long* story, with a really complicated history," Alden muttered.

I crossed my arms. "We're not in a rush. *Spill*," I commanded. I realized I was speaking confidently, something I had never done before. Something I had never been *allowed* to do before.

Alden wiped some sauce from the corner of his mouth and coughed, trying to delay the story. "About forty years ago, there was this guy named Waldron Hawkridge."

Hawkridge, I thought to myself. *Like Holly.*

"He was from a wealthy family, one of the richest in Lana Ilu actually. In fact, you've already met the wife, Lorelei, of his nephew, Reginald Hawkridge. Lorelei opened the door for you at Lucas's sector's mansion. Also, you live right by Holly who as you have probably figured out is also part of the lineage. But back onto the main plot line—Waldron. A while back, he worked as a mechanic at the Palace of Time, which was strange from the beginning because his family was worth billions and billions of dollars, so why did he have such a small job? But anyway, he started preaching some insane ideas about wanting to take over the Idum-world right after he started working there. He literally argued that with our advanced technology and greater minds, despite Gradiens making up a tiny fraction of Idums, we could *rule and command* their population. Yeah, he was such a Gradien supremacist that he only referred to himself as a Suprem, which is basically the most grossly elitist thing you can say. The rest of the Hawkridges disowned him after that and cut him off from all of their money. To add on to Waldron's problems, he was fired from the Palace of Time and put on temporary government supervision."

Alden took a deep breath and shook, like he was recalling a nightmare. "Then he got even worse. He said that while working at the Palace he overheard that the Queen, our beloved Queen Prima Imamu, had a relationship with an Idum and gave birth to an Idum child before marrying her Gradien husband, which by the way, was 100% condemned for the Royal Family. Now, investigations went on and the Queen admitted it was true. Most of Lana Ilu forgave her because she was and still is a great Queen who has dedicated everything to this city, and we get that people make mistakes. But Waldron and a group of lunatics he gathered were not part of that. Right after everything was found out to be true, he planted a bomb at the Palace. Luckily, it was found and nobody got hurt, but before going to jail, he declared he was doing it to 'provide the best city in the world with a more capable ruler.'"

Alden paused again. "He wanted himself on the throne, but he was the worst person Lana Ilu has ever known."

"Dead now?" Lucas asked, suddenly intrigued in the story.

Alden laughed and pushed up the sleeves of his shirt. "Dead to the city. But unfortunately, no, he's just in jail. On the bright side, our prison makes Alcatraz look like a kiddie park. He's getting what he deserves," Alden grumbled.

"But what does this have to do with me?" I asked, grinding my teeth.

Pandora jutted in. "Keira, you know how everyone told you that you are the *only* one in Lana Ilu of your era?"

I nodded, scared for what she would add.

"That's a lie. You are just the only one besides Waldron Hawkridge."

CHAPTER 8

DROPPING MY FOOD WAS NOT OVER-dramatic.

"What?" I stuttered, spilling over my own words. "Why do people even care about me? What did I do?"

"Nothing, of course!" Alden exclaimed. "Just, it's what you could do..."

"Oh, not you too! What exactly is it that I 'could do?'" I screamed. Heads turned from the nearby tables, giving us attention we did not ask for.

"No, Keira, I'm not one of those people scared of you. I *promise*. It's just, every city has its superstitions and when you are the first one of this era in over sixty years, it is hard to ignore that you may not just be a coincidence. I mean, maybe you could be a sign of his escape and you're here to protect us. We don't know, and it could be nothing," Alden said.

"Is there a prophecy or something?" I sneered.

Alden shook his head. "No, but there are a million people terrified of the exact same thing and that can be a whole lot stronger than any word of God."

Hearing that only made me feel worse. My whole life I knew I was different, I never fit in with anybody, so that wasn't a difficult conclusion. Finding out that I was from some alternate-dimensional city actually made sense in a way, like an explanation for why I was always made to be the outsider. Being of the farthest time just seemed to go with the package. But I didn't ask for any of this 'prophet-stuff' that was being pushed on to me now. I'm the fourteen-year-old daughter of divorced college professors from Ithaca who would have probably failed her next math test and loves salt-and-vinegar potato chips more than anything else in life. That doesn't exactly sound like the recipe for a hero.

Pandora scanned my face and slowly made contact with my crazed eyes. "Keira, it's all just superstition. Alden's just got a lot of bias against the Hawkridges and has some paranoia about them, too."

"I do not!" Alden protested.

Pandora rolled her eyes at him. "What, are you going to deny that your family has a total Romeo-and-Juliet situation with the Hawkridges? You know, minus the romance?"

"Why, uh... Romeo and Juliet?" Lucas asked. I was quickly realizing this boy could channel all my confusion for me.

"Don't." Alden began to urge before Pandora cut him off.

"Alden hates the Hawkridges and all their billions so

much because his family, the Fischers, is just as rich and powerful as them." Pandora shoved his shoulder. "And our boy here is very sensitive about whatever kind of competition he is involved in."

"Pandora, you're being unfair!" Alden fought.

"Your sister's name *is* Juliet, in my defense."

While Lucas was laughing at their debate, I had to hold my breath for a second. I was sitting in the presence of a kid from one of the richest families in the world. I mean, Alden had the vibe to him, but part of me was still not ready to accept it. I don't know why it shocked me, as it seemed perfectly natural for Holly. But I felt like Alden was becoming my friend, and the two of us had something in common that nearly all of the world didn't. I could relate to Lucas, but not even time travel could put me in Alden's shoes.

"Next?" Lucas pushed, breaking the tension.

Alden nodded, obviously eager to escape any talk about his family's social status. "The Colosseum is definitely an amazing place. There's actually a dance competition going on there right now which we might be able to get some late entry tickets to." Alden ducked his head. "And I'll pay for everyone."

I wanted to refuse and offer to get my own ticket, like I had seen my parents do whenever they went out with others, but after learning exactly *how* much money this guy had in his pocket, I knew he was being more responsible than considerate. Suddenly, I felt the urge to ask more about Alden's family before we moved on. I had never gotten to know a billionaire this well before (or well at all because he was the first I ever met).

"I can't help but be curious, Alden. What does your family do?" I inquired.

Alden's shoulders fell. "Generations after generations of international, interdimensional, interannual business masterminds. And consistently knowing how to get a high-ranking job in the Palace of Time. Keira, no offense, but can we leave this topic?"

I was silent for a moment, still a bit dazed from all these realizations, but then I apologized. Following the agreement, our group cleaned up the table and started heading for the famous Lana Ilu Colosseum in a taxi.

THE LANA ILU Colosseum looked exactly like what I had seen of Rome in photographs, that is, if they were taken two thousand years ago. Dusty limestone caved into itself, forming uniform blocks and stately arches. Lucas and I stood there together in awe, our eyes wide. Both of us shoved each other's shoulders as we noticed each new thing, like the crowd of thousands or the fact that the top seating went beyond our easy view. Meanwhile, Pandora and Alden were busy arguing with a ticket vendor about what seats were available. To be honest, I felt a little sorry for them, especially Alden. I would never want to reach a point in Lana Ilu where even the most impossible of accomplishments failed to astound me.

Pandora and Alden came running back, saying that they had found us seats but the next round of performances was starting soon. We rushed inside and sat down in the middle of the Colosseum upon perfect marble. For the most part, it looked pretty fitting, with the ground covered in dirt, not turf, and without any hotdog stands.

Still, there were about four different t-shirt cannons. Some things are just more important than historical accuracy.

A couple of groups performed, the first dressed in 1800's American clothing and the second in patterned skirts of Egyptian origin. I thought their skills were incredible but from their scores, the judges definitely believed otherwise.

Soon, a new group stepped forward, larger with six members. Each was dressed for a different era and country, one wearing a 1920's flapper gown, another in a metallic edged jumpsuit, a third in 90's baggy jeans, the fourth painted in rows of numbers, the next clad in a medieval gown and finally, the sixth in a ballerina's tutu made completely of stones. The final member, Ms. Rocky, walked to the center of the arena and shouted: "may our Queen be immortal" to the stands. Pandora and Alden, along with thousands of others in the stadium, clapped heavily and many stood up and recited the exact words. But I did notice a few lingering silent ones, just still.

When Pandora sat back down, I poked her shoulder to turn to me.

"Yeah," she said, still focused on the dance group.

"What do they mean, you know... by *immortal*?"

"Well, obviously they don't mean it literally. We have had countless scientific achievements here, but avoiding death is not one. Basically, since we're time travelers and can go to anytime we want, it's our job to spread some sort of legacy of Queen Prima everywhere. Having your name always be known is basically the same as being immortal."

I nodded, a little perplexed, but when would I not be? Also, I began wondering if I would ever see this worshipped Queen Prima. Did the people of Lana Ilu get to meet her?

I turned my attention back to the dance group which now had a background reading *The City's Dance: danced by* ∞. Yes, their name was the infinity symbol. It seemed fitting for the costumes.

A humming sound began, a strange whisper of music. I could not trace it to any time I knew of or place for that matter, but it did not stop. The humming did not change to a piano or techno scream, but just continued purring. But nobody else in the audience looked confused. Instead, they bobbed their heads, like this soft monotonous cry was the catchiest song they knew. Finally, the dancers began to move. To my surprise, the woman in a tutu began to do some robotic kind of dance, shifting her body without a smooth step. Then the jumpsuit moved onto his toes and began to twirl, like he was in Swan Lake or something. And just like them, the remaining members continued to dance in any way possible that conflicted with their costumes. The medieval girl began to break dance while Mr. Baggy Jeans began slow dancing with an invisible partner. The 1920's girl jumped and flapped around in some movement I could not begin to understand, while the coded man swayed his hips to a waltz.

Every dance was unique. There was no music to back any of the members, just the humming that still sang in my ears. At first, they looked like a group of friends at a school talent show that all of them had purposely not prepared for. Then I noticed Alden nodding along with the dance, obviously impressed with the performance. I wanted to join in with him, looking proud to be a member of this city of whatever, so I tried to look closer. Then,

I noticed a very important detail I had been ignoring. Their feet, at one time the right, then the left, would hit the ground in perfect unison. In fact, the humming even changed pitch for each stomp, ever so slightly. This dance was not a mess, it was the most precisely choreographed yet. It was amazing.

The humming slowly quieted as the dancers halted, earning a round of applause even greater than their first. The judges gave all tens, a perfect score. More groups came and went and the judges gave their critiques and their scores. They changed numbers and boiled down to the smallest details, like I had seen in TV shows. Then, the top groups came to the arena, with ∞ unsurprisingly among them. After a few minutes of anticipation, the host walked up to the groups and announced the winner. It was ∞, to which the audience cheered. I clapped with everyone else, Lucas joining in with me.

Soon enough, the crowd filtered out and the four of us went with them. The way we left reminded me of the Yankee games I had gone to, the ones where they had won. Nearly everyone was grinning and laughing, glad about who the winner was. But just like after the pledge had been announced by ∞, a handful of attendees were silent or even grimaced. I guess not everyone truly wanted the Queen to be "immortal."

"So, we have that competition once a year and people train until March for auditions. The winner gets to perform in Las Vegas, yeah in the Idum-world, until next year's contest," Alden informed me.

"And that infinity team won last year," Pandora added.

"And the year before."

"So, very popular?" Lucas asked, crossing his arms.

"The city's favorite. Their lead dancer, the girl in the rock tutu's name is Beni Estrella, and she's one of Lana Ilu's sweethearts. Behind our Princess, of course," Alden assured.

"Princess?" I asked. "Is she the Queen's daughter?"

"Granddaughter, actually. Queen Prima has a son, Oladayo, but he's kind of nerdy and in his 40's, so not exactly a heartthrob type. Prince Oladayo and his wife, Princess Bahati, have twins who are a year older than us, the Prince and Princess, and they're the ones everybody cares about. There's Prince Trevor and Princess Avarielle Imamu. They're both incredibly famous and well-liked in Lana Ilu, but Avarielle definitely takes the prize, since she's older and will get the throne. Take the most famous girl in the Idum-world, and you have Avarielle. I mean, stores here will give her anything to be a model for them, because if she supports a brand, basically everyone supports a brand. And she's only 15!" After explaining all this, Pandora turned slowly to Alden. "And Alden knows Avarielle pretty well, doesn't he?"

Alden blushed. "Pandora!"

"You can't deny it!" she jeered.

Alden's face stayed red. Very, *very* red. "I mean, I guess..."

I so badly wanted to ask about his connection to Avarielle, the freaking Princess of this city, but I realized I had already interrogated him enough. I knew that if I kept being so invasive, my chance of being friends with him (and Pandora for that matter) were going down the drain. Nobody likes someone who can't mind their business and if this friendship worked out, I would learn more about Princess Avarielle Imamu anyway.

"So, what next?" Pandora asked.

"How about the Alloys?" Alden suggested.

"Ugh, I hate the Alloys," Pandora complained. "Oh wait, I know! Holographic Habitat is honestly the coolest place here. I know exactly how to get there."

CHAPTER 9

L ET ME TELL YOU, PANDORA WAS absolutely correct about Holographic Habitat. It looked like some sort of post-modern techno playground for every age, not just a toddler on monkey bars. In the area stood rock-climbing walls, spiral slides that went ten stories high, and swings that hung from bars suspended in thin air. But the most mind-boggling parts were the massive illusions that decorated every play area. The rock wall gave off the appearance of dripping lava and, incredibly, man-eating sharks. The slide looked like it was carved into Mount Everest, while the swings flew over vast cities. But it all took up less than an acre and of course, was fake. Still, it took me a million looks to settle upon the truth.

Soon enough, after exploring more of Lana Ilu's museums and floating restaurants, the sky began to darken as it even does in parallel universes.

"Hey!" I called to my new friends, who already beat Harper, Taylor and Sadie in every way possible. "I promised Theo and Holly I would be back for dinner on my first night. But really, this day was definitely one of the best of my life, if not number one."

The three of them beamed and Lucas pointed to himself in agreement. Pandora gave me a hug goodbye, her embrace warm like a friend's should be.

SEEING THAT IT was still a few minutes before 7:00, I decided to see if I could walk with Theo and Holly to dinner. I headed to Theo's apartment, #1 on Katali Road, and raised up the same way I had done for mine. Within a minute, that red hair that I had only just gotten to know confronted me again. Behind him, I noticed Holly reclining on the couch. She wasn't watching TV or fixing her hair, but was perusing what looked to be a scrapbook. It wasn't glimmering with 3D magic, but instead was glued together with photographs and frilly paper, like an Idum-world collection. She was smiling more than I had ever seen anyone smile.

They're inseparable, Mr. Handal had said.

"Keira, we were just about to head over!" Theo exclaimed. "You had a good day?"

"The best!" I answered. He was grinning at me with the same brightness Holly held.

"I know, the first whole day in Lana Ilu always is. You'll have to tell us all about it over dinner. I can't wait to hear!" Theo turned around towards Holly. "Holls, you ready?"

She stood up, sweeping her black hair over her shoulder. She walked over to Theo and placed a hand on his shoulder. "Keira, you'll have to give me *all* the details of your day. I never got a first day here, and it's been so long since Theo had his as a little eleven-year-old." Holly clicked her tongue and laughed. "So, I'll just have to live through you."

I nodded, but couldn't help looking at her differently. If it weren't for her family history, I would be focused on the immense amount of money and the mansion this girl just chose to leave, but there was so much more. Waldron, his evils, his hatred, his *era*. No wonder she looked at me with more fear than others. It was in her blood where everything went wrong.

I shook the idea out of my head and smiled back at her. We left the apartment and began our short walk. Theo threw his arm around my shoulder and ruffled my hair, a brotherly move of sorts that honestly surprised me. Holly squeezed my arm to add to the support.

"Don't you just love it here?" Theo charmed, hugging my shoulders again. "It is really the best place in the world."

"I'm still getting to know it, but of course."

Holly scratched at her polished nails. "Take it from somebody who was born here, you will never stop loving it. Oh, and I have to ask, who did you spend your day with?"

"This boy Lucas," I started. "I met him right at the Idum Inductees building so he was sort of my first real friend here. Also, this girl Pandora and another boy named Alden."

Holly tilted her head at me. "Alden as in *Alden Fischer*?"

I was reminded of Alden's reaction to Holly's family. He detested every little thing about the Hawkridges, from their history to their entitlement. I could see now from Holly's expression that the hatred was reciprocated.

"I know him and his whole family quite well," Holly added. "His sister Juliet and I once did a school project together, we're the same age. Alden's got an older brother named Orville too, and he's already eighteen." She paused once again. "Yes, I know them quite well."

Noticing the tension, Theo hurried us to the Handals' S-shaped home. After he knocked on the door, an older woman slid it open. She had a gray scarf tied around her head and wore a matching dress. I knew this was Mrs. Handal, her smile wider than anyone's I had seen that day.

"Hello!" Mrs. Handal cried. She clasped her hands together as she looked at me. "Oh, you must be the famous Keira Sun! My husband has told me all about you, including the little era thing, but that is no problem. Oh, you are just so beautiful!"

She moved to Theo and Holly. "And as for you two, I haven't seen you all day. I trust you were being perfectly responsible and not getting into any trouble, right?"

Theo grinned. "Of course, Mrs. Handal. And could we ever get into any trouble when we're under your watch?"

She scoffed. "Occasionally I doubt I still have any watch over you. I mean, you are teenagers who know this entire city very well and I get nervous. Oh, you two didn't go anywhere near the Alloys, did you?" Mrs. Handal began to panic just a bit.

"No, we would never!" Holly asserted, but I could hear sarcasm in her tone. Alden had mentioned them before, but in a way where they seemed inviting. But Pandora was disgusted by the place. Maybe rich kids here like Holly and Alden liked to escape to places their parents, or anyone who watched over them, would be angry about. *Rich kid rebellion* was famous in the Idum-world and it would only make sense to exist here, too.

We entered the Handal abode, which just had narrower rooms than most houses, and made our way to the dining room. Mr. Handal was bringing the final plates of food from the kitchen. The platters were covered with spiced green beans, roasted chicken, and delicious-looking potatoes. My Mom rarely cooked at home, and my Dad was never around at his place to put something together. Recently, Clarke had tried to make dinner for us when we were over, but the tension between her and Willow was always too high for comfort. I wasn't exactly used to such a nice, family meal.

Mr. Handal grinned widely under his dark mustache. "Keira, I'm so glad you joined us. I'm sure this will be the first of many dinners with us all together. Please take any seat you want!"

"And *eat* as much as you want, there's plenty left in the kitchen!" Mrs. Handal cheered. "I always rather you go to sleep beyond stuffed than even a little bit hungry."

Theo rubbed his stomach dramatically. "Mrs. Handal could feed this whole city in one night's cooking if she put her mind to it."

Mrs. Handal cocked her head towards Theo. "Are you implying I don't usually 'put my mind to it,' Mr. Chevalier?"

Holly gasped and made a sort of *oh no you didn't* hum. She shoved Theo's shoulder and raised her eyebrows at him, almost like a warning. Then again, she was also laughing, so I didn't see any real urgency.

Theo put his hands up, his brown eyes wide with

fear like a kid who had just yelled at his mother. "No I would—that is not what I was—I am... "

"Oh, stop it," Mrs. Handal chuckled. "I'm just messing with you, Theo. Now please, take a seat."

The five of us all sat down at the table, with the Handals each at one head. I knew not to sit between Theo and Holly, who had already plopped down next to one another. I noticed for a second that they were holding hands, and I couldn't help but smile. In middle school, every couple is a joke because it's well, *middle school*. And to be honest, the same went for those in the school above me as most high school relationships didn't last more than a few months. Still, I had to admit that I could see Theo and Holly being together for years to come. I found the chair next to Holly and sat beside her, and surprisingly she moved her focus from Theo to me.

I smiled at everybody, trying to figure out how to describe my day. I wanted to make a good image on my first night here, especially after the problems I had already had with Holly. Leaving out meeting her mother definitely seemed like a good idea. "So today, my new friends and I got tacos at Antonio's."

"Oh, I eat lunch there all the time! I work for the Idum-Gradien Connections department, and half the office is bringing in tacos every day!" Mr. Handal added.

I beamed, happy to see them so engaged by what I was talking about. "Yeah, they were amazing! And then we went to this dance competition at the Lana Ilu Colosseum where this team actually called Infinity but just with the symbol won and everyone was cheering. Then, we went to this place called Holographic Habitat. It was like the playground I had been looking for my entire childhood.

Then, there was a cool floating tapas place and a Renaissance museum." I took a breath after my rambling. "It was just all so amazing."

Mrs. Handal beamed at me, her head tilted to the side. "That makes me so happy. This is the most incredible city in the universe, it should be enjoyed."

We ate quietly for a few minutes, and I had to admit, it was the most delicious food I ever had. Everything was warm and comforting and tasted of spices that I was positive didn't even exist outside of Lana Ilu. I could have stayed at this table for years.

"So, Keira, starting at a new school in Lana Ilu is way different than anything you would do in the Idum-world. Outside, you would just join a class in the middle of the year and pray to God the past place caught you up. We don't trust that here. You will do independent classes, taught to you by a computer simulation that will read what you know and what you don't in order to help you. There's also meetings with teachers and such, but mostly you're on your own. Oh, and you still have tests! Lucky for you, you probably only have to do this for less than two months before the next school year rolls around," Theo said.

"And Lana Ilu education is better than any other in the world! You still mostly learn history in terms of present and past, but there are some future elements. I mean, the teachers are so good at language that Frenchy over here is perfectly fluent in English," Holly commented, raising her eyebrows at her apparent boyfriend.

Theo scoffed. "And Spanish, Japanese, and some Arabic. Also, I learned a lot from immersion, so give me credit for that."

Holly rolled her eyes, but couldn't hold back a grin.

All the while, I was just trying to take everything in, from the information about the new school to the fact that I was a little embarrassingly obsessed with Theo and Holly's relationship.

"So how many schools are there here?" I questioned.

"Two, one for the east side of the city and one for the west. You will go to the latter," Mr. Handal told me. "Hope to be in the same as your friends?"

"Definitely! Would you know if I told you where they lived?"

Mr. Handal laughed. "I could map out every inch of this city from memory, Keira. Of course, I can tell you."

"Well, there's the 2900 BC, 2418 and 1300's areas," I offered.

His face lit up. "Well, don't you have good luck! I bet you will see them all in your classes."

I felt myself beaming at that, a surprising sensation. Considering my experiences back at Ithaca Middle School, I wasn't used to being excited about being in classes with my friends. I guess that's because before Lana Ilu, I never really had friends. Even Theo and Holly, two years older than me and obviously more obsessed with each other than they would ever be with me, were still so much closer. At least they had made me laugh.

"So, Keira, you're probably going to see your Idum family again tomorrow," Mrs. Handal told me. "The city helps you travel back in time a bit so your family does not worry that you went missing. Are you excited?"

Part of me wanted to shake my head and scream at her *no!* I had no interest in going back so soon, especially if it meant confronting my parents, which it *would*. I had finally found a home, but I realized that meant I needed to burn some bridges with the old one.

All of a sudden, I recalled the one person I truly did want to see—Willow. What was I going to say to her? How was she going to feel when I just left for another world before her eyes? I guess it's not all that different than college. That's what I would tell myself. We were both going to be leaving, one for university and one for an alternate universe. Even the words sound the same. *No difference at all.*

We chatted for the rest of the dinner, telling hilarious stories and reminiscing over things barely anyone knew. It was warm in the Handal household. It had a warmth I had never known, not even when my parents were still married. It was a warmth I was grateful to be welcomed into.

As it neared 9:00, Holly, Theo, and I readied ourselves to go. I waved goodbye to Mr. and Mrs. Handal, thanking them for the wonderful meal. As I paced the sidewalk with the two other teens, I noticed they were definitely more absorbed in one another, but I didn't feel left out. It was nice seeing two people so happy.

When we approached Theo's apartment, I saw Holly quietly kiss Theo goodnight. After she ran back to me, I saw that her cheeks were noticeably red. She was looking down at the ground, her hair slightly covering her eyes.

"Is this a secret or... " I whispered.

Holly laughed. "Supposed to be, but everyone knows."

"Well, Theo's really nice and you seem great together," I said.

For the first time, Holly showed some affection towards me. She wrapped me in a hug and, right before leaving for her apartment, looked me straight in the eyes.

"Keira, please don't let our rough start ruin our friendship. I really can't wait to get to know you better."

I hugged her back, clenching her shoulders a bit tighter. "Me too, Holly. Me too."

CHAPTER 10

IHAD TO SAY, WAKING UP IN A BED
that moved with me as I shifted was a nice change for the mornings. I tried to be a "morning person" back in Ithaca, but life was never as nice back there. I had something more to wake up to in Lana Ilu.

I hit down on the alarm clock supplied to me, a silver disk levitating in the air. Most of the hovering objects had no reason to hover, they just did. Seeing that it was 6:30, and wanting to make it to breakfast in an hour, I went to try out my new shower. In the bathroom were three pearl white towels left for me, soap, shampoo, conditioner, and a guide on how to use what looked like such a confusing shower that hotels would be jealous.

I read through the instructions, which told me certain voice commands to activate the shower. First, I yelled "shower on" and water began to fall from its ceiling.

Smiling, I yelled again "shower off" and the water immediately stopped flowing. I kept going about that routine, *on* then *off, on* then *off.* I would have continued for the rest of the hour but the ingrained command of my Mom to "quit being reckless" stopped me on my last *on.* After saying "water hotter" a couple of times I reached in my hand to check the temperature and saw that it was perfect.

I showered using shampoo and conditioner that smelled like all the flowers from the Royal Gardens combined, and brushed my teeth with the rest of the Lana Ilu supplies. Finally, I dressed in Lana Ilu's orange tank top and shorts, feeling ready for the day. I looked one last time in the mirror before heading out in my Lana Ilu washed hair and Lana Ilu brushed teeth and Lana Ilu styled outfit.

After I walked over to the Handals' house, I was surprised to see not one of them, but Holly, open the door. Her clothes were very different than before, her crimson skirt traded in for leggings, heeled boots for sneakers, completed with a tank top. For some reason, maybe because of the rich-girl vibe or her maturity, I couldn't imagine Holly wearing anything that wasn't top fashion. But then again, no person has just one side.

"Keira, glad you're here! Mrs. Handal made pancakes," Holly said, gesturing me inside. Theo and the Handals were sitting at the dining room table, scooping up breakfast minutes before I thought the meal even started.

"Am I late?" I arose, nervous I had made a mistake.

Mrs. Handal laughed. "Of course not, darling! You are right on time! We're just a group of early risers."

I grinned at the explanation, though knew I was never going to be able to meet that lifestyle. Mornings were the worst time of any day, and no alternate universe was going to change that.

I took the same seat as last night at the table and began to fill my plate with pancakes and berries. It was all so refreshing and delicious that even the morning didn't seem *that* bad. I was still not great as my eyes still fluttered closed now and again, but the food did help.

All of a sudden, Mr. Handal yelled, "Theo son, put those notes away and eat your breakfast!"

Theo kept his hand steady on his work tablet. "I'm sorry, Mr. Handal, but I have the last science exam before the final today and I *need* a good grade after my last one."

Mr. Handal did not look satisfied. "Holly has that same test and she's spending time talking with us."

Holly went over to ruffle Theo's hair. "Yeah, because I didn't procrastinate until yesterday at 11:00 at night and then keep a poor innocent girl up asking her about biotechnology."

"I forgot what Ms. Espinoza said on that topic. You're such a freaking bully, Holly!" Theo huffed.

Holly rolled her eyes and sat back down, finishing up her own pancakes. I struck up conversation with her about the fascinating shower in my apartment. She told me that she had unlocked some "secret" commands like *pulsing light* or *scented water* which she would show me later on. I was truly ecstatic.

Just as I was settling in to breakfast, Mr. Handal piped up towards me. "Keira, I have to take Theo and Holly to school, but right when I get back, some Idum Inductees agents will be over to help you time travel for the first time. You have to go home and tell your family about who you are and where you will be living from now on. I'll see you in half-an-hour."

And with that he, along with the two teens, were out the door and off to another part of the city. I croaked a bit, wanting to hear more details about the return, but I would just have to wait.

Mrs. Handal rolled her eyes. "My husband always does that, leaving people on cliffhangers. It does get quite annoying."

I chuckled, trying to keep the mood lighthearted. I had never been great with talking. "So, Mrs. Handal, is it really cool being of this era and all?"

"It would be if I were, but I am actually not. I moved here to live with Omar, particularly because I like the remote atmosphere. I'm really only from a couple decades into the future at the moment, but I'm a Gradien nonetheless."

"Did you grow up in the sector for that time?" I asked, suddenly very interested.

Mrs. Handal nodded, now taking a seat at the table with me. "Yes, I'm an Idum-born from Egypt. I came here when I was eleven, so that's why I don't have much of a distinctive accent anymore. I still have a lot of connection to my homeland, though. You can have more than one home, you know."

I cracked my knuckles. "Maybe for you, Mrs. Handal, but I cannot see myself connecting again with Ithaca other than my sister."

She smirked. "You'll find comfort there when you least expect it, sweetheart. Now, would you mind helping me bring in the rest of the silverware? I know I could buy a robot to do that for me, but nobody can be that lazy under my roof."

"I get that, my Mom would say the same... and my Dad probably the opposite."

"Well, your mother is a wise woman and your father needs to shape up. I'm guessing your Mom runs the household?"

I bit my tongue, remembering the *little details* of my parents' relationship. "Not since I was a toddler. They've been divorced since long before I can remember."

Mrs. Handal tucked a lock of dark hair into her olive-green hijab. "I'm so sorry, Keira. It must be difficult growing up with separated parents. It is easy to give up on love when you see that for so many years."

My face heated. "Oh, Mrs. Handal, I'm *way* too young to think even a *little bit* about love."

"I guess that's true."

Mrs. Handal picked up a few serving spoons and brought them into the kitchen, before coming out with a cloth to wipe down the table.

"Keira, I never asked, but who did you see the city with yesterday?"

"Oh, um, this boy named Lucas who came to Lana Ilu the same day as me, another girl who's lived here for about a year and a half, named Pandora, and this boy Alden, he's Gradien-born."

Suddenly, Mrs. Handal turned sharply, staring at me right in my eyes. "Alden... like Alden Fischer?"

"Uh... yeah." *Gosh*, it seemed like every person in this city could tell who he was by a picture of his hair.

Mrs. Handal chuckled, shaking her head. "Well, I won't make any assumptions or anything, for all I know you could secretly hate the boy, but I think I need to make it known not to develop any crush on him. His parents would shoot it down before *you* even knew about it. I know they make pretty children, but those kids are not up for grabs by just anybody," Mrs. Handal heeded, like a warning.

"Why?" I asked. "Not that I like him or anything, I don't! I'm just curious about all the secrets of Lana Ilu that I still need to learn."

Mrs. Handal scooped up a platter. "Let's just say his parents started planning his wedding to our Princess Avarielle the day he was born. Poor boy will never have a choice in anyone if his family ever has anything to do with it."

Now I knew exactly why Alden got so embarrassed when Pandora brought up the Princess. I would be so weirded out if my parents thought about who my spouse would be when I was only fourteen.

I decided to brush off the past conversation and help Mrs. Handal clean up the remainder of the table. But after a little while, her husband finally came back through the door.

"Keira, I have company. Are you ready to get going?" Mr. Handal announced from the entrance hall.

I tensed up a bit at the alert. "Yes, sir. I will be there in a moment!" I quickly said my goodbyes to Mrs. Handal and raced to the front door where Mr. Handal stood with a woman in a simple sheath dress, fitting in exactly with the outside world.

"Hello Keira, I'm Mrs. Hammerstein and I am here to give you your first time travel lesson. I know it may seem a bit jarring, going to a whole other day in a matter of seconds, but it will become second nature in no time."

"Do we need to go anywhere?" I questioned.

"Your apartment should be just fine. There is no equipment required for Gradien time travel. All you need is your mind!" Mrs. Hammerstein answered.

"SO JUST LISTEN carefully to my instructions. As soon as you begin to put yourself in the other time, you will get a sensation similar to that of when you first came to Lana Ilu. But do not worry. It will definitely be a much calmer feeling. You will see a dim light and feel a bit of vibration, but nothing uncomfortable," Mrs. Hammerstein coaxed. "So now, in your mind, keep repeating *Ithaca, New York; May 12th, 2018; 7:00 a.m.* and then just visualize your home. Really, you must grasp the details."

"And then what?" I fretted. I had thought about cities and times constantly, but never physically moved there!

"Just visualize yourself there and let go. Your brain is a Gradien one, with energy fueled from the entire cycle of time. It will understand what you are doing if you really put yourself in the other world. That's how our energy works. Actual days on a calendar, places, they are all artificial to time itself. You have to feel the deepest of connections to make anything happen but your brain will understand," she added.

The thing was, my brain did not understand what I was doing because *I was my brain.* I couldn't sense any energy whatsoever flowing through my body. It felt closer to when the teacher tells you to find imagery in a standardized test article about the benefits of genetic engineering of bee pollination on daffodils. Sure, I could draw the legs of the bee or the petals of the flower in my mind, but where was the sound? The touch? The smell? Mrs. Hammerstein was asking me for those last three things.

"Keira, I will travel there, as well. I am going to appear at your home to speak with your mother not long after you arrive. Now, just let go and repeat the place and time. Finally, simply close your eyes and put yourself wherever in your home you please. Before you know it, a light will come to you," Mrs. Hammerstein informed me, her smile now obviously forced.

"I will try again," I told her. Then, just like instructed, I shut my eyes and repeated *Ithaca, New York; May 12th, 2018; 7:00 a.m.* Then I thought about that little yellow house, 26 on that street. It was there, the familiar scent of air fresheners and the touch of over-fluffed pillows. I could taste my favorite salt-and-vinegar potato chips. I could hear Willow's groans of waking up. I could feel myself sitting in the bed that I had learned not to hate.

Then, just like I was told, a faint light surrounded me. My nerves shook ever so slightly and I suddenly could not sense the cool floor of my Lana Ilu apartment. In an instant, I was wrapped in those pale, yellow walls I had memorized every detail of. I checked my cell phone which sat upon my old wooden nightstand. The date read *May 12th, 7:00,* two days earlier than where I should be living. *I had just time traveled.*

The bed was still unmade from when I had woken up, which, though it felt like days to me, was only a few hours at this moment. I noticed a lump of my clothes, the

exact jeans and t-shirt from Friday, on the ground as I had
been too lazy to throw them in the hamper. There was
even an empty bag of salt-and-vinegar chips sitting on my
sunflower patterned rocking chair. This was definitely my
room from Saturday morning.

The light in the hallway illuminated, a soft gold so different than the piercing white I was getting used to seeing.
Willow was humming some alternative indie song as she
brushed her teeth. *Classic Willow.* Even just sitting in the
room over from my sister, I could not believe how much
I missed her. And it had only been two days. How was I
going to feel when we were separated for months at a time?
At least that would have happened with college anyway.

Realizing that Willow or my Mom could open my bedroom door at any time, I knew that I should change into
some convincing pajamas and probably mess up my hair
while I was at it. I threw on the closest t-shirt and pants I
could find and shoved my hair onto a pillow and whipped
it around, allowing my straight locks to fly over my head.
Finally, I rubbed my eyes over and over to give them that
red, half-asleep style that I so wanted to achieve. For the
end of my act, I hopped into my bed, so uncomfortable
now compared to the one in Lana Ilu. I hoped this costume would mask the fact that I had just spent the past
two days living in a city full of time travelers, getting my
own apartment, and learning that I shared the same era
as a super villain.

Just as expected, the bedroom door slid open with my
Mom behind it. I had wanted to see Willow. She had her
bulky brown glasses on instead of her regular contacts
and hair flat down her back. This was a tired Mom look.
She wiped her forehead before peering at me tucked into

my covers. "Keira, do you want an omelet? I'll make you an omelet," she said groggily.

My Mom always made omelets on Saturday mornings. It was one of her only traditions. I loved the little act of hominess and comfort my Mom's Saturday omelet gave, stuffed with our favorite cheese and vegetables. I mostly loved this small chance of getting to share some time with Willow and my Mom, all of us too tired to argue and too awake to ignore each other. It was almost as distant from my regular life as Lana Ilu was.

"Of course, thank you," I answered, faking the best tired voice I could. I would have to pretend I was still hungry after such a filling breakfast from Mrs. Handal. Then again, food was food, so it wouldn't be such a hard act.

I pulled myself from the bed I had only been laying in for a few minutes and walked downstairs, slowly, taking in every detail. It was so strange being home again and having to pretend nothing had happened. An old broken clock hung on the wall and not a single thing levitated. My sector would be absolutely repulsed. But what bugged my eyes the most was my great grandmother's amulet. So brilliantly green, the same green that had burst into light and sucked me into another universe, just sat calmly as my Mom cooked. The case was not broken or even opened. Not a single object around was scorched from the burn or a piece of furniture out of place. Nothing had changed. Now I felt like I had been dreaming. I must have been dreaming. Such an incredible, impossible thing could not have gone down in my living room and not made a single dent in the world. Everything, my era, my apartment, my *friends*, had all been a figment of my imagination. I almost began to cry at the realization that it was a dream until

I recalled that my Lana Ilu clothes were still in my bedroom. If they were still there, it had been real. *They had to still be there.*

I raced back up the stairs and stumbled into my room, searching for the orange tank top and shorts I had never owned before. I dug through piles of clothes left on the ground and threw apart my bed sheets until I saw the glimmer of clementine. They were there. Lana Ilu was real.

Calm again, I headed back downstairs where Willow was now digging through her first omelet of the morning. She always liked hers with mushrooms and gruyere. I used to mock her for acting all fancy-schmancy, but I was friends with not one, but two billionaires now so I wasn't one to talk. Before sitting at the table, I peered at the (working) clock and saw that it was 7:30. Mrs. Hammerstein would be here to explain everything, everything that would change my family's lives forever, in just half an hour.

"Keira, I had the craziest dream!" Willow chirped after swallowing a mouthful of egg.

I smirked, knowing it could not be half of what I had been through. Still, I listened. "Tell me!"

Willow grinned and spread out her hands. "Let me lay the scene. I am in a field full of crabs, not flowers or trees, but *crabs*! Then, out of nowhere, my old kindergarten teacher, Mrs. Haverford, appears and starts complaining to me about my poor performance in crayon drawings. Then, to top off all the insanity, I just sprouted wings and flew away from the conversation, but also decided to kick Mrs. Haverford in the face while doing so." Willow turned to my Mom in the kitchen. "Hey Mom, did you hear any of that? Do you know what it means?"

My Mom groaned. "You're the one interested in therapy, Willow. How about you practice for once?"

Willow looked down and bit her lip, trying to decipher the messages in her vision. She moved her glasses off her eyes and looked into the lenses, as if she were trying to make a crystal ball out of the simple glass. She scratched her nose and finally lifted her chin. "Before I leave for college, should I confront Mrs. Haverford again as a last goodbye... but make sure to show off that *sassy* personality I have developed through the years?"

My Mom placed an omelet in front of me. "I suppose, but I saw more that you're a crabby girl who likes to ignore her own problems instead of dealing with them."

Willow huffed at the interpretation. She was never one who liked to talk about her own problems, though she loved other people's. Her whole life she has batted away any sort of confrontation about difficulties with friends, a break-up, an essay turned in late, you name it. Maybe that was why she wanted to go into therapy so much, though I thought that chair would never fit her.

All of a sudden, my Mom placed a cold hand on my shoulder. "Keira, about the test coming up, I am going to look into getting you a cheap tutor. Maybe one of my students will be enough, because this just cannot go on any longer."

"Are-are you really mad at me?" I squeaked, feeling the oddness of an Idum-world issue.

"Well, I'm certainly not happy. This is a problem that we need to work through. It's true that I do not like your teacher, that Ms. Summers or whatever, so you are not 100% to blame," my Mom commanded.

"Alright, I understand."

Just as my Mom took a seat, she pulled the conversation on a whole other path. "You girls will not be going to stay with your father this week. He called me and said he and Clarke have their honeymoon. So *please*, don't be reckless over here, since this is double the time that I am used to having you. Then again, you are definitely in better hands with me than that idiotic ba-" she stopped herself. "Just be neat and quiet."

Willow and I both nodded silently, just as we were used to when our Mom brought up our Dad, or vice versa. I had heard of divorced couples that were able to stay friends or at least somewhat close after the separation. My parents were the polar opposite. Sometimes I wondered why they ever got married. I don't even remember them loving each other when they were still together. They would fight constantly and often sleep in different rooms, then spend the next day like nothing had happened until the cycle would repeat again. A couple of times, my Dad went on "work trips" where I'm pretty sure he cheated on my Mom but, in all fairness, she had probably done the same. I hated to think it, but in ways, Mrs. Handal was very right. If I had lived here in Ithaca until I turned eighteen, I probably would have given up on love. I had never seen it with my own eyes.

Sensing the tension, Willow tried to bring up a lighter conversation. "Mom, I found out that there's another kid at my school going to Princeton, you know, other than Gillian."

My Mom didn't look up from her breakfast. "Who?"

"David Shapiro. I think you know his Mom."

She nodded. "I do, she's a nice woman. I've heard she's very passionate in the school board meetings. How well do you know David?"

"Not very well. We're in some of the same classes."

A bit bored by the conversation, I looked up at the clock and read that it was now just a minute before 8:00. Then, a long-awaited doorbell rang, humming through the air like a gong. I began to tap my foot on the ground, more excited to see Mrs. Hammerstein's face than I thought possible. It was coming. They were all about to find out that I was a Gradien. But wait, how was I going to explain all this? How would they believe me? How would my Dad learn about the situation? What if my Mom made me stay in Ithaca? Now I was nervous.

My Mom stood from her chair and tied her silk robe around her tightly. "Who could that be so early on a Saturday morning?" she grumbled.

I peered through the room, eyes fixed on the door. Here it was, here it was, here it was...

"Hello?" my Mom answered.

"Hello, Ms. Sun. I am Julia Hammerstein and I have some very important information to share with you about your daughter, Keira. I promise everything is perfectly fine, but may I come in?" she charmed.

My Mom straightened her back. "What 'very important information'? And how do you know my daughter?"

"I am from a city called Lana Ilu, which I am sure you have never heard of. You see, Keira belongs there and I would love to speak with you about the arrangements."

"She's not adopted, she is from Ithaca. I think you have the wrong household, ma'am."

But just as my Mom tried to shut the front door, Mrs. Hammerstein held up her hand to stop it. She held up an identification card reading her name, the signature of her department head and the Queen, along with what I assumed was the Lana Ilu insignia, a clock with an infinity symbol for hands. "Ms. Sun, I must come in and speak with you. Please, this is urgent, and I know it means the world to your daughter." She peered inside. "Keira, isn't that right?"

I smiled wildly. "Yes, Mom, I know her! Please let her in!"

My Mom hesitated, but then opened the door the whole way. "You can have a seat on the couch. Would you like any water?"

"No ma'am, but thank you very much. I would rather just move onto business."

While my Mom joined Mrs. Hammerstein on the couch, Willow came over to me and grabbed my arm. "Keira, what is this? Who is that lady?"

"She's going to explain it in a moment, just wait," I said.

"Can I trust her?" Willow stressed.

I laughed, forgetting that they had never met. "Yes, definitely! I already met her."

Willow fixed her glasses back on and strolled over to the couch, curious about this whole situation. It felt so odd to be the only one in the family *in on* something so important. I usually just felt clueless.

"Ms. Sun and Willow, it is so nice to finally meet you. What I am here to tell you is quite hard to believe, I understand that, but very worthwhile. After our initial conversation, I would like to have Keira's father over, since he is also her legal guardian and needs to know."

"Well, what is it?" my Mom near yelled.

Ms. Hammerstein set her hands in her lap. "The reason you have never heard of my home, the city of Lana Ilu, is that it exists in an alternate dimension. It holds a race of people we call Gradiens. I am one of them, and so is your daughter, Keira. You, as well as almost all humans, are Idums. Now of course, you must be wondering what these Gradiens and Idums are. Well, Idums are people whose energy is completely singular and has not changed. The energy you live with now, that runs through your body, is from the exact same year in which you were born. You are a balanced, regular human, which is perfectly great. But a Gradien is very different. We, as in Keira and I, live with energy, or a soul if that is what you believe, from a different year than our body was born. Because time is a circle and not a straight line, it surrounds everything and everyone. When two people in two different years are born at the exact same fraction of a fraction of a fraction of a nanosecond, beyond splitting the atom, their energy will pass through the force of time in perfect sync, switching bodies. Keira, for example, traces her energy to over 200,000 years from now, with the last of humanity. Her energy, from 200,004, is with another human far into our future, although this does *not* change the fact that she is your biological daughter and sister! But to add on, this change of energy throughout all of time gifted your daughter and over a million others with the power of time travel, no machine required. Her energy passed through time, so she is part of it. Get all that?"

In short, Willow and my Mom did *not* get all that. They both sat dumbfounded, their eyes wide and jaws open. My Mom was shaking her head in disbelief. "You must be kidding! How do you expect me to believe this? Is this some sort of drug thing, has my daughter gotten involved in drugs?!" she screamed.

"No, this is all very real and for hundreds of thousands of people, they were raised in the beautiful city of

Lana Ilu. It is a great place with the best schools in the world, wonderful food and a terrific apartment for your daughter to live in until college. She may attend one in Lana Ilu or the Idum-world."

This time, Willow spoke. "Has she, I mean, has Keira time traveled yet?"

I couldn't help but smirk at the question. When I looked over my shoulder, I saw that Ms. Hammerstein had done the same. "Yes, just about an hour ago for the first time, in fact. You see, Keira has been living in Lana Ilu for the past two days-"

"Two days?" my Mom exclaimed. "My daughter has been living with you strange people for two days?!"

"Yes, and she has been in perfect safety, Ms. Sun. We needed to bring her in to let her know who she was before any of this could happen. And before you ask, to bring someone into Lana Ilu, we apply energy to an object 'out of its time' per say, and the amulet in your house worked wonderfully. Do not worry, no harm was done to the valuable object," Ms. Hammerstein assured.

"I don't... what proof do you have about this *Lana Ilu* and time travel nonsense?" my Mom demanded.

Ms. Hammerstein pulled a newspaper clipping from her dress pocket and held it before Willow and my mother. "With this, a newspaper from a week from today. I will channel my energy inside it as you hold on and will take you to Lana Ilu. But first, I must have Keira's father over to tell him the same information."

"Her father is not important."

Willow shook her head. "He is one of our legal guardians, I will admit." She looked over to me. "Keira, can you call him?"

"He's going on his honeymoon," my Mom mumbled. "He probably won't be around, but I guess you have to try."

I ran upstairs for my cell phone and came back down with my Dad's number typed in. Finally, I called. After a series of rings, the other line picked up with some sort of classical music playing in the background.

"Keira, hello?" my Dad said.

"Dad, I need you to come over to Mom's right now. It's urgent."

"Is everyone alright, Keira? This has to be an emergency for me to stay in the same room as your mother and you know that. And anyway, I'm packing for my honeymoon so it's not the best time," my Dad grumbled over the line.

I knew he was not lying about refusing to come over if it were not an emergency. As much as my Mom hated my Dad, he often hated her even more. The last time they were in the same room was Willow's orchestra concert, where they sat in opposite ends of the auditorium and did not speak even once. They even assigned times of when they would congratulate my sister so they would not have to see each other's faces. So, I would have to make up a story to get him here. It was all I could do and after convincing my Mom and Willow, two of the smartest people I knew, that I had been in my bed all night, I could do anything.

"Dad, Willow went into a mental breakdown about leaving for college. She's just so scared that she's doing the wrong thing with her life. Please, she needs to talk to more than one parent but she's refusing to leave her bed or go on the phone. Please Dad, I am so worried about her and you know you are a better speaker than Mom."

I threw in that last bit because my parents *loved* to hear horrible things about the other.

My Dad mumbled something to who I assumed was Clarke. "I'll be there in fifteen minutes. Just wait and tell Willow not to stress."

I grinned. I really was getting good at lying. This was a dangerous power, but I was glad to know I had it.

"SO, WHAT DO you mean there's no 'Willow mental breakdown emergency?'" my Dad hollered. "Keira, why did you lie to me?"

"Because you would never believe me if I told you the real reason," I persuaded, or at least tried to.

"You're not trying to get me back with Mei, are you? That is *never* going to happen, Keira, and you know it."

My Mom let out the loudest, most deep laugh I had heard from her in years. "Nice one, Peter. That might be the only funny thing you've ever said, other than that you expected your second and now third marriages to go well."

Willow burst into the room. "Stop arguing, you two! We get it, you're divorced. But guess what, you got divorced ten years ago so you need to start putting it behind you, alright? You have tortured Keira and me for our whole lives. Right now, there is a lady in Mom's living room who has something *very* important to tell you Dad, but you are too darn full of yourself to care a bit. Now, Dad, just go into the living room and listen to what she tells you. If you don't, I really will have a mental breakdown."

Slowly, my Dad agreed. Willow was going to be a good

therapist. He entered the living room he had not been in for about a decade. There, through the walls, I heard Ms. Hammerstein give him the entire talk Willow and my Mom had just received. He did not act any differently. At last, Ms. Hammerstein called the rest of us in and said she was ready to bring them to Lana Ilu, with me as the only one who could stay there.

"Just place a finger on the newspaper and the energy will begin to do its job. You will see some bright lights and feel a bit of tingling, but nothing uncomfortable. Are you ready?" Ms. Hammerstein said.

"Definitely," Willow inputted. "For Keira."

My parents looked at each other begrudgingly but forced smiles. "For Keira."

Then, like I was beginning to get accustomed to, the light returned. I tried to look at my family's expressions but I forgot how fast the trip was. In just a second, we stood not in the cookie-cutter lobby I had known first, but next to my apartment. The city was bustling with life, people working and shopping and going to school. I had only been gone for a couple hours, but it felt like weeks. I just wanted to go bundle up in my new bed or meet up with my new friends. I just wanted to really be home, but maybe with Willow here, too.

"How..." they all said in unison, more dumbstruck than I ever imagined seeing them.

"It is real, just like we said," I told them. "Isn't it amazing?"

Willow scanned everything within her eyesight. She was grinning, near laughing as each new thing, a levitator or the bubble-like homes, came into view. "It is, Keira. It is!"

"So, this is real... are you sure we're not dreaming?" my Mom cried.

I couldn't help but laugh at the question. I had asked myself it a couple days ago and earlier this morning, but had learned to stop. Lana Ilu was *definitely* real and full of more life than Ithaca ever was. Did they ever question if Ithaca was part of a dream, maybe some sort of nightmare?

"Yeah, Mom, it is. And I live here now, it's the best home I could have ever imagined having," I asserted. I noticed a tear bud in Willow's eye, despite her obvious amazement at the moment. We were going to live separately anyway and we could still have contact all the time. Wait, I hope she didn't think that when I called Lana Ilu the 'best home' it was because of leaving her. *That* could not be farther from the truth.

Out of nowhere, my Mom threw up her hands. "Alright, alright. I see that this place is real. But I will *not* let my daughter live here. She needs her family and a regular life..."

"Ma'am, I hate to interrupt, but life here would be much more comfortable and 'regular' than in Ithaca. Lana Ilu is filled with over a million other people of her kind. She could time travel easily and get the best education from our teachers. She's already made some good friends here. I'm sure she will be able to relate better to them than anyone she knows in Ithaca," Ms. Hammerstein tried to reason.

My Dad let out a grunt. "Keira, you have to be kidding with us about staying here. You know I hate to agree with your mother on anything, I would fight her on ketchup or mustard, but this is no place for you. To be honest, I still don't think this is a place at all."

Before anyone else could intervene, Willow wiped her eyes and wrapped her arm around my shoulders. "Keira, have-have you really made friends?"

"Yeah, a bunch already, Willow. I hope somehow I can have you meet them one day."

"And have you gone any cool places that you like?" Willow hugged me again at that.

"Definitely! There was a colosseum and museums and a really cool playground with holographs..."

Willow lifted her chin and looked my parents right in their eyes. "Then it's decided. Lana Ilu is very lucky to have a new resident. Keira, I know this city is going to be better because you are in it. You already did it for our world and you can do it for any other." She stopped and gritted her teeth. "And don't fight me on this, Mom or Dad. You know she belongs here. We should get going before our visit expires."

"Willow, do you honestly think you have the authority to make this decision?" Dad brandished, shaking his head at my older sister. "You are barely an adult, you are not either of her parents, stay *out* of this!"

Willow stood behind me and hugged my shoulders, her forearms like a shield from our parents. "It's really, *really* bold of you to actually own up to being one of her parents right now, Dad. Just out of curiosity, why didn't you every time she was sick or had been bullied or maybe just wanted her Dad to say goodnight to her the two nights a week we're at your house? No, it's been me, always me." Willow took a deep breath and smiled down at me. "And I was always glad to, but I know Keira better than you ever will, even if you spend every last second of your life talking to her. I only want her to be happy and she is happy here and that is that."

Mom did not look satisfied. "I appreciate all you've done in raising your sister while her father was too busy with whatever to notice his own daughters, but Willow, this is insane. I do not trust this place and even if I did, Keira could never make it on her own here."

Then Willow laughed, she chuckled, her eyes wide as she glared at my parents. "You know what, if you will not accept what I'm saying, I will take you to court and become Keira's legal guardian to get her in Lana Ilu. I am more than willing to go that far. How's that sound?"

My parents peered over to each other until my Dad headed over to my Mom. They spoke for a few minutes before my Dad turned back to us. "She can stay."

Willow hugged me tighter and beamed.

"Thank you, I love you so much," I whispered to my older sister. My arms had chills and tears had budded in my eyes. I felt like I could have run faster than any levitator here just out of pure excitement. I looked back to Willow. I wanted more than anything for her to stay. It would have made Lana Ilu the perfect place.

"What... what do we tell her school?" my Dad asked.

"Our schools are certified in the Idum-world with replicas to "fool" the outside. We will send forms to your house to hand in, no worries. Also, please do not call Keira for the next few days. There are a few time travel complications and she still needs to get settled in her new home. Afterwards, all phones work! Oh, we will send you any contact information you might need, and Keira may come back to collect some clothes and things. Until then, let me help you back home."

And then, with a flash, she brought my family back to Ithaca, back to their home. And though I got to stay in mine, I couldn't help but feel a strange tugging at my heart.

CHAPTER 11

"PANDORA?" I SAID OVER MY MULTI.
"Hi."

"Hey Keira! Nice to hear from you! Did you meet with your family yet?" her perky voice responded.

"Yep, they left the city a few hours ago. It was... a lot," I admitted.

"Tell me about it. Mine threw such a fit but it didn't really matter. We're both meant to be here in Lana Ilu. It's our home."

"Yeah," I whispered back.

I heard a light humming sound on the other side until she picked up again. "Keira, would you want to go out for a little?"

I grinned, still not very used to be invited places. "I would love to! But uh... where? That cafe from before?"

She chuckled. "I was thinking something more along the lines of, er, the Alloys?"

"I thought you hated that place. At least, that's what you told Alden."

"Come on, Keira. We pick and choose who we tell our secrets to. So, I'll see you there in ten minutes?"

I wanted to ask why she would reveal her liking of the place, the most mysterious and dreaded place among a lot of Gradiens, to me. But just like she said, not everyone gets to hear secrets. I was lucky enough to be in on this one.

"Yeah, I'll see you."

THE ALLOYS WERE ugly, like *really* ugly. From what I had seen of Lana Ilu, it appeared to be the most beautiful place the world could ever craft. Every culture, every year had contributed something wonderful. And then there were the Alloys. The Alloys looked like the project everyone attempted but gave up on. It was the abandoned part of a great city. The Alloys was just a staggered tower of large metal boxes which looked like storage compartments. Some of them were occupied by people smoking or drinking or kissing or whatever. The entire grounds smelled of sulfur and expired milk. I had no idea why Pandora wanted me to come here or why Holly winked at me about the place or why Alden wished to visit. It was, frankly, *disgusting*.

To the right of the structure was Pandora, wearing her blonde locks in a high ponytail. She was wearing a yellow shirt to match her hair, accessorized by white sneakers detailed with green. She probably was the polar opposite of my fashion sense, or sense of anything at all for that matter.

Pandora waved for me to come over and pointed to a rusted staircase winding between the boxes.

"Let's head to the top," she suggested.

I looked up at the formation, rising high above us. "The *top*? It's like 15 stories high!"

Pandora grabbed my arm and pulled me towards the staircase. "Yeah, I know. That gives us the best view in the city and it's also a great place to talk. You did want to talk, right?"

Heading closer to the stairs, I gave in. Fifteen stories of walking were a very small price to pay to have a sincere conversation with a true friend. I would have walked 100 stories if I could have gotten the chance long ago.

We marched up the stairs, dragging our feet behind us like any lazy teenage girls would. I couldn't help but breathe heavily as the steps increased, letting out a gasp with each one. On the other hand, Pandora was speeding up. I guess she had been up these stairs many times, though I had no idea who she had been with since she told Alden she wasn't interested. She must have had other friends or at least been comfortable in her independence. I wish I could relate.

At last, we reached the final row of boxes, one of which had a dent in its left side. Of course, that was the one Pandora chose. We entered through a door from the back side of the compartment, yet what shocked me was that there was no fourth wall. If you stumbled, you could easily fall out.

"Isn't that a safety hazard?" I asked Pandora.

She nodded and sat at the edge, her legs swinging in the air. "Only if you're not careful. Now come sit."

Begrudgingly, I sat by her, carefully letting my shins sway in the air. Pandora pulled two lollipops from her pocket and handed me one wrapped in neon green. "Apple lollipop? These are my favorite."

I took one and unwrapped it in unison with Pandora before popping it in my mouth. I had never really liked apple lollipops, but I had to say this was delicious. Not too sweet or sour, but a perfect Goldilocks combination. *Absolutely* perfect.

"So, what is this place?" I questioned.

Pandora kept the candy in her mouth. "It belongs to the 3000's district, a time when a bunch of new metals were discovered or created. That's why it's called "The Alloys." It was supposed to be a monument but the guy in charge was found to be in some sort of alliance with Waldron Hawkridge and lost a ton of money. So, it was going to be painted and turned into a great tourist spot, but then it just got abandoned. Now it's where drug addicts and teens whose parents don't approve of their partners come."

"Well, and people like you," I said.

Pandora laughed and took a big lick from her lollipop. "Yeah, and people like me and Alden and basically anyone who needs to get away from anything."

"What are you getting away from? Seems like you're doing pretty well here. Better than the Idum-world."

"Exactly, and my Idum family calls me all the time and if I'm here I feel better about not picking up. Also, as much as I love Alden, not like a crush, don't get the wrong idea, he can be... intense. Not that I blame him because of his crazy, monarch-obsessed, billionaire family, but alone time never hurts," Pandora droned.

"He doesn't seem bad," I mumbled, not exactly sure how to respond.

"Oh yeah, he told me about that whole 'beautiful boy' thing! That was actually pretty hilarious. I gotta give it to you, I'm going to use that to make fun of him for years!" Pandora blurted out.

I blushed. "I didn't mean it like that."

"No, I get it. And hey, can we stop talking about Alden? I feel a little weird saying things about friends behind their backs if I don't need to."

"Sure," I started. I paused for a second, wondering how to continue with this conversation. I loved talking to Pandora and I wanted to build a friendship with her more than anything, but that also made the stakes for messing up so much higher. "So, what's your family like? Where are you from?"

Pandora rolled her eyes. "I think I give away the whole story when I say I'm from Beverly Hills. By the way, when I tell you about my family, you're going to think I'm a whiny rich girl, which I am, but don't look at me like that."

I practically hollered. "Hey, honesty is the best policy."

She grinned, holding my hand for a second. "You'll know who my parents are. Their names are John and Gwyneth Dailey."

"John and Gwyneth Dailey?" I screamed. "*The* John and Gwyneth Dailey? That's so cool, they're like two of the best actors in the world!"

"They're really not, Keira. They're just two of the most *famous* actors in the world, and that's very different. And trust me, it's not cool either. The paparazzi basically camped outside of my old house each night. It would have been better if my parents had tried to shoo them away, but they welcomed them in. Even famous actors lose the spotlight, so they did anything to make the front cover," Pandora spat.

"I've seen your sister Cherry all over the internet—and some of your brothers too. I get that Cherry is a model and is popular for that but like, did you ever get harassed?" I pushed, not being able to help my curiosity.

Pandora wiped at her eyes, but I saw no tears. "Constantly, because I was the *fat one*. It was like, how could my mother, the symbol of Hollywood beauty, have a *fat* daughter? My Mom would always try to get me thinner for the big 'transformation' picture in all the magazines, like she wanted me to go on a raw diet or something. And all this when I was even younger than fourteen!"

This time, I reached for her hand. "Hey, you know you don't have to go on any of those diets, right?"

"Keira, if you're going to say 'oh you're not fat' just stop, because I've heard... "

"No, Pandora, I was not going to say that. I just wanted to tell you that you look healthy and happy and beautiful and you're great to talk to, so don't let your celebrity parents make you think you need to change anything. I've just known you for a day and you're already probably the best friend I've ever had, so anyone who thinks being chubby makes you bad or gross could not be more wrong," I assured her.

I noticed Pandora smile wider, this time her white teeth showing. She was playing with her hair now, almost looking more confident with herself. Maybe I *had* said something right. "You're a really good friend too, Keira Sun... so tell me about your family."

This time, I was getting hesitant. "Well, for starters, my parents are as divorced as two people could get."

Pandora rolled her hand. "Go on."

"They separated when I was only three and fought all the time before that, so I don't really think they ever loved each other. I live with them both technically, but mostly just with my Mom. My Mom never remarried but my Dad did twice, his most recent just a few days ago." It was so odd explaining this to Pandora, someone who knew almost nothing about me and yet more than anyone else. Telling her the basics made me want to show her so much more.

"I'm sorry, Keira. You deserved to have more happiness in your life before. Do you at least have a sibling to help you with all of that?"

I nodded. "My older sister, Willow. She's the best person in the entire world, and I say that with 100% honesty. She hates them just as much as I do, sometimes more, so we confide in each other about that. She's so funny and smart, I mean she's going to Princeton in the fall, but I wish I could really bring her to Lana Ilu. She's studying to be a therapist but she's *not* an office person." I stopped for a second, thinking. "Can Idums *really* not time travel at all?"

Pandora sulked. "No, sorry. You can still bring her back little things if you're careful though. Willow seems worth it."

"She definitely is... Pandora, can I rant about something?"

She turned to me, swinging her legs back over into a criss-cross position. "I love rants. Spill."

I took a deep breath, knowing that once I began letting out every little frustration I had kept in for so long, I would not be able to stop. "My parents have always been abusive, just mentally, but still awful. My Mom would always ignore me or shoo me away and make me feel like it was my fault that I got excluded. She pegged failed tests on the fact that I was stupid and made fun of the way I dressed. She was relentless and I don't even know why. She never really cared about my Dad, so I don't know how much of the anger was from that, but, oh God, was it awful. And then my Dad always had to make up an excuse to not spend time with me. He would be working or fixing something or tending to his other marriages or dating or whatever. And the few times we sat down and talked, he refused to listen to my stories. It *always* had to be about him. But earlier today when I was telling them that I wanted to stay in my true home, Lana Ilu, they suddenly freaked. My parents cried about wanting to protect me and care for me, two things they had never done before. For the first time in my entire life, my parents claimed they wanted me because now, I got to show I didn't want them. How is that right?!"

Pandora shook her head. "It's not, and my parents did the exact same thing. It's just another one of their abuses. Bad parents make their kids feel like the villains instead of the victims all the time, so when they can't control us, they pretend we are controlling them. Don't give in, Keira. This is where you are safest." Pandora took another lick from her lollipop. "I guess all we can do as kids of awful parents is promise to do better than them when it's our turn."

I shrugged. "Yeah, that's true. I just want my future

kids to like being with me, and if their parents weren't divorced, that would be a big help."

"You better find someone good to marry then. But you don't have to worry about that yet, you probably haven't even met them," Pandora input.

I wanted to keep my tirade going and move on to my awful old "friends" next. But something about it seemed like such a waste of time. I might never see Harper, Taylor, or Sadie ever again. They tried to ruin my life constantly and never really apologized for it. Why would I talk to a girl who actually cared for me about them when I could work on something new? Lana Ilu was about all of time— in the universal sense, and in certain cases, some of that time had to be forgotten. Those "friends" back in Ithaca were part of that.

Instead, I decided to take another route with the conversation, something small but funny and warm. "Random question, are there TV shows here?"

Pandora gasped. "Yes, oh yeah! We watch a lot of stuff from the Idum-world just because there's more material, but the few shows we have are *so* good. There's this one sitcom that *everybody* watches, I have literally never met anyone who hasn't. It makes fun of time travelers. It makes us look like that cheesy 1950's style with time machines that look like toasters or whatever, with the most bland time travel type thing. Like, they only go to boring places like Ancient Rome and the future is all flying cars. The best part is that they film here in the city, not the actual eras, so it looks really fake. But that's what makes it so funny! Other than that, we have news and game shows and stuff, but that's really what you need to tune into."

I smiled and took a lick from the lollipop. "Sounds great, I will. Oh, and I have to tell you, this lollipop is *amazing*!"

She pulled me over so my legs were no longer dangling either (I had forgotten how terrified I was) and looked me straight in the eyes. "One thing you're going to learn about me, Keira, is that I *never* steer my friends in the wrong direction." She stopped and twirled a loose curl in her hair. "Not on purpose, at least."

CHAPTER 12

M RS. HANDAL OFFERED TO TAKE ME shopping in order to replenish both my closet and my refrigerator. It was amazing to have all these points given to me by Lana Ilu to just pick *whatever* I wanted. Every item I chose was for me, not my Mom or my Dad or even Clarke. It was liberating, just like the half-dozen bags of salt-and-vinegar chips I bought.

My day had been going smoothly and quite well (besides my parents' attempt at overprotectiveness) until I got a surprise call from Alden. I wasn't upset to hear from him at all. I just thought we still were "developing" one-on-one terms.

"Keira, are you available right now?" he asked.

"Yeah, I spent some time with Pandora and went shopping so that was my 'getting out' for the day."

I heard Alden huff on the other end of the line. "Would you be willing to go out again?"

Immediately, my interest was piqued. I had to say I was wondering where billionaire kids took friends. It's not that I only look at him for his money, I'm just curious! I promise, I am *not* materialistic. "Where were you thinking?"

"The thing is, I told my parents about meeting you and your era, which apparently they already knew about from gossip or whatever, but they want you over for dinner. Could you make it in an hour and a half? Oh, and if you do come, just dress a little fancy. My parents are a little stuck up about that kind of thing."

"Sure, I'll be there." I was quite nervous to go over. These people were a different kind than me and I was not sure how to talk to them. Hopefully Alden would guide me with each step. "What's your address?"

Alden did not respond at first, but I could hear deep breathing. "Just, just tell the driver you're going to Fischer Mansion. They'll know where it is."

Typical, I thought. *Rich people always get their names on wherever they want them.* Part of me wanted to make a snarky comment back at Alden, but I could hear a tinge of guilt in his tone, like he was afraid to tell me that. I guess there is a feeling of shame when you have as much money as Alden does, especially when you made none of it yourself. And anyways, he still seemed really nice. Being nice back was the least I could do.

"Tell your parents I'll be there later, Alden. Thanks for the invite."

Afterwards, I immediately started fishing through all

of my new clothes, figuring out what exactly fit into the category "dinner with time-traveling billionaires."

WHEN I GOT into the taxi in my new silver dress and heels that were definitely too high for a girl my age, I could tell the driver understood I was going somewhere fancy. When I added that it was Fischer Mansion, I just confirmed all his suspicions.

"May I ask what you are going for? It's an exclusive house," the driver said, trying to make conversation.

"I was invited for dinner," I informed him.

He let out a chuckle. "Well I can tell you that you are about to have the fanciest food in the world, both Idum and Gradien. The only family richer than the Fischers is the royal one. Actually, the Hawkridges and Sharmas probably have something on them, I don't know."

I was not quite sure how to respond to that, I already knew they were rich, so I just forced a laugh. I was honestly too panicked about meeting the Fischer parents (why did they really want me over?) to focus on any other conversation. I knew I probably sounded rude, but I was sure the driver would get over it.

After a few more minutes of driving, Fischer Mansion came into view. Crafted from a selection of multi-colored stones, each shaped perfectly into the next, the house stood nearly half as tall as The Alloys. The front doorway was a towering arc, painted in white flowers. Each window was detailed by stained designs and balconies guarded the upper floors. The yard was peppered with aromatic flowers and fountains, many with statues in front. This looked like a tourist stop.

I paid the taxi driver and headed for the walkway, which I half expected to hold a red carpet (it didn't). Once I reached the entrance, I felt my finger hovering over the doorbell, wondering about when the right time to ring it was. I said "hello" a million times to myself, trying to decide on the right pitch for eating with billionaires. I had to tell myself to stop stressing. It wasn't like they were the Royal Family.

At last, almost as if a gust of wind had hit me, I pressed down on the doorbell. In a second, a man in a butler's outfit opened the door.

"Keira Sun?" he asked, his gloved hands still held tight on the doorknob.

I grinned. "Yes, sir. I am here for dinner."

"Just this way, Miss. The Fischers are already seated at the dinner table."

Following the butler through the hallways, I inspected every little detail of the home. The walls were covered with stunning art, both from the past and future. The finest china filled every cabinet, grounded by exotically carpeted floors. Looking at all the decor, I knew there was no reason for people to have anywhere near as much money as the Fischers did, yet it sure did look like a lot of fun.

When we reached the dining room, lit by a crystal chandelier, I quickly saw that I misunderstood what Alden meant as "dress fancy." What he meant, at least in my family's terms, was "look presentable." Alden wore a dressy button down, similar to his older brother and father. His sister was clad in a blouse and girl's slacks (which I could never pull off) and his mother in her business dress. Meanwhile, I looked like I was going to middle school prom in my outfit.

Nice way to start off the night, Keira.

The first to stand up was Alden's mother, Ms. Fischer. She held her arms open as if for a hug, which was intimidating and comforting at the same time. "Keira, it is *so* wonderful to meet you. And no worries about the little clothing mix up, the dress is lovely," she said. I wanted to believe she was authentic in her words, but I had heard that tone before. A tone that reeked of *I'll be nice to who I need to be nice to.* I felt it could easily fade away.

I noticed the only empty seat was at the edge of the table, directly next to Alden. I was glad I could sit aside him, since he was the only person here I knew at all. He smiled at me when I sat next to him, a welcoming smile that I desperately needed. Other than being terribly intimidated by the Fischers, the thought of why they were so eager to meet me kept tugging at my mind.

"So, Keira, where are you from?" Alden's father asked. He looked a lot like his son, with those same shocking blue eyes. Alden's older brother shared the same color, though his sister (Juliet, if I remembered correctly) peered at me with midnight irises, similar to her mother. I guess only the guys in the Fischer family got blue eyes.

"Ithaca, in New York," I told him. "It's very different than Lana Ilu for sure."

Mr. Fischer let out a deep chuckle. "Well of course. I've heard of Ithaca, it's a small city, barely a city. Other than their universities, not much happens there. You are very lucky to be part of a world, of a *people* that let you escape that little place."

Though I had thought (and said) basically the exact

same thing Alden's father had just announced, it felt awkward and damaging to hear it from him. Bashing Ithaca was *my* privilege. I had lived there for years and dealt with the monotony of awful kids in school and each day revolving around whatever the Cornell administrators chose. But Mr. Fischer had been living lavishly in this mansion since before I was born, getting the adventure of time travel and luxury of wealth for years. He knew *nothing* about Ithaca. He knew *nothing* about any of the Idum-world. For the first time since I had arrived in Lana Ilu, the outside world felt a little more like home.

I could tell I wasn't the only one who uncomfortable with his comments. Alden, his face lowered, was bright red but not in his usual blushing fashion. He was burning with embarrassment and anger. I even heard him mumble under his breath "Just shut up, Dad." I recalled Alden wanting to visit those hated Alloys. Now I knew that his rebellious side, which would probably bloom as I got to know him more, had to be hidden within the walls of this mansion.

Piping in next was Alden's mother, who I already knew just wanted to piggyback off her husband's statement. "It is always so fascinating for me to hear about Idum-borns, Keira. You know, my family has been in this city for twenty generations, so I know nearly nothing about your kind. Tell me, was it upsetting for you to come to Lana Ilu and see all the knowledge, all the innovation and experience you had been forced to miss out on? I mean, you are one of us, yet you were cooped up in the Idum-world, deprived of your true character. You must feel so refreshed."

Again, not feeling amazing about how his parents viewed Idums. They were not some basic, undeserving people. They were just different than we were, with *fewer* resources. Part of me wanted to retort, but Alden shook his head softly. I knew that meant to stay quiet.

"Yes, it was a little upsetting to see this amazing world I had missed for so long, but at least I have so much to learn now," I answered. I hoped that met some kind of middle ground.

As the conversation fell quiet, servants began to bring platters of food out. The plates were filled with edible gold, caviar, truffles, lobster, every fancy thing you could imagine plus some foods I had never seen before. I had not tried in my life most of the things before me, so I was eager to get a bite. But after I lifted a couple of spoonfuls of caviar and lobster into my mouth, I was longing for Mrs. Handal's famous chicken and spiced potatoes. Sure, the food the Fischers gave me was good, sweet, soft, and salty, but what it couldn't give was the warm sensation of being full. To be honest, I felt more like I was eating money than dinner. That was not as satisfying as you may think.

Putting aside the meal that I still had mixed feelings about, I tried to stir up my own kind of conversation—something a little less insensitive to the majority of the world.

"So, what do you two do for work?" I questioned. Immediately, I saw that it looked like I was searching for the source of all their money. I wished I could take it back.

Both of Alden's parents opened their mouths to speak, but his father held up his hands to halt. "Penelope, you go first."

Ms. Fischer sat a bit taller in her chair at that. "It is a long-held tradition in my family, the Fischer family, to work either for the family trade business, as a diplomat, or an advisor to the reigning monarch. For me, I am in the third position. So, I basically work as the Queen's right-hand woman, helping things go smoothly in our city as well as with years across the Idum-world. It is a wonderful job for me since I am the leadership type. Ulrich," she flaunted.

"And though I just married into the family, I went with choice number two. I am the diplomat for my era, the 1910's. It was World War I back then, so it is quite a bit of work making sure we Gradiens can keep relations. But it is an honor to have the title."

"And the responsibility," Alden's sister grumbled.

Mr. Fischer grinned. "Yes, and of course the responsibility, Juliet dear."

Juliet rolled her eyes at his addition, obviously annoyed by her father's entitlement. She was a very pretty girl who looked a lot like a female version of her brother, minus the aqua eyes, of course. Her brown hair was tied back in a long ponytail, so sleek that I could barely see her tresses behind her. She wore heavy makeup, very well done I should add, and its darkness seemed to match her personality.

I expected the talking to shift back to me soon, as I was the guest of honor, but it quickly felt like I had just been invited to fill up the table. Alden's older brother was mostly quiet, along with his sister, but his mother definitely was not.

"Juliet, did you get a chance to... " she started.

"Talk to Trevor? No Mom and stop it! Trust me, it's never going to happen," Juliet interrupted. Her tone was harsher than I imagined her parents usually allowed with company. I wondered if I was acting as a shield for these kids.

Again, Ms. Fischer said, "Alden, how about you with Avarielle?"

He stared down his fork while the words floated to

him. I couldn't help but notice that Alden's shoulders were tense. "It's difficult because we go to different schools."

"But did you?" his father shouted. Quickly realizing he had raised his voice in front of a guest, Mr. Fischer rubbed his son's head, just slightly messing up his chocolate hair. "But son, did you?"

"Yeah," Alden breathed. "We did some homework together at the library. We both have a math test at the end of the week so we helped each other study a bit for that."

"Talk about anything else?" his Mom pushed.

"Mainly just math, Mom," he admitted. He looked defeated as he said it, his shoulders slumped and eyes closed.

What was the problem with just *math?*

"Well, that means there is more up for conversation tomorrow, sweetheart. Remember, the clock is ticking so stop being so shy with her. She's a *nice* girl and we need her to *like* you, Alden," Ms. Fischer continued, her voice slowly growing more aggressive with each word.

"Mom, I'm not shy, really... "

Mr. Fischer set his glass down on the table, rocking the board a bit. "You heard your mother, Alden. *Stop* being so shy."

He nodded and went back into his food, pushing some fancy vegetables around the plate. He had looked so excited to talk to me and Pandora and Lucas yesterday, like he couldn't wait to show us every spot in the city. I realized that Alden needs to use every precious second he can find to be himself. He looked like he was sticking to a script at this dinner table and the director yelled at him every time he forgot his line. Unsure of exactly how to help him, I just moved to pat Alden's shoulder in as subtle a fashion as possible. Thankfully, he smiled at me in return.

Across the table, I saw Alden's mother nudge the shoulder of his brother, Orville. Orville was incredibly handsome, I had to admit. His hair was a shade darker than Alden's, much closer to black and combed carefully across his head, not slightly curling like Alden's did. His eyes were a blinding blue and he sat with a presence that made it look like he wished to be head of the table, pushing his parents aside. He peered at me every now and then, his colorful irises seemingly trying to uncover one of my secrets. He was paler than Alden, though. I guess he didn't get outside much.

"So, Keira," Orville began. "I'll be the one to address the elephant in the room. Everyone in the city is talking about you, The Girl from the End of Time. I bet my brother or someone else has told you why it's such a big deal."

I began tapping my foot against the floor, now sure of *why* I was invited. I was an item of fascination to the Fischer family, like a strange fish whose tank they wanted to tap. The whole family wanted an insight on Lana Ilu's newest obsession. Also, I was surprised that they had already created a name for me.

"Yeah, Alden and our friend Pandora told me about it. Guess I just need to build a better reputation for the era," I said.

Ms. Fischer laughed. "Dear, you will truly have to go above and beyond for that to happen. Waldron Hawkridge is a kind of evil that few can ever redeem. I would distance yourself from your year—your so very late year—as much as possible. Nobody wants to spend time with what could possibly be Waldron's lasting legacy. It's better for you, Keira."

Now *that* got me angry. I didn't care who else in the entire world shared my era, it was still part of me. I would work my entire life in this city to match the time over 200,000 years into the future to my name, not Waldron's. It was not anyone's place, especially a random lady that I just met, to tell me to disown myself. I wanted to leave this dinner so badly, but Alden looked as miserable as I did. He wouldn't face either of his parents and was grinding his teeth. Then, out of nowhere, he spoke up, too.

"Mom, Dad, is it alright if I show Keira around the house? There's a lot of cool art stuff for me to teach her about," Alden pleaded, glancing over at me as he spoke.

His parents glared at each other, silent for what seemed like hours. But finally, they both nodded. "Be back in ten minutes, Alden. You're not usually supposed to leave the dinner table," his Dad informed us.

Immediately, Alden stood up and guided me into a side hall I had not seen before. Just like the entrance, the walls were blanketed in paintings and pottery. Gold lined each window and door, making the home seem like a slightly smaller Louvre.

"So where did your family get this?" I pushed, trying to make conversation about a sculpture until Alden shook his head at me.

"Keira, do you *really* think I asked to be excused from dinner for art?" he mocked.

I bit my tongue. "No..."

Alden brushed a hand through his hair, leaving a few strands out of place and scattered over his forehead. I'm sure his Mom would have killed him if she saw that.

"Listen Keira, I am so sorry. I knew they would be asking you about that."

"Then why'd you take yes for an answer if you knew?" I shouted.

Alden held up his hands in defense. "I just hoped they would be more civilized about it and I really wanted you to come over. It was wishful thinking with my parents and Orville, but I just wanted to believe they would." He paused and wiped his eyes for a second. "They do this with all my friends. Pandora went through the Idum-born talk and Kabir Sharma got totally pushed around for being from one of the other top families. I have this friend named Charlie who wears glasses, *glasses*, and my parents asked him why he didn't bother to get surgery to not have to wear them. And that was the first thing they said to him when he was over and we were *seven*! Just don't take it personally."

I crossed my arms but smiled at him. "Don't worry, if anyone knows that kids aren't their parents, I do. My Mom and Dad are crazy divorcees who like to ignore my existence unless they need to use me for something—ranting, guilt, getting the remote—you name it. I would never want to be anything like them."

"I'm sorry, Keira, but at least we can relate somewhat on that. Well, my parents don't ignore my existence. They ignore that I'm my own person, but sometimes I just have to deal with it. Also, trust me, some kids *definitely* take up every little aspect of their parents. Look at my older brother, for example. He just wants to be a copy of my Dad. I mean, he even dresses and cuts his hair to look like him. It's creepy!"

I laughed a bit there. "At least you know how to be

yourself a bit..." I wanted to ask him again about Avarielle, something I had pushed aside before. It was surely something personal, something awkward as it was about marriage and he was so young, but we were complaining right now so what could it hurt?

"Alden, I heard about your 'relationship' with Avarielle from my supervisor's wife. How, why, and again, *how* do you handle all that pressure?"

Alden dragged his palm down his face. "Um... I barely do. But that's one thing my parents ask of me that I'm really trying. It may sound weird, but marrying into the Royal Family is something my ancestors have been working on for centuries. And I've got a real shot, so I would like to make my family proud in that way."

"But that's so... weird! Don't you just want to make choices for yourself? And do you even like her?" I knew right after that this question sounded super awkward. Why was it my business to know who Alden may or may not have had a crush on? Maybe it was because I had never been let it on this type of gossip in Ithaca so getting even a sliver of a chance was appetizing.

Alden heaved. "It's not weird when you've grown up with it always part of your life, Keira. I know it sounds weird, but it's started to make sense now. And yeah, she's nice and *crazy* pretty and there's worse things than being a Prince in the future so sure, I like her. We should probably be heading back anyway, Keira."

I could see in Alden's darkened eyes that I had overstepped. He was willing to rage about every little issue with his family until it came to Avarielle. He complained about feeling controlled and how embarrassing they were unless we were on the topic of what I would think should be the epitome of both of those categories—arranged marriage. And the worst part for him, it wasn't even guaranteed. My parents were the worst in every possible way but being forced to like a certain person from the day I was born without knowing of any reciprocation? They wouldn't go that far.

Just as we began to walk back, Alden stopped me. "Keira, I need to ask because it's going to be uncomfortable for us if I don't. Are you upset by the Avarielle thing because of what you called me when you first came to Lana Ilu?" He looked down, but I saw that his face was bright red. The red of blushing, a color that had been absent the entire dinner. "Keira, you don't *like* me do you?"

Now my face was burning. I had never been asked this before and even though the answer was *no*, I didn't feel any better. "No, oh my gosh, no! I just thought I was dreaming then, please understand that, Alden. I don't like you at all—I mean I do like you, but not like that—you're still cool just… you know."

Alden snorted. "Ok, ok, I was just making sure. But I'm still going to use 'beautiful boy' against you the whole time we're friends, ok?"

I rolled my eyes. "Yeah, I know. Just wait until I get something for you, though. You won't even see it coming."

After our little clarification, from which I still had sweaty palms, we took our seats at the table. We didn't talk much. Alden's sister was lazily chattering about some geography assignment in school. Juliet seemed more like Alden than his brother, with a much more rebellious spirit. I had heard the way she casually called out her father for his greediness in his job and the glare she held during each exchange with her parents. She also was dealing with her parents' obsession with the Prince and Princess, as I had heard them connect Prince Trevor with her name.

"You're back!" Orville announced, too dramatically. "Keira, you like any of the art?"

"Yeah, I showed her some of our Rafael's and Yoshida's," Alden answered for me.

When I didn't respond, Alden nudged my shoulder with his, making me pipe up. "Yeah, it was super cool learning about their use of colors!"

Alden grinned at me a bit mischievously. I looked over to Juliet and she was sending the same expression. Even though Alden shared so many features with his brother, it was really Juliet whom I couldn't tell apart from him.

The rest of the meal went much smoother than before, considering we had already gotten over all the things Alden's parents hated about me. Maybe next time I was over, they would have a new list, but until then, I think I was safe. Dessert also tasted a lot better than the savory courses, with a delicious red velvet cake.

Through a mouthful of the rich cake, I jokingly asked Alden, "Do you ever eat salt-and-vinegar chips around here? Or do they make you like common folk?"

Alden shook his fork at me. "Only in dark alleyways when I get them from my snack dealer." he mumbled. "But I think my parents are starting to figure it out."

I gasped. "Well, then, you either need to quit or find a quieter snack dealer."

"Trust me, I've been looking but the market's small," he joked.

We both laughed at the idea and I could tell Alden took joy in mocking his parents right in front of them. Juliet snuck over to our side of the table to scoop another dollop of whipped cream and carefully put herself into the conversation.

"I enjoy your peaceful act of rebellion," she whispered. "But you may want to be a little quieter like you want your future snack dealer to be."

Alden and I snickered after hearing that, but kept our voices down. I didn't want his parents to scold him before bed for eating salt-and-vinegar chips. My parents had actually done that a handful of times. It was not something to look forward to.

When dinner ended and I was about to go home, Juliet was the first to say goodbye. She wrapped me in a small hug and then smiled, a warmer smile than I had seen at the beginning of the night. "It was really nice having you here, tonight. I can tell you're going to be an awesome friend for my brother and probably me, too. Also, I love your infinity necklace. Very true to the city!" she chirped.

"My sister actually got it for me a long time ago, way before I knew I was a Gradien," I told her.

"Well, then your sister either can tell the future or just has *really* good taste."

"Oh, it's both."

Juliet then waved again, but just as I was heading out the door, Ms. Fischer kept me inside. She peered down the hallway intensely, stretching her neck to check the entire path. Then, with her near black eyes she scowled at me.

"Don't think I don't know what you are doing, young lady," she slammed.

"I, I don't," I tried to croak out.

"As I'm certain you could catch from the conversation at the table, Alden and the rest of this family is working immensely hard to seal a future marriage between my son and the Princess. And I've had this talk with Pandora and all the other girls he's been friends with, but now that Alden is older, I see that you are the one to worry about. I saw your little side conversations and all the shoulder nudges and laughing. Do *not* distract my son with that pretty little face of yours or I can assure you that you will never see Alden ever again. Is that understood?" Ms. Fischer threatened.

"I'm just Alden's friend ma'am, I barely know him..." I was nearly quivering.

"I said *is that understood?*"

I nodded quickly. "Yes, Ms. Fischer. It is very much understood."

Then, with a bright red smile, she wiggled her fingers in a friendly wave and guided me out the door. All I could think was poor, *poor* Alden.

CHAPTER 13

T HE NEXT DAY IN LANA ILU WAS MY
first day of school, or whatever school was for a newcomer. Mr. Handal owned a levitator (which was painted
bright blue!), so it was basically the coolest ride to school
I had ever experienced. We had run a bit late after breakfast because Theo spilled oatmeal on his shirt and Holly
declared that she would "never besmirch her good name
by walking around with a filthy boyfriend." That was also
the first time she had called Theo her boyfriend, which
he smiled at for the entire morning. So, since Theo and
Holly were sure they were going to miss half of their first
period class, Mr. Handal cheated the speed limit and
flew the levitator a level higher than the rest, practically
zooming through the sky. I couldn't help but laugh at the
cars driving below us.

After the thrilling ride, we arrived at the *West School*, a towering clay stone building etched with domes. The inside was brightly lit and students passed through the halls endlessly. I had seen it before over the weekend, when it was more of a hangout spot than a school. But now it was buzzing with academia, everyone with a book or tablet in hand.

"Keira," Mr. Handal said. "Just walk straight in the building and you will see the main office. In there, they will tell you how the remainder of the school year will go. And my wife is busy today so you'll need to find your own way home, alright?"

"Alright," the three of us answered in unison.

As we headed up the main path, still crowded with late students like ourselves, Theo and Holly grabbed my shoulders.

"Make new friends," Theo said.

"Focus in class," Holly added.

And then together, "Be good."

I stifled a laugh. "I think I figured that out on my own already."

They both shrugged at each and nodded, both sent me a smile before they headed to class. It was a small goodbye, just enough for me to know they were only gone for the day.

Just like instructed, I walked directly into the school and didn't make a single turn until I saw the main office. It was illuminated by a series of mini chandeliers, some classic and others modern, glittering in the middle of the day. There were several desks inside, each occupied by someone busy working. I went to the first desk I saw, metallic like the Alloys. It had silvery sheets and screens. Others were covered in parchment.

"Hello, I'm Keira Sun and I just arrived in Lana Ilu a

few days ago. I know this is supposed to be my first day at school here but I'm not sure where to go."

The man looked up from his desk, wide eyed like so many others I had encountered. "Keira Sun, the... Yes, um, one moment."

He searched through one of his devices before facing me again. "You will be in the outdoor library today."

I thanked him and went back into the hallway, asking teachers and other students for help on my way. I soon found myself outside, where stacks of books piled into stone racks. There were scattered desks about the cobblestone floor, most occupied by a working student. I noticed Lucas reclining in one of the chairs and rushed over to the empty desk beside him. He smiled when he saw me.

"Get yours," he said, pointing at a computer-like object on his table. "This is school... in now..."

I stepped up from my desk and walked over to where a young man was seated, a single computing device beside him. Seeing that everyone else in the library, a couple dozen people, had one of the devices, I picked up the final one for myself. Hearing the light clank against his desk, the proctor looked up at me.

"Oh Keira, you're here," he said. "That's the last Magistone here so it's already set up for you. All you need to do is turn it on and scan your eyes so it can connect to your ears and let you hear it."

"Why would I scan my eyes if it's for hearing?" I asked, holding the gold tablet in my hands.

The proctor took a sip of his coffee. "I don't know really. Just... technology."

Considering this man was working at one of the two schools in Lana Ilu, I would have figured he would have been a bit more knowledgeable, or at least cared about learning in some way. But he seemed incredibly unfocused about watching the library and answered my question with 'just... technology.' I thought everyone in Lana Ilu was experienced with the greatest in innovation.

I headed back over to Lucas and sat down beside him.

"Late," he joked, raising his eyebrows at me.

I stuck my tongue out. "Be quiet. We're in class."

Lucas rolled his eyes and pointed back at the proctor. "You think he looks? Keira... "

"Fine, I guess you're right. It's fun to slack a little sometimes, anyway."

He squinted his eyes at me and bit his tongue, trying to decipher what I had just said. Again, I felt guilty for either talking too fast or using words he might not have known. Growing up in upstate New York, even though I got to see all kinds of people at Cornell and had plenty of people who spoke Chinese in my family, I still took it for granted that everyone knew English. I hated myself for just assuming that, something for my own benefit.

"What did you do..." I moved my thumb back to symbolize *yesterday*.

Lucas shook his head at me, laughing. "Keira, I *know* what yesterday means, you know, that what you are saying, correct?"

"Yeah, sorry..." I mumbled.

"And I went to uh... a basketball game with Alden after his school. It was for two teams here and it was really fun. The basketballs... they go to players after uh... the hoop, just them. No people throwing."

I grinned at him. "Sounds fun! Did you see your family, too?"

Lucas put his head down. "Abuela and my sisters. They, I think, understand."

"How about your parents? Shouldn't they have found out that you're a Gradien."

Lucas looked down and rubbed his palms slowly together. "Um... Keira, my father is dead from, uh, car accident and my mama is in the hospital with cancer. Abuela will tell her."

Quickly, unsure of how to respond, I leaned in and hugged him. Thankfully, he wrapped his arms around me, too. "I'm so sorry for bringing it up Lucas, I had no idea. You're really strong for keeping going and..."

"Yeah, I know, thanks. I, I love them, so much." He ran a hand through his espresso hair. "What did you do yesterday?"

A million thoughts ran through my mind when he asked that question. Yesterday felt like enough to fill an entire month. My parents pretending that they ever truly cared about me, having to leave Willow, learning Pandora's life story and possibly finding my true best friend, and don't even get me started on the Fischers. They were an entire different tale in themselves.

"Told my parents and my sister that I was a Gradien. My sister, Willow was great, but my parents... not so much. Then I hung out with Pandora..." I cut myself off, realizing I was about to share her love for the Alloys. That seemed like something secret, for us. If she wanted Lucas to know, she would tell him.

"Um, we just went to the park. Then Alden's family had me for dinner which was a lot. Those rich people..."

"Yeah, I saw his house. Why do people need really big place?"

"Oh, the answer is that they don't. It's just for show, probably not even comfortable to live in."

Lucas nodded, though when he was about to respond, the proctor came over to us and put a finger up to his lips. "Do your work."

We laughed and turned back to our tablets. Just like I was told, I held it up to my eyes and felt a dim light run a scan. Suddenly, I heard a ding in my ears. After I chose English as my language, an entire lesson plan popped up, with designed periods for each topic. The class started with math as the Magistone's voice instructed me on those angles I had left on. To be honest, I think I finally understood it. The day went on as a mellow female voice taught me from nearly exactly where I dropped off in Ithaca, from cell biology to grammar. There was a lunch in between where Lucas and I headed to the nearby sandwich shop, but other than that, I actually wanted to be focused on my academics. *That* was definitely a change. Part of me wanted to go tell my parents, particularly my Mom, that I was finally liking school. But I wanted this to be for me. My love of learning was my own and no one else's.

Finally, the proctor let us out and Lucas and I met up with Alden and Pandora in front of the school.

"How was your first day?" Pandora inquired. "Learn a lot?"

"Yeah, the Magistone is cool," Lucas answered. "Better than some teachers."

"Lana Ilu ones included, I can tell you that," Alden added. "At least the Magistone never yells."

"I have to say, she was nice to listen to. Hey, can we stop by *Dolce's* for those Clock Cookies? I could *really* go for those," I suggested.

They all agreed and we made our way to the cafe. By the time we got there, even though school had just been let out, the place was already crowded with students. Friend groups hung out at tables, sipping coffee and hot chocolate, while couples found space for their after-school dates. The few adults there looked greatly annoyed by all the *youth* around them, shutting their eyes and complaining to each other about the noise. Generation gap was a universal thing.

After getting in line and purchasing our cookies, the four of us found a half-occupied table that we had to share with a group of high-school seniors discussing their upcoming prom. But right as we sat down, Alden started grumbling at his multi.

"My Dad just told me I need to get home now. Sorry, guys. You stay here and hang out, though. Don't worry about me," Alden told us, sulking. Cookie in hand, he left the busy restaurant and started heading down the street to his mansion.

Though Lucas and I were definitely feeling bad for him, Pandora seemed desensitized to the whole situation. I guess she was just used to it at this point.

"So, Lucas and Keira, I *need* to tell you guys about something that happened in my gym class today."

"Keira?" A voice behind me rang. Surprised, I turned around to see a boy close to my age, with short coily curls and dark-toned skin, surrounded by a dozen other guys. He wore a dressy button-up and pants, too mature and fashionable for a kid probably leaving high school.

"Yeah?" I asked, a little annoyed that I had been interrupted. His friends all laughed and the people standing by watched firmly, scanning me like I was some sort of prey.

"Are you Keira Sun?" The boy said again, his group staring from behind.

"Yes, why?" I was nervous now because I knew this was about the whole *Girl from the End of Time* thing, which I was already over. But I was also a little scared of getting attention from such an obviously popular guy, especially one that was pretty cute.

"Hey, everyone's been talking about you, especially in my house." There was laughter around his friends at that. "How's Lana Ilu treating you?" he charmed.

I felt my face turn red. "Oh, it's really nice here, different from my old home. Who are you? Sorry, I don't know..."

His friends hollered, but he forced them to stay quiet. "I'm Trevor Imamu, it's nice to meet you finally. You're everything people talk about in Lana Ilu right now."

Trevor Imamu, I thought. *This was the Prince and he was talking to me!* I suddenly felt more star struck than I had ever been and I once met Bill Nye the Science Guy!

"Oh, you're, you're the Prince!" I screeched. Embarrassed, I calmed down and tried to lean back on my chair for the "relaxed" look. "I mean... hey..."

He smiled at me with his *incredibly* white teeth. "Yeah, I'm the Prince," he admitted, waving jazz hands. "You seen the city yet?"

"Yep, most of it," I said, pointing back to Pandora. "My new friends showed me around, so a lot."

Trevor gestured towards the front door, away from his now growing squad. "Could I talk to you for a second?"

Hesitant and definitely a little scared, I peered back to Lucas and Pandora. Both of them were gawking at me due to the shocking attention, but they shared grins. Pandora mouthed *Go* at me while Lucas shoved his hands in the air, simulating pushing my back. I guess it wasn't common that the Prince or any of the Royal Family took interest in regular Gradiens, so everyone in this whole cafe was taken aback.

"Sure, of course," I answered, walking over to meet him by the door.

CHAPTER 14

TREVOR LOOKED BACK AT THE CAFE
smiling, his russet eyes scanning every person inside.
He looked quite wary for a Prince, who would usually
have had bodyguards at every turn and the entire city on
look out if he was ever harmed. But then again, he entered
Dolce's with his only protection being his popularity and
crowd of friends. Now, leaving the restaurant with only
me, he was unshielded, but his apprehension lowered. I
could tell he was unique.

"So, I'm guessing you haven't seen much of the Palace
of Time," Trevor supposed.

I started to twist my infinity necklace around. "Yeah,
just the outside, but it looks like something out of a
dream. I mean, those rotating towers and that strange
shining glow! How is that even possible?"

Trevor shrugged his shoulders. "Keira, I was born there

and I don't even know. I doubt my Grandma even truly does. But you're soon going to see within those walls."

Peering at the Prince, at *Trevor*, for just a moment, I saw that I needed to ask why I was today's lucky guest at the Palace. He was looking forward at the road, seemingly distracted from me, but every now and then his dark eyes would face my way.

"Uh... Trevor, just, are you only taking me on this tour because you know, I'm the Girl from the End of Time?" I halfway interrogated.

"I'm not going to lie to you and say no," he responded.

I scoffed. "I appreciate the honesty, trust me. I haven't seen it much."

Trevor laughed. "Well, everyone deserves honesty, but you *are* Lana Ilu's biggest obsession and headline and from being the city's Prince, I know how it feels to be in the spotlight. For all of the attention you have and will be dealing with, you at least deserve to see some cool stuff all those annoying people don't." Trevor smirked at me. "It's just solidarity."

'Thanks, that actually means a lot."

"Keira, I saw Pandora talking to you and I know her a bit. Who was that other guy you're friends with?" The Prince asked.

"Oh, his name's Lucas Acosta. He arrived here the same day as me."

Trevor nodded. "Make any other friends while you've been here? I know it hasn't been that long but we've got some good Gradiens here."

I clicked my tongue. "The only other one besides the two people around my age living in my sector is Alden

Fischer. I know his family's status is pretty high, *very* high actually, so I'm sure you know him."

"Yeah, he's one of my closest friends! He's the greatest, I'm glad you know him," Trevor said, giving me confidence about the friendship. But all of a sudden, Trevor's head sunk and he began to wring his hands together. "How, how'd you meet him?"

"Oh, he was my welcomer. It was really awkward for both of us... I was freaking out and thought I was either dreaming or being kidnapped, but he had never welcomed an Idum-born before, so he had no idea how to calm me down. Then we kind of just started shouting at one another and then he just sort of hugged me, which was also awkward."

"His family wants him to marry my sister and my Grandma likes him so he's probably going to," Trevor snapped. "Just so you know that about him."

I nodded. "Yeah... I've heard." I wasn't interested in staying on that topic anymore. I had already heard enough about Alden's unfortunate arranged engagement and decided to go in a completely different direction. For me and Alden, and for Trevor, because his clenched fists did not look promising. I guess he wanted a different husband for his sister. "So, what's your year, Trevor?"

Trevor's face lit up, though his eyes were still dim. "Oh yes, my energy is from the year 3000. I guess it's a pretty cool time considering it's about a thousand years into our future."

"And it's an even number. All those zeros give it a good ring," I charmed.

Trevor shook his head. "You don't need to try and flatter me or whatever just because I'm the Prince."

Eyes wide, I waved my hands in defense. "I was not trying to do that, I promise. I sincerely thought it was cool..."

Not responding to what I had said, Trevor started to walk faster to what I noticed was in fact the Palace of Time. Just like a couple days ago, crowds of people still closed in the structure, taking photographs or sitting down, scribbling in notebooks. It looked like too busy a place to write, but I wasn't a writer anyway. A girl in my grade started writing a book and every teacher was all over her determination and creativity and whatever, but I was just amazed she had the time. I mean, what kind of person writes a book *and* does homework?

Anyways, the moment Trevor took even the slightest step with his polished loafers onto the castle grounds, every head turned. Kids began to pull at their parents' clothes and a couple cameras began to flash in my eyes. There were a few shouts at the fact that Trevor was walking into the Palace with a girl, or a guest at all that had nobody had seen before. Then, the inevitable happened.

"Guys, it's The Girl from the End of Time!" a voice yelled.

"Keira Sun? Her?" Another screamed back.

"And she's with Prince Trevor!" a third person announced.

The people in the crowd began to push into one another, trying to catch a glimpse not of Trevor but *me*. I heard the snaps of photographs and typing on tablets, screams of gossip, and the movement of pens.

Suddenly, Trevor grabbed my arm and pulled me through the dozens. I could tell from his forward stride that he was *very* used to dealing with public craze. I guess I had to learn as well.

As we neared the castle doors, which had been opened

by guards already for us, Trevor leaned in close to my ear. "The crowd really loves you," he joked.

I rolled my eyes, but I knew he hated the attention just as much as I did. Oh, and on that note, for anyone who is yearning to be in the spotlight, *stop*. It's the worst. At last, we entered the reflective platinum doors, which shut immediately behind us. Amazingly, there was no *boom* or *thump*, but a mellow hush as the doors joined together. Again, it's just Lana Ilu stuff. Even at this point, I still wanted to call it magic.

The indoors were how I imagined any fairytale castle to appear. Portraits painted with dozens of styles lined the golden walls and the floors were lined with diamonds. The rugs were velvet and woven with what seemed like pure light, which I was pretty sure was impossible. It was not much quieter inside the Palace, with servants bustling through the corridors and advisors rushing to their respective office. A few of the people inside greeted Trevor, only to send me a shaking *hello*, as well.

"So, what do you want to see?" Trevor asked. "The library? The dining hall? The ballroom?"

"The ballroom!" I answered. "That sounds amazing!"

He showed me the way through what seemed like a dozen more hallways, this castle really had no ending, until we were confronted with brass doors. After pushing them open, glass floors and crystal chandeliers reflected rainbows about the room. Five thrones, the most stately in the center, stood across from the entrance. There was a velvet rope in front, yet I was sure it was much more than an exhibit. The entire ballroom looked big enough to fit two hundred thousand people. Then, my eyes drifted to an object Alden had mentioned to me not long after

I arrived in Lana Ilu—The Golden Grandfather Clock. Just like its name said, the structure was made entirely of shining metal, like a star in the night sky. It stood at least one hundred feet away, and every tick of the second hand echoed through the hall.

"Lana Ilu is a perfect circle, 161.803 square miles, and that amazing clock is right in the center of it all," Trevor informed me.

"Did your ancestors, you know, the Royals of the past, do that on purpose?"

Trevor shrugged his shoulders. "I mean, where else would they put it?"

"So, do you have real balls here or is this just for show?" I asked, still incredibly curious.

"Well, there's parties all the time, but we do have one major ball each year. In the very beginning of September, the entire city is invited to the Royal Ball. Of course, that's about a million people, but usually only a fifth of that comes. Lots of people instead watch it on their TVs or have their own parties, or go time traveling or... don't like my family. It's a great ball, though."

I clasped my hands together and jumped, deciding to ignore Prince Trevor's *don't like my family* addition for the time being. "Oh gosh, I can't wait to go! I've *never* been to a dance other than like a family wedding or something in elementary school, so that's going to be a refreshing change."

Trevor raised his eyebrows. "I have to go every year, so I'll see you there, Keira. Now come on, I want to show you the observatory."

As Trevor went running to the opposite side of the ballroom, I raced to keep up with him, not wanting to get lost. This Palace itself seemed bigger than all of Ithaca and I was sure one wrong step could take me to a part the Royal Family themselves probably never knew of. Seeing Trevor going up marble stairs, I followed him level after level. Then, out of nowhere, Trevor halted in his steps. I bumped into him from the sudden stop.

"Grandmother!" he exclaimed. "I didn't realize you were coming downstairs now."

The woman, whom I realized was Queen Prima, chuckled. "Trevor sweetheart, I come down whenever I please. Now, no more running in my staircases, understood? I was going down to gather some books from the library for my lesson with Avarielle and you are lucky you ran into me before I was holding them."

Trevor sunk his head. "Of course, Grandmother. I won't do it anymore."

The Queen looked past her grandson and onto me, giving me a better view of the older woman. She wore her hair in her an afro, the black curls highlighted by the occasional silver lock. Despite her being in her sixties, Queen Prima shone with youth, her skin still golden and barely wrinkled. Her makeup matched her hair, metallic and dark and perfect with her skin tone. She wore a beautiful red gown, topped with short sleeves and a jeweled belt. The most shocking was the soft smile she gave me, despite not knowing what I, a strange girl, was doing in her home *with her grandson.*

"Dear, are you Miss Keira Sun?" the Queen asked me, tilting her head at the idea.

Nervous, my eyes widened as I froze. As anxious as I was when I met Trevor, that feeling was amplified a thousand times in the Queen's presence.

"Yes, Your Majesty," I quivered. "I know my name has become quite famous recently."

Queen Prima fluttered her eyes and grinned again. I knew the gesture was intended to be comforting, but the fact that she still stood what seemed a foot taller than me was not helping. "That it has. I was actually meaning to call you into the Palace to get to know Lana Ilu's new star, but it seems my grandson has done that instead."

Trevor blushed for a moment, but kept his head down.

"Trevor, if you do not mind, may I take Keira for the remainder of the afternoon? I would love to speak with her on, well, both the obvious and the not so obvious," the Queen requested, as if she ever had to request anything. I mean, she was the *Queen.*

Trevor nodded. "Yes, Grandmother. I was going to start my homework soon anyway."

Queen Prima patted her grandson's head, combing her fingers through his short curls. "Thank you, you may go now. And Keira, please follow me to my study."

Shaky, I watched Trevor rush off the stairs as quickly as possible, until he remembered to stop running and immediately took up a slow pace. In her diamond heels, the Queen walked back up the stairs, though I noticed she had not gone back for a single book for her lesson with Avarielle. I was sure not to correct her, though. Like I said, she was the *Queen.*

At last, we reached what I believed was the fifth floor of the castle and it was even more stunning than the first. But what caught my eye the most was a girl around my age, impatiently tapping her foot against the floor. I could tell immediately she was Princess Avarielle, Trevor's sister, Alden's 'hopefully' betrothed and Lana Ilu's second in line.

Though Avarielle was dressed casually in wide leg corduroy pants and a fitted white blouse, she looked nothing short of a Princess. Her hair was braided in three intricate plaits, all winding upon one another over her scalp, forming the shape of a flower. Within the shape were threads of pure gold. She looked quite a bit like Trevor, with his same dark eyes and skin. She had a commanding look to her stare, though, that I had not seen in him, a glance that could kill and soothe all at once. I might have been even more nervous to meet her than the Queen.

"Grandmother, you're back...-" Avarielle started before looking down at me. I felt her eyes decode me, reading into exactly who I was. "The Girl from the End of Time," she stated. She did not ask or wonder. She knew. She made sure *I* knew that she knew.

"Avarielle, I am so sorry, but I will have to postpone our lesson for about half an hour. Keira Sun is here and I have very important topics to discuss with her," Queen Prima said.

Avarielle crossed her arms, but kept her lips shut. She too knew not to argue with the Queen. "Alright, Grandmother. I'll just... *review* what we did last time *again*."

The Queen nodded and continued towards her study, but I was terrified to pass by Avarielle. Her eyes were like lasers and I knew she had good aim. And, just as I feared, Avarielle did lean into me as I crept closer to the study.

"We'll talk after."

CHAPTER 15

DESPITE THE FACT THAT THE PRIN-cess, who may I remind you is my future leader as well, had terrified me beyond reason, I continued on with the present Queen into her study. The room itself was half the size of my old house, each wall completely coated in books. I had seen plenty of futuristic technology in Lana Ilu, practically everywhere I turned in fact, but Queen Prima seemed to prefer older styles. While the Palace itself had some postmodern elements, her study was devoid of a single piece of technology with the exception of a few lamps. Even the air conditioning was just her open window.

When the Queen took a seat at her desk, I kept standing though she told me to sit in the other chair. It was odd being at the same level as Queen Prima. I expected her chair to be more like a throne and mine a beanbag, considering our difference in rank, yet we sat nearly eye to eye.

"So, Keira, how have you enjoyed discovering that you are a Gradien, something I'm positive you never heard of before?" the Queen asked, relaxing in her cushioned seat.

"It was great, it's nice to know who I truly am."

Then, increasing my worry that I was saying every possible wrong thing, the Queen began to shake her finger at me. "No, Keira. You discovered you were a Gradien, not who you truly are. Few ever discover that and it requires much more than biological identity."

I nodded. "Of course, Your Majesty. I realize that now."

"Oh Keira, don't act so nervous and proper. You sound like my grandchildren and *goodness* do those two need to lighten up around me," the Queen said, laughing quietly.

I had noticed both Trevor and Avarielle's apprehensive behavior around the Queen. Every word they said shook despite sounding like they had rehearsed it a million times. They walked on eggshells around their grand-mother, like any slip up would disgrace her entire name. It was odd that she wished to me that they would stop.

"So, I trust every person you have met has brought up your year. You *do* have a name for it, too."

"Yes, I have heard it constantly, wherever I go. To be honest, it has gotten quite annoying," I admitted to the Queen.

Queen Prima rested her chin upon her hand. "It may seem that way at first, dear, but you will value it soon. Having a name given so long after birth is an item of power. Use it as you see fit."

Unsure of exactly how to respond to such a statement,

I just supplied a simple "yes," but the Queen saw right through my reply.

"I know my words are confusing at first, Keira, but I see us talking quite a bit in both our futures. You will learn to understand me without a dictionary."

Still pretty confused and shocked that the Queen wanted to speak with me beyond today, considering the fact that I was not exactly a terrific conversationalist, I just sat there quietly. I knew of one question I wanted to ask her, but I still felt worried about letting a single sound roll off my tongue.

"Um, Your Majesty..."

"Just call me Queen Prima, Keira."

"Queen Prima, there must have been some reason you wanted to talk to me, something deeper than what anyone else has said. What is it?"

The Queen stood up and pulled a book that appeared to weigh half a ton off one of the shelves. Then she slid it down onto the desk in front of me. The novel was bound with leather, in the fashion of books written centuries ago. But something about it felt perfectly new.

"Keira, I want you to understand that I do not fear you because of your shared era with Waldron Hawkridge. Though that man terrorized me, I more than anyone else understands that a person is not their birth. My father, the King, hated me for being his only Gradien child as all my siblings are Idums. He wanted a son, but he never got one that could live in Lana Ilu. He treated me like an inconvenience until the day he died, forcing me to marry and have a child even though I protested." The Queen walked over to the end of the desk and picked up a photograph of her when she was younger, in a white wedding dress. Beside her was a tall, dark-haired man, looking at her fondly even though she only faced the camera. "My husband, Anthony, passed a few months ago. I did not want to marry him, but he was a very good man. A caring husband who never hurt or betrayed me once. It was arranged by my father so I cannot blame Anthony for the haste of it all. He was there for me for over 45 years." The Queen peered at the ground. "It wasn't love but it was enough."

Sitting back down, the Queen looked wistfully out the crystal window. Then she faced me again. "As I was saying, Keira, I do not see you as I saw Waldron Hawkridge, whatever you may think. Just as I did, I trust you will make your own name."

"I will definitely try, Queen Prima."

The Queen grinned, her red lips curling up towards her ears. "Just in those words, dear, you already have begun." She took a sip from a glass on her desk, filled with a drink I could not see. "You know, my year is 35,816 *BCE*. That is quite long ago. Humans had not even begun farming. And you, dear, are the furthest this city and entire world knows before humans die out. From that fact, you would probably think we are worlds apart, but Keira, we are more similar than anyone else in this city."

"May I ask what you mean?" I asked, continuing with my streak of bewilderment.

"Yes, of course, I'm not here to keep you in the dark. What I mean, Keira, is that we are from the two most curious peoples ever to roam the Earth. For me, the people barely existed as we humans do. We were just primitive animals, surviving every day as best as we could. There was no writing or language or society. It was just existence. Back then, humans knew so little that they were forced to be curious to live. If they had not been curious, we would not know which berries are poisonous and that fire is and will be the greatest discovery of all time. The world was just big to them, they knew not of continents or straits or rare animals on the other side of the world. They were curious about the dirt beneath their feet. For your people, time has already run out for them. They are not even completely human, being more fit for water than land in all those years. You know, after the next Ice Age, water disperses differently, flooding even more than we have now and forcing humans to be semi-aquatic. They know of every equation and pattern and star in the sky. Your people have explored every centimeter of the ocean and millions of galaxies. They can construct working brains from recycled plastic and speak with life lightyears away. They know *absolutely* everything, so as humans die off, they leave curious of whatever they possibly could have missed, no matter how small."

The Queen took a deep breath and looked out her window once again. This time she spread her manicured hands along the windowsill and sighed against the glass. She was looking down on the city's gorgeous architecture and diverse people. Her mouth was straight but her brown eyes shone with delight. "Keira, I have always hated the phrase 'curiosity killed the cat': how disrespectful to both parties! Curiosity might be dangerous, but in all honesty, it is the greatest item of creation. Curiosity *built* the universe because without it, humans would have sat on this Earth without ever asking about what was beyond their blue sky. To think, the universe would have never existed to people without curiosity and someone had the nerve to call it a killer of the purely innocent."

"I guess we are similar in that way," I whispered, before repeating it louder for the Queen to hear. Then, I looked back down on the mountain of a book on her desk. Now, I saw that the title was *History of the Universe*. I was sure it was at least five thousand pages long, which was quite short for all eternity.

"I have a copy in every language," Queen Prima said. "Please open it to the first page."

Lifting the ten-pound cover, I dropped it back onto the wooden desk. I kept my eyes shut when the parchment first met my glance, maybe out of fear, maybe out of respect. Something about this book felt holy, like the meaning of life was hidden inside it. Finally, I began to read.

Things happened.

That was it, just two simple words in the center of the first page. I flipped through several dozen more, but they were all completely blank. It must have been some kind of joke or a replaced copy. The Queen would never own something like this.

"It... " I croaked out.

"I know, a bit surprising, huh? How could one *ever* have a book titled *History of the Universe*? I'm a time traveler who could go to any year she wants and even I know there are new things discovered with each passing second. It was pointless to edit the book every day, so I settled on the best summary of history I could find. *Things happened*, because they have and always will. Even without life, *things happen*."

Then, all of a sudden, Queen Prima began shuffling me out the door. "I'm sorry, Keira," she said. "I did promise my granddaughter that we would have our Queenship lesson today and it's not right to keep her waiting for too long. It was wonderful speaking with you."

"It was wonderful speaking with you too, Queen Prima," I responded.

Afterwards, I swung open the door of the study to see Avarielle standing with her arms crossed in front of me. She was still tapping her foot against the floor, even though I had already left the study and she was free to enter. But she did not move a step.

"How was your conversation with *my* grandmother, Keira? She enrich you with the secrets of the world and all that?" Avarielle teased.

"No, I wouldn't put it that way, but the Queen is a very smart woman," I said, trying to coax Avarielle into no longer being mad at me. But trust me, it didn't work.

Avarielle batted her eyes. "Oh yes, I know that. In fact, *I* was supposed to get some of that wisdom in my lesson which is now starting late because of you. You see, Keira, I am the future Queen, which is closer than you may think because my father plans to abdicate the throne as soon as he gets it. My Grandmother is the *only* teacher that I can trust and I don't appreciate you taking up my precious time with her. And also, whatever she may have told you, the Queen really did want to make sure you were not the next Waldron Hawkridge." Avarielle began to inspect her fingernails. "I guess you passed."

"I'm sorry, Princess, but Queen Prima did speak to me about much more. And she clarified that me being evil was not one of her worries."

Avarielle began to walk into the study but looked back at me once more before entering. "Keira, I hate to break it to you, but sometimes people say what they need to say to make friends with who they need to make friends with. My Grandmother is no exception."

I wanted to believe that Avarielle was lying, that she was just jealous and wanted to hurt me. But there was a look of sincerity in her eyes that I could not brush off.

CHAPTER 16

TODAY, FRIDAY, AFTER ALL OF US HAD
gotten out of school, Alden's family and Pandora had
been invited to a birthday party. It was being held by the
fourth ultra-wealthy family of the city, the Sharmas, for their
daughter Sonam's 14th. Alden decided to bring Lucas along,
while I was Pandora's guest. I had met the father before when
he was the doctor that conducted all of my era-scanning
tests, the lasers still ingrained in my brain. Apparently, he
rarely ever participated in the actual tests and rather managed everything medical in Lana Ilu, but stopped in from
time to time. Part of me wondered if he'd had a suspicion
that I would be The Girl from the End of Time.

It was outdoors at Imamu Park, obviously named for
the Royal Family. The Sharmas had rented it out for the
night and a crowd of two hundred people were there. All
of Alden's friends' families would be there. This meant

that, for the first time, I was going to stop being shy. Pandora suggested I practice my talking skills on individuals in a huge crowd. If I messed up, there was always someone to move on to.

We arrived at the lush park. A massive gazebo sat right in the center. We were early so most of the party had not arrived yet, though there was a large group of kids who looked no older than five sitting in a circle on the lawn. There was an older girl in the center speaking to them. I realized it was Princess Avarielle. I was still scared of her.

After a few minutes, the group of kids broke apart, running to adults waiting for them on the other side of the lawn. Avarielle began walking in our direction, one of the children still hanging onto her leg.

"Thank you for the class, Princess," a little boy said. "My family can take me to see Ancient China now!"

Avarielle beamed down at the child. "Of course, Ben! It was my pleasure to teach you all about time travel. I mean, it is the most important thing to all of us Gradiens." She ruffled his hair after saying that.

Ben nodded. "Yes, and I know so much now! Have a nice day, Princess!" the boy cried before heading off to his mother.

After her conversation, Avarielle started to walk closer to my group, a wide smile spread across her face. I hadn't talked to her since that day in the Palace of Time, which I still wake up from nightmares about. It wasn't that I was exactly terrified of Avarielle or worried she would hurt me, but rather I was scared of how smart she was. Avarielle seemed like she could discover one's darkest secrets by just hearing their name, and I suddenly wondered if I had anything to hide.

"God, I love kids...Hi Pandora," Avarielle said first,

waving to my friend. "Did you ever get your group to finish that biology project?"

"Barely. I *still* had to take over like always," Pandora complained.

Avarielle grinned back at her before scanning me like she had in the castle. She cocked her eyebrows but continued to pass on to the next person, acting like she hadn't even noticed I was there. Where her eyes settled next was Alden, whose face had already begun to blaze. I wondered if he knew how much he blushed.

"Hey, how are you, Alden?" Avarielle asked.

"Um... I'm good, Avarielle," he stuttered.

Avarielle pushed a loose curl out of her face (her hair was unbraided today) and whispered something to Alden the rest of us couldn't hear. He smiled back at her and said, "thank you," making me even more curious about what she had told him.

Then, before leaving the group, Avarielle faced Lucas, still not making any eye contact with me. "Hi, are you new? What's your name?" she questioned.

Lucas nodded, looking as nervous speaking with the Princess as I had with the Prince. "Yes, I lived here for three weeks. And I'm Lucas."

"Well, Lucas, I'm so glad to have you here. See you guys later at the birthday party, ok? I have to somehow get all dressed up to celebrate with one of my closest friends in twenty minutes."

Pandora, Lucas, and Alden all laughed and wished her luck, but I stayed silent. She still hadn't said a word to me. Avarielle moved on like she had noticed a pile of animal droppings amongst where my friends were standing, just wrinkling her nose at the sight.

"So, what did Avarielle tell you?" Pandora asked, supplying my question.

Alden shrugged. "Just to tell my parents that we spoke a lot today, to make me look good."

Pandora rubbed his shoulder. "It's really great that she's here for you about this all."

While Alden looked appreciative of Avarielle and Lucas was still near heart-eyed from the encounter, I could not brush off the way she looked at me. I assumed when I met her that Avarielle was just obnoxious to every person she met, considering that even though I was a complete stranger she still ridiculed my every move. She was defensive and angry, yet joked with Pandora about school. She welcomed Lucas, *sincerely*, and told Alden he could lie about her to make sure he didn't get yelled at tonight. But what really *was* her problem with me?

Deciding that I needed to confront this before it got worse, I ran after the Princess. She walked with long strides, seemingly clearing more ground in a step than I could do in three. She still scared me.

"Princess Avarielle!" I called. "May I talk to you?"

"I already told you that I was busy. I have to get ready and I'd really love if you stopped delaying everything I need to do," she said, not even turning around.

I caught up to her, practically having to gallop across the park, but got the Princess to face me. Her eyelids were low as she glared at me, with her lips pursed. She was rolling her hand, telling me to get moving on whatever I was 'wasting her time' with.

"Avarielle... "

She stopped me immediately. "It's still Princess

Avarielle to you or Your Royal Highness if I'm in that kind of mood, but continue."

I had to keep myself from rolling my eyes. "Well, *Princess Avarielle*, I mean no disrespect, but you're really confusing me. When I first met you, I'm sorry, but you were so mean to me. You blamed me for your Grandmother's choice and made it seem like *I* was threatening your success as the future Queen and you said that Queen Prima was lying to me. All of those things were just kinda... obnoxious and I know you're definitely smart enough to understand that. Then I see you today and you seem really nice. You volunteer with children and welcome my new friend and support people going through things and whatever. So why do you hate me so much?"

Avarielle's eyes widened, obviously surprised by my confrontation. "Ok, first of all, nobody is nice to everybody. People who are equally friendly to every person they meet are the worst kind of people, because they are never authentic. Also, I don't hate you but I do have a problem with you, Keira, one I think you can figure out."

"You said you didn't think I had anything to do with Waldron Hawkridge though."

"And I still don't. You really need to stop with your whole 'but I'm not him' pity party, ok? Nobody really thinks you are his shell or whatever. I just think you're taking things for granted."

"How could I be taking things for granted? I hate all the attention! You're the Princess of the richest family in the world, so I'm sure you've taken much more for granted than I have."

"Don't assume people are so one-sided, Keira. There's always another story, and trust me, you have your own.

You just walked into the city and *everybody* knew your name just because of some year you had *no* control over. People just care about you because of your birth and I don't respect that."

"Oh, you're one to talk," I scoffed, shocked that I was allowing myself to talk like this to my future ruler. "All your money and fame and love from Lana Ilu is because of your birth as a Princess."

Avarielle nodded. "Yeah, that's true, but I made a name for myself. That class with the kids? *I* organized that. I travel all over time with people who don't have anyone else to go with. I've done research to help my father with the schools. I have learned every possible thing about this city because I love my people and I want to be the best Queen possible for *them*, not me. I know I'm the only one in the entire world fit to lead Lana Ilu after my grandmother, so I'm working to show that. My year is 1349, in *Europe*. Do you know what was happening in 1349 in Europe? Just constant, disgusting rat death. That's all they teach about. I understand I would be nothing if I were not Royal, but I *don't* take it for granted."

"You haven't even given me a chance to show that I deserve fame or whatever for more than just my birth," I proclaimed.

Avarielle clicked her tongue. "Then prove yourself, Keira Sun."

And with that, she was off towards the Palace, leaving me with quite the mission.

"HAPPY BIRTHDAY TO you, happy birthday to you!"
sang the entire party. "Happy birthday dear Sonam,
happy birthday to you!"

There was a round of applause as the chorus finished
and Sonam blew out the candles on her 13th birthday
cake. Her friends were huddled around her, hugging
Sonam and continuing to sing to her. Pandora even went
in to personally wish her a happy birthday. Apparently,
they'd been friends for a few months now.

I couldn't help but feel like an intruder at the cele-
bration, considering I had never met Sonam before. I felt
guilty with every bite of cake I took, like I was just using
some connections I made for a night out. I really just
wasn't used to being invited to birthday parties.

Out of nowhere, Pandora began dragging my arm
towards the center where Sonam stood. I took a look
at Pandora's green dress, which still stood as my least
favorite color. But after seeing my new best friend wear it
every other day, it was growing on me. *I* would never buy
anything of the tone, but seeing Pandora gush about her
new green earrings always made me smile.

When we reached Sonam and her friends, the birthday
girl immediately looked over at me.

"Hi, happy birthday!" I said to her. "I'm Keira."

"Oh you're The... " she stopped herself, looking at the
ground for a moment. "You're Pandora's friend! It's so nice
to get to meet you."

Just hearing her quick change was the most refreshing
thing I heard all day. People were still, even after three
weeks, making endless comments about my era and Waldron Hawkridge and whatever else they could dig from

the source. Sonam was one of the few who looked at me as a regular person, or at least tried to.

Afterwards, Pandora introduced me to Sonam's older brother Kabir and then we headed back over to Alden and Lucas. Lucas was chatting with another kid I had seen in our "Magistone class." I think his name was Ken Kimura. Meanwhile, Alden was playing some sort of football game with a few guys and one I recognized as Prince Trevor.

Nearly out of breath, Alden ran up to Pandora and me. "I hate playing any sport with Henry Wilkinson," he groaned, putting his hands on his knees. "He's so much better than me."

"I mean he does play all the time, and is the captain of the middle school's football team. You should train more if you're going to complain like that," Pandora ridiculed.

"But Pandora... This is Lana Ilu, the city with the greatest technology in any universe. Isn't there some sort of medicine I can take to just be better at sports?"

I smirked. "Alden, we actually have those in the Idum-world. They're called steroids."

Just as the three of us began laughing, Lucas joined us and asked what was so funny. After I filled him in, he began laughing, too. The four of us were just standing in the middle of someone's birthday party laughing at a joke about steroids. I couldn't have been happier.

Out of nowhere, Alden was toppled over by one of the kids from the football game. From his sheer size, I guessed he was the football team captain, Henry Wilkinson. He was a burly guy and definitely looked too old to be in middle school, but I didn't ponder upon that. He looked like the stereotypical football team captain, even wearing those coats athletes always wore in the 1950's, despite it being around seventy degrees outside.

"Alden, why'd you leave the game?" Henry complained. "It was just getting started."

Alden looked at a loss for words. He stood silent for a moment until eying Lucas and me. He turned back to Henry and spread his hands out, prepping for an explanation. "These are my new friends, Henry, and neither of them really like football. I promised I would spend time with them at the party, you know, because they don't know anybody."

Lucas and I shook our heads slightly, knowing that we had tons of people to talk to. But we played along with the lie to keep Alden out of the game. I was worried that if he went back in for even a second, he would pass out.

"Oh ok, that's fine," Henry responded. Then, he pushed a fist towards Lucas. At first, my friend eyed Henry in confusion and even leaned back a bit, before realizing what he was asking for. Lucas too created a fist and pushed it against Henry's, making it the most awkward fist bump to possibly ever occur in human history.

"Welcome to Lana Ilu, Lucas," Henry said. Afterwards, he looked over towards me. Just from the fact that his mouth hung open I knew he was going to bring up my era. His eyebrows were wrinkled, like he was deciding the least offensive way to bring it up.

"Wow guys, you're friends with the Waldron Hawkridge girl?" Yeah, he somehow chose one much more offensive than I expected. "Gosh, that's cool. So, like... do you have telepathy with him in jail or something? Like do you know his plans? Is he coming back? 'Cause my Dad says he is and he's gonna be way stronger this time around. You're not really bad or anything, right?"

Now it was my turn to stand with my mouth hanging open. Henry Wilkinson, with his light brown hair falling in his face with every word, had reached a new level that I had not seen before. Honestly, I was entertained. "Please don't call me the 'Waldron Hawkridge girl' and no to the first two questions. I have no clue if he's coming back, I mean, he is in the world's most guarded prison. And well, I hope I'm not bad."

Henry pulled his mouth to one side of his face. "But I heard even the Queen..."

"You know what, Henry?" Alden interrupted. "How about you go show me where you scored that touchdown again?"

I mouthed a *thank you* his way to which Alden imitated tipping an invisible cap. Part of me knew that Henry had good intentions, but when you get *really* bothered by someone, it doesn't really mean much.

"Hey Keira, I'm going to go introduce Lucas to Sonam and a few other people. You alright just hanging out here for a while?" Pandora said to me.

"Sure, I'll find something to do."

I began to wander around the park, watching as the birthday party continued. Sonam was playing some sort of yard game with a large group of friends, and I saw Avarielle and Alden's sister, Juliet, among them. Juliet and Princess Avarielle seemed to be laughing on the sidelines, watching their younger friends with their heads resting on each other. From that, I only wanted to get to know the Princess more, to get to see the good that was so obviously in her.

There were over a dozen girls and a few guys in the group, all racing with their ankles tied and attempting to win a massive game of Jenga. Sonam's parents, one of whom I recognized as Dr. Sharma, were engaging in what was probably the wealthiest conversation in existence. Both of Alden's parents, as well as Mrs. Hawkridge and a black-haired man I assumed was Holly's father, were chatting over glasses of wine. There was also a third couple who both shared a great resemblance to Avarielle and Trevor. I assumed that was Prince Oladayo and his wife, Princess Bahati, the middle generation of Royals.

On the other side of the party, the football game had ended, with the players still sparsely hanging around. Prince Trevor was standing alone by one of the towering trees, strange for such a popular guy, so I decided to go over to him. I had talked to him here and there since we met, but usually in a group of either his friends or mine. I had barely mentioned to him that I had met his twin sister.

I began heading over towards Trevor and as soon as he noticed me, a smile spread across his face. He waved towards me and began walking, meeting me halfway.

"Keira! I didn't even see you here? Who brought you?" Trevor asked, adjusting the collar of his shirt as he spoke.

"I'm Pandora's plus one. Otherwise, I would have never gotten into such an *elite* party," I said.

Trevor shook his head. "Sonam, Kabir, well really the whole Sharma family, are the nicest people in the entire world. I haven't met a person at either school who isn't at least a little friendly with them." Trevor leaned in closer to my face in order to whisper. "They're so nice it surprises me that they're rich."

"Isn't that weird for you to say, *Prince* Trevor?" I pushed.

"Keira, Keira, Keira, I know best that it is next to impossible to be nice and rich. Rich people walk in and out of my home every day, whether they're in my family or not. I mean, my parents are pretty good people but... well, you met my Grandmother. She's not evil, but she's not even close to a sweet old lady, either," Trevor continued to mumble, as if he was worried she would hear him from the Palace of Time.

Nervous to continue with any serious bashing of the Queen, I redirected the conversation to any other member of his family. I picked Princess Avarielle. "You know Trevor, I met your sister a few weeks ago. And we also just talked before. She's... extremely smart."

"Well, doesn't the future Queen have to be? She would never want our city led by anyone with an insufficient IQ." I heard tension, *resentment* actually, in Trevor's voice. He was grinding his teeth and his fists, his entire body straight. Then, his shoulders relaxed. "Avarielle is a great leader, though. I'm very excited for her."

I smiled in agreement, wanting any talk of the Royal Family to end. It was really not my place to be in it.

"So, how has school been?" I asked. "I haven't gotten an opportunity to see what it's really like in Lana Ilu. Are the teachers at the East school as good as those at the West?"

Trevor didn't answer at first, obviously still lost in whatever he brought up about his family. His chin was tilted up towards the sky and for the first time since we had first met, I realized how cute the Prince was. Like, I knew all princes were stereotypically supposed to be handsome, but he really did have a beautiful face. Princess Avarielle did, too. I guess the Imamus just had really good genes.

Finally, Trevor's throat cleared. "Yeah, yeah, it's good. It's always weird being the Prince but people get used to it. And I would definitely say the teachers are on par with each other, so don't think that either West or East is at a disadvantage... Keira, do you want to leave the birthday party?"

I coughed. "Um... why and to where, exactly?"

"Just, I know everybody here, and Friday nights are the best time for adventure!" Trevor exclaimed.

"But you're the Prince. You already know everyone in the city, anyway." I felt a little nervous. I liked Trevor a lot, don't get me wrong, but we weren't exactly friends yet. He was the Prince and could do absolutely anything he wanted in Lana Ilu without worry of making a mistake or overstepping a boundary. I was the girl everyone was either curious about or terrified of. I couldn't afford what he could. And anyway, I wasn't ready to leave somewhere without the three people I had become closest with, especially considering walking around with the Prince would only lead to more rumors I wasn't ready to handle.

"Yeah, I know everybody, but I barely know you. Come on, we could go to the Alloys or something. I'm sure you haven't been there yet."

What was it with rich kids and the Alloys? I had been and if Pandora wasn't there to speak with me the entire time and give me lollipops, I might have thrown up from the sheer smell. It just looked like rusting metal, and there were few people I could ever imagine returning there with. I was not sure if Trevor had made the list quite yet.

"Trevor, I've been there and..." I mumbled out.

He grabbed my hands and I realized that my palms were covered in sweat. "Then let me take you time traveling! We could go the past, the future, whatever you want! I just need to go somewhere and I'd like to with you."

When he said those last words, I realized something that had never happened to me before—Trevor had a *crush* on me. A *crush*! I honestly couldn't believe it was coming from anybody, let alone the Prince. He *liked* me and maybe I liked him, but I was not ready to deal with that, especially with the entire city watching.

"Trevor, I haven't had my proper time travel lessons yet and I still have more people to get to know. I... I think you're great but maybe another time. I probably need to head home with Holly and Theo anyway. But, have a good night, alright?" I coaxed.

Trevor grinned. "Goodnight, I'll see you soon Keira. And don't worry about this, I have plenty of things to do anyway. You just do what you want to."

CHAPTER 17

IN SCHOOL THE NEXT TUESDAY, THE four other kids who had come to Lana Ilu the same day as me, Mark Highsmith, Rosie MacGregor, Aaron Williams and of course Lucas, were brought into a separate classroom to learn some extra information about time travel. The extremely bored class proctor we had been stuck with before had somehow been assigned to give us the lesson. I hadn't thought it was possible, but I was less than excited to learn about passing through the existence of time.

The proctor's name was Bob. He didn't even give us a last name. Part of me thought the reason was because he didn't have one. He was holding a pile of folders, though his expression towards them indicated none would be opened.

"Ok, so you all are going to start time traveling soon because we're Gradiens and that's what we do and all that," Bob said, not even looking at us, despite being his temporary students. "Ok, first of all, if you are under the age of sixteen, you cannot go time traveling without an adult. Any person over eighteen is fine—does not need to be a city official or anything. Next rule, you have to go check at the main office of the Time Travel Safety building and see if there are any Zanarees, or what we usually call Watch Dogs. Those things are these massive energy creatures that *will* try to kill you because they're protecting Varem and they want your energy. Varem are what we usually refer to as Time Cases, crazy objects that can delete time if not destroyed correctly. The bigger the Watch Dog and Time Case, the longer they have existed. One that is just a second old would be about the size of your fingernail, but one millions of years old could be the size of many skyscrapers. If there is a Watch Dog there, you need to get a Preserver sent out to kill it. Preservers make sure time can't get deleted, so that's why they have that name. You can also get your own Watch Dog trackers if you don't want to go to the office. Also, I have a votan for each of you, which is a weapon used to destroy the Time Cases, just in case somehow you encounter one. Stick it in the center of the Watch Dog's chest where the energy is highest, because that's where the Time Case is. Each votan is programmed for your specific energy so don't lose it because no other will work as well."

Aaron raised his hand. "But you said we would be able to know if there's a Watch Dog, because of the tracking and all that, and one of those Preservers will deal with it…"

Bob shrugged. "Even Gradiens have technical difficulties, but don't worry, 99.9% of the time we find a Watch Dog beforehand. A surprise encounter is incredibly rare, just happened once before. Now, just come here and take these things," he said, gesturing towards the votans in a steel container."

He began handing one to each of us, with me again the last to receive her's. Bob was shaky as he plucked mine from the box, as if he were terrified about dropping it. Like the others, it was a dark metal bar, probably a little under a foot long. But while the others were relatively dull, mine shone with sparks. Electricity was racing through the object, yet when I touched it, I felt no shock.

"It's highly positive to match with your era, Keira," Bob told me, for the first time a change of tone in his voice.

Not knowing how to follow, I just nodded. "Thanks."

When I returned back to Lucas, he was waving around his votan like a kid playing with a toy airplane.

"Votans don't shoot lasers, Lucas," Bob said. "It's not a lightsaber."

"Then what's it do and how do you use it?" Rosie inquired, jumping as she said it.

I noticed Bob roll his eyes. "It's full of positive energy and Time Cases are full of negative energy, just like Gradiens' negativity. But our votan functions in a different way. Just use it like a knife and stick it in the Watch Dog. Depending on the size of the creature, you need more higher-powered votans but don't worry about that now."

I winced at the thought of carrying anything even close to a knife, especially knowing I might have to kill with it. I had watched tons of mysteries and horrors, and stabbing was *always* my least favorite part. The gush of blood and ripping someone open made my stomach churn. I hoped those Watch Dogs felt more like light bulbs than animals.

After I got over that revelation, Bob handed us all nearly transparent, minuscule objects that looked like hearing aids. He instructed us that we would hear with them as translators when time traveling, though they sometimes lagged. I was grateful because nobody, even with Lana Ilu's superb education system, could learn every language that ever existed.

Afterward, I looked over to the one person who had not spoken at all to me or Bob—Mark Highsmith. He had been especially quiet from the moment all of us arrived in Lana Ilu and had not changed a bit since. All the students here had lived in Lana Ilu for about a month, and everyone besides Mark looked to have adjusted. I had seen Rosie talking with a group of other girls in her Magistone class and knew that she was always hanging around Holographic Habitat with them. Aaron had become incredibly close with Ken Kimura. The two were always studying together. And, of course, Lucas and I had found our people. But most often, Mark sat alone and pushed others away when they approached. As everyone else was trying to get some quarter of an understanding of their votans, discussing them among ourselves, Mark just let it hang down by his side. His eyes were blank.

"SO, I HEAR you got your lesson on time travel," Pandora said to Lucas and me as we waited for Alden to come out of the school. "You think you two are ready to really go?"

"Hopefully," I answered. "I'm kind of scared."

Lucas mumbled through a bite of a sandwich in agreement.

Pandora laughed. "It's not scary, I promise. I've gone

time traveling like twenty times. It's really no big deal at all. You can go anywhere in the world, anytime in existence. Be excited instead of scared."

"But the Watch Dogs…" I pushed.

"Watch Dog, smotch dog," Pandora mocked. "Literally, like once in time travel history has the tracker ever made a mistake. I know we'll be fine and I really want to go exploring with you two. I *promise*."

"When?" Lucas asked. "You know, the time?"

She rested a finger against her temple. "Let's wait to decide that with Alden. That slowpoke should be coming out any moment."

As if she prophesied it, Alden came out the front door of the West School with Henry Wilkinson, who was continuously shoving Alden's shoulder. Waving goodbye to Henry, who still looked like he had a million things to tell Alden, he snuck out to our group.

"I was going to talk about the English test with either Marco or Alice, you know, the top students in the grade. It's one of those essays on a book from the future, which means it's so much harder, because even in Lana Ilu, we still are more used to the past. *Buuuuut*, Henry is still trying to convince me to go out for football next year, which I'm never going to," Alden complained.

Pandora crossed her arms. "I bet your parents would like it if you played football. It's good for popularity and isn't that all they care about?"

Alden shook his head. "Like I've said before about football, it *will* kill me. I don't think my parents want a dead son."

"Uh, your parents have… other son. They will be good," Lucas joked.

Alden threw his hands into the air. "Pandora, you put him up to this, I know you did! I thought I had a real friend for once with Lucas. You still like me right, Keira? At least more than Pandora and Lucas?"

"Oh, don't worry, Alden," Pandora sighed, wrapping an arm around each of our shoulders. "You're still such a *beautiful boy*. Isn't he, Keira?"

Though Lucas was laughing uncontrollably, both Alden's and my own face were hot.

"I *really* wish I hadn't told you that she said that," Alden grumbled, obviously trying to hide his tomato cheeks.

"Trust me, I wish I hadn't said it but we need to move on because I thought I was dreaming and believed Alden was not a real human. Can we just focus on something else, please?"

Pandora rolled her eyes. "*Anyway*, I want to take Lucas and Keira time traveling for real, for their first time. But they're too freaking scared of Watch Dogs to leave Lana Ilu. Alden, any ideas?"

He pushed his hair out of his face before saying anything. "First of all, you guys need to get over that. *Nobody* ever accidentally finds a Watch Dog. Our technology is really too good for that. But since I guess you still need to break in all that Gradien stuff, we don't need to go to a time that is too far away." Alden stopped for a second. "Pandora, what do you think of the late 1960's?"

"Could we go to Hollywood at that time? Like 1967?" Pandora added. "Also, I'll cover the adult supervisor thing, there's this nice woman in my sector, she's 23 and I can ask her."

"Sure, are you guys in?" Alden asked, peering towards Lucas and me.

The two of us glanced at one another, still nervous about the trek. Those Watch Dogs, and the crazy Time Cases they protected, sounded nothing short of terrifying. Just thinking about them made me feel like I was a second away from death, especially if I encountered one. Then again, I had not even been told what a Watch Dog looked like, so how bad could the threat be? I mean, since I was lucky enough to be one of the few Gradiens in the world, I should at least participate in what it meant to be one.

Lucas nodded at me, showing that he and I had gone through the same thought process.

"I guess we're going to the Sixties," I answered for us.

Pandora grinned. "Ok, we'll meet up where I live, Saturday at ten. Also, Lucas and Keira, make sure to go buy some Sixties-era clothes to fit in. I'm excited. I've never been."

CHAPTER 18

A S SOON AS I WOKE UP THAT upcoming Saturday morning, I raced to put on my outfit for the Sixties trip. I had bought it with Pandora, who helped me in finding black which, unlike in modern fashion, was pretty scarce in the Sixties themed shops. People in that decade *really* loved their colors, so I hoped to just look like a fan of Wednesday Addams in my black dress and tights. I think The Addams Family was around in the Sixties.

I was not much into the idea of wearing my hair two feet above my head, so I hoped just tying it into a ponytail would do the trick. I also wondered if I needed to smell a certain way to blend into the Sixties, like flowers or a Beatles album or something. I knew I would need to check every little aspect about myself following breakfast. Like, nobody ate kale in the 1960's, and if I had *any* in my teeth, some people might think I was interested in eating leaves.

Finally, I headed over to breakfast. I noticed that Lana Ilu was pretty busy on Saturday mornings, even in my tiny little sector. Families were out shopping or grabbing breakfast at one of our cafes and some people were even heading out to time travel, which I noticed as I saw bodies zap out of thin air. I wondered how in the world my friends and I were going to be able to arrive in 1967 and leave without completely baffling some unprepared pedestrian, which would be all of them. Even worse, I was scared it would inspire some sort of science-fiction novel. If anyone were to write a book about us Gradiens, it probably would not help our secrecy.

As I continued walking towards the Handals' house, I noticed Sean Rockford and his husband, leaving their home, just across the way.

"Hello, Keira!" Mr. Rockford called. "You're up early this morning. We never see you on our jogs."

"I'm going time traveling, like for real today. I've never been before so I couldn't really sleep and wanted to get an early start!" I answered.

Mr. Rockford gave me a thumbs up. "Early bird gets the worm! When and where are you going?"

"Hollywood, in 1967!" I yelled back, as we were still on opposite sides of the street.

"That explains your dress. I hope you have a great time!"

I sent a smile and waved after the couple as they continued on their run. As for me, even the beautiful mornings of my *beloved* city could never make me wake up early to exercise.

At last I went into the Handals' home and saw that

everybody was there for breakfast. For the most part, Holly and Theo didn't come to weekend breakfast because they slept in, as exhausted high schoolers all do. At this point, since it was well into June, the two of them were preparing for finals and joined us. I think exams were scarier than any thought of Watch Dogs.

"Keira, love the dress!" Holly announced as I came into the room. "Let me guess, you're time traveling today."

I nodded. "To the Sixties, 1967 to be exact." I took a seat beside her and began to pile some of the breakfast on a plate that had been left for me.

"So why are you guys up so early?" I asked Theo and Holly.

Theo put down his fork. "We're also using our Gradien abilities today, except we're going to the future. What year was it again, Holls?"

"Just 2999 and then 3000. I want to see the beginning of the next millennium." She said it so matter-of-factly that an Idum might have dismissed what she said as something as normal as a vacation to Florida.

Theo snapped his fingers. "Yep, that's when. You know, Keira, when I went time traveling for the first time I went like 50,000 years into the future because I was curious if the world still even somewhat existed like before, and it *did not.* Good choice on time traveling to a closer era. It will help you learn a lot more."

Holly rested her hand upon his. "Yeah, somehow an eleven-year-old version of this guy convinced one of the school interns to take him *way* into the future. Even though we're Gradiens and time travel is literally rooted in our genetics, it's still dangerous. Take it slow, Keira."

"You know to be especially careful about concealing

your identity as a Gradien, right?" Mr. Handal pointed out. "Do *not* bring your cell phone or wear any clothing that indicates a later year. The *only* objects that you should be carrying that are from beyond 1967 are your multi and a votan, both of which you should put into compact mode so that they can fit in a small pocket. That's all you need to channel your energy through to get back to Lana Ilu, nothing more. There is no loud talking about anything after 1967 unless you are sure you are in private. Keira, just because Gradiens are a strong and advanced people does not mean we cannot be in danger. Idums out-number us drastically and we *cannot* risk any exposure. Who knows how many of them could invade and take our inventions and knowledge for evil purposes? Do you understand?" he commanded.

I gulped and clutched the table cloth. "Yes, sir. I promise I'll be careful."

All of a sudden, Mrs. Handal rubbed my shoulder. "Don't let him stress you out, Keira. Any Idum who hears you talking about the future will probably forget about it anyway. Everybody is nervous to go their first time. Who will they meet? What will they do? Will they ruin the entire cycle of time? Will they run into a Watch Dog and have to fight for their lives? Trust me, I had those same worries and for the last two questions, the answer is *always* no, as long as you check the Watch Dog tracker, which I'm assuming one of your friends has."

I smiled. "Pandora called me this morning telling me everything was clear."

Mrs. Handal sat back down at the table. "Then you are perfectly fine. Now finish up so you can go have fun!"

AS SOON AS I had eaten all my breakfast, I began walking over to Pandora's apartment in the 2900 to 3000 BCE Sector. Inspired by the clay bricks of Egypt, the buildings were many. They were all short, designed for having just a few apartments instead of compacting all who lived there into a couple of buildings. The windows were carved out, with a sheer blind due to weather. I knew she lived in the sixth apartment building on the left side of her street. It was a tiny structure, only two floors high, with two apartments each. She had the first floor.

I entered the building and knocked on the door of her small home, hearing rustling on the other side. Then, all of a sudden, a boom crashed against the ground.

I was concerned until the door flung upon, a shaken Pandora balancing against the frame. "Hey."

"Hey," I responded. "You alright?"

Pandora began to scratch her scalp. "Yeah, I just fell as I was coming here. I was in the middle of getting my hair together and then you came and... well, you get the story."

I peered behind her, noting that Pandora was not one to keep her home neat. I had been to her apartment before, and it was always more disorganized than the last time I visited. Clothes were always left on the floor and half used dishes sitting on the counter. In all fairness, it was partly Lana Ilu's fault for thinking they could allow a fourteen-year old to live alone. But considering Pandora's highly organized sense of style, a color and shape scheme each day, I expected the look of her apartment to follow.

Pandora was dressed in a lemon colored, short sleeve dress that exactly matched her long hair, with white buttons running down the front. Standing across from her, between our different hair and dress colors and probably our attitudes as a whole, we looked like night and day.

"So, you're trying the whole beehive hair, then?" I asked, only partly joking.

Pandora shook her head. "Of course not, that would be impossible! I just want a little height to blend in better." She scanned my outfit. "I need to cover for both of us."

I stomped my foot at that. "You bought this dress with me and I *like* black!"

"I know, I know, but truthfully, nobody was wearing black back then, Keira. You look great, but you're going to seem like the Grim Reaper or something."

"Well then, I'll start a trend," I said, going into her apartment and plopping down on her couch. "Where are the guys?"

Pandora ran into the bathroom to grab a comb before responding. "They'll be here soon, or you know, on time. You're early, Keira."

I smiled at Pandora as she began to comb her hair upwards, eventually adding a few inches to the style. "I'm just excited, and you should be happy about that. By the way, do you have any plans for our day in the *Sixties?*"

She hesitated, but nodded after a moment. "Kind of... Alden said he had some places in mind, so we'll listen to him later. *But,* I really want to go see my house so I can know what it looked like just a few years after it was built." She fished into a pocket in her dress, causing a ringing sound. Then, she pulled out a pair of brass house keys. "I'm going to try to get in, too."

"Pandora, there's no way our supervisor is going to allow you to do that. And anyway, do you really think the locks didn't change after fifty years?" I sighed.

Pandora crossed her arms. "Keira, one thing that you really need to learn is that you'll never know until you try."

A minute later, a knock sounded at her door, which Pandora again rushed to answer. I thought it would be the guys, but instead stood who I assumed was the girl who was coming with us time traveling, well, the girl we *needed* to come with us. She had on cropped pants and a t-shirt, both definitely styled like the Sixties. She wore her jet-black hair in a pixie cut.

"Hello, you must be Keira!" she exclaimed, grinning. "I'm Huilang, I've heard so much about you from Pandora."

I smiled back at her and noticed that her name was one I had heard in China. I hadn't really met that many other Chinese people in Lana Ilu, though I knew there were many, so it made me feel a little more comfortable to know she would be going back in time with us. I was pretty sure Hollywood was more diverse and socially aware than a lot of places back in the 1960's, but it was easier to not have to think about that alone.

A couple minutes later, Alden and Lucas stood at the other side of the door, having walked here together. The two of them had really become incredibly close friends, which I had to admit made me feel a little accomplished. I mean, *I* was the one to introduce them. Lucas was wearing a green short sleeved shirt with plaid pants, while Alden was dressed in a more formal button down. They both introduced themselves to Huilang before coming over to Pandora and me.

"So, do you all know what you're doing today? I

remember when I was your age, I wanted to ignore my time travel supervisor as much as possible, so I'll just stay to the side, let you guys hang out and keep you from blowing up something if needed. Just let me know if you need anything," Huilang said.

"We don't want to ignore you, you're great!" Pandora exclaimed, knowing her much better than any of us did.

Huilang laughed and crossed her arms. "It's ok, Pandora. I won't be offended."

After that, we directed our focus back to getting our trip ready.

"You guys almost ready?" Alden asked. "I think we still need to convert our points into money for the Sixties. They won't accept any dollars from later because you know, it looks impossible and like counterfeit money."

Lucas cocked his eyebrows. "Counterfeit?"

"It means the money's fake."

Lucas snapped his fingers. "Word of the day."

"Well, anyway, there's some places I want to go when we're in 1967," Alden started. "There's an old Italian restaurant called Miceli's that is actually still open but I want to see it when it was *kind of* new. Of course, there's the Chinese Theater with all the old stars on the Walk of Fame, and uh, we can't get in but there's this club called Pandora's Box that we can't miss."

Pandora, *our* Pandora, huffed. "Oh, because of my name?"

"No, because it's historic! Sharing your name is just by coincidence. There were riots there the year before with tons of people, even that guy from The Shining..."

"Jack Nicholson?" Lucas piped up.

"Yeah!" Alden said, grinning in surprise. "You like scary movies, Lucas?"

"They are my favorite, always good at night. I think they are very scary only at night."

"Well, we'll stay late in 1967 to go to one of the cinemas. I think Night of the Living Dead is from around that time," Alden added.

Lucas shook his head and nudged Alden's shoulder. "A year after, but close, so not too bad."

"Loving the bromance I'm seeing here," I said to the two boys, "but I think we should probably go get some money for the trip."

Everyone agreed and we headed over to the nearest bank, Nulmendar. I knew that Mr. Hawkridge, Holly's father, had recently taken over it after his Dad stepped down. Despite the place bringing Holly and her family tons of money, she only ever had bad things to say, like it was *exhausting* or *fake*, neither of which I understood. Then again, I didn't get a lot about these really rich kids.

After we traded in our points with some money for 1967, we gathered beside the bank to time travel.

"Votans?" Lucas asked, reminding us all to check if we had stored them. We all patted our bags, assuring him we were prepared.

"Remember," Pandora began, "just say, *Los Angeles, California; June 10th, 1967; 11:00 a.m.* and then think about the Chinese Theater as best as you can. We should all be there in an instant."

Then, together, we closed our eyes and focused. I could hear some mumbling amongst the four of us as we each verified exactly where, and of course, *when* we were going. There was no room for error. Just as I had experienced before, a pale, mellow light enveloped me and ticklish shocks raced through my arms. With another blink, I was there, 51 years away from home.

I was standing on the bustling Hollywood Boulevard, but instead of tourists snapping pictures with iPhones, they used polished Nikons. Girls wore floral mini dresses and skyscraping hair, matched with boys in brightly colored sweaters. Couples stood in front of the Chinese Theater for photographs, pictures that kids I went to school with might have looked back at with their grandparents. Others were loudly singing tracks from *Sgt. Pepper's Lonely Hearts Club Band*, which had just come out a few weeks ago. I could tell from much of their careless caroling and lack of attention to notes that these people were probably not completely aware of their surroundings. I then remembered that, er, experimental substances were quite popular in this year.

I looked over to my three friends, who were all just coming to their senses as well. I was shocked that nobody seemed to stop and stare at the four kids who just materialized out of nowhere, as we had just appeared in many peoples' walking paths. Then again, I know this time was famous for experimental substances and those substances may have helped in diluting the image.

"So, this is it," Pandora said. "I'd really never been."

"It's incredible," I gasped.

Lucas put a thumbs up. "Yes, Keira."

Looking much less bewildered than the rest of us, Alden picked a direction to begin walking in. "Come on guys, let's start moving." He lowered his voice. "Remember, just *blend in*."

I nodded harshly, wanting Alden to know I understood. Even though Pandora had lived in Lana Ilu for almost two years, it was still Alden who had experienced the Gradien life since he was born. I knew I had to trust him here.

"So, are we going to see the stars?" I asked.

Alden looked over his shoulder at me. "The ones on the ground or the actual people?"

"I meant the Walk of Fame stars but real celebrities would be amazing! Who do you think we can see? Elizabeth Taylor? Audrey Hepburn? Any of the Rolling Stones or *The Beatles*?"

He shrugged. "For the ground stars, probably. I have no idea for the real people."

I walked forward to catch up to Alden, forming a straight line with my friends on the sidewalk. "You don't seem too excited," I mumbled.

"No, I am. Just, celebrities really aren't that cool. They're just people. But I am excited to be here with you guys, trust me on that."

"Some people are really cool though, Alden. You have to admit that you and Audrey Hepburn are not on the same level," I retorted, laughing.

Alden shoved my shoulder. "You aren't either, Keira. We're just both simple, boring people."

At that, Pandora struck up a new conversation. "So, do you want to go catch lunch first? Time traveling when you're hungry is never a good idea."

I had eaten breakfast not long before, but the excitement of being so far away from my home, farther than I had ever imagined I could, had definitely taken a toll on my stomach. Not that I threw up or anything! It was just constant butterflies.

"Food, *yes*," Lucas answered. "Where is the restaurant?"

"Miceli's is..." Alden lost track of his thought. "Sorry guys, I don't remember. It can't be too far from here, it's part of the busy area of Hollywood."

I looked over to Huilang. "Do you know where it is?"

She shrugged her shoulders. "Really sorry, no, I actually haven't been here."

Pandora grumbled under her breath, which I hoped was more directed at Alden not thinking ahead than Huilang. "I'll just ask someone." Pandora looked around for people who were not walking by too quickly. There were plenty of people dancing in the street or parents trying to handle their rambunctious children, so unfortunately, we were a little short on options. But near us was a young couple, probably just a few years older than us, just chatting against one of the buildings.

"Babe, I have to take you to one of his speeches. Dr. King is a revolutionary and I would have thought a girl like you would have seen him in person," the guy said to his girlfriend. She was an incredibly tall young woman, which was just added to by her heeled boots and towering afro.

"Lonny, I would love that, I really would. Maybe we can find a time," the girl responded.

After their interaction, Pandora stepped up to them. "Hi, sorry to bother you two, but do you know where Miceli's restaurant is?"

Lonny scratched his chin. "Uh, I think it's a few blocks down, so just walk on straight. But it's on the side, so you need to turn. Can't help much besides that," he said, pointing beyond the theater. "Oh, and you need to cross this street right here before going on. That any help?"

Pandora smiled. "Yep, thank you so much, have a nice day."

Lonny's girlfriend wiggled her fingers in a wave as we headed to lunch. There was something a little familiar about her, but I couldn't figure out what. But I was fifty years away from when I existed, so there was no way I knew her.

We walked along the path that Lonny had directed us to, which was pretty vague, but we connected the dots. As we continued down the streets, I absorbed more and more of the Sixties feel. There were hippies wearing their flowing dresses and girls with wide eyes from British influence. I even saw some of those stereotyped go-go boots and checkerboard skirts, which I had to remind myself were not part of a costume.

There was a group of four teenage boys to my right all dressed in casual suits like the Beatles and others in their heavily ironed polos I'm sure they waited on their moms to finish. The guys, some adults and others, even little kids, ranged from having sophisticated combed down hair to incredibly unflattering bowl cuts.

I tapped Alden's arm, gesturing towards one person with the round hair. "Do you think your hair could do that?" I jested. "I mean, it's long enough."

Alden frowned at me. "Keira, something impossible will have to happen for me to wear a bowl cut. Like, so impossible, I cannot even think of an example—it would be that impossible."

I smirked. "Well, I hope something impossible happens."

The thing I tried hardest to focus on was everything the people, the true people of this time, were saying. I could tell from words of Martin Luther King Jr., like I heard from Lonny, as well as Angela Davis, Cesar Chavez, and Gloria Steinem that we were in a hub of activism, though I think that was not too different from Los Angeles in my time. I felt that amongst that talk, I was living in history. True, real, *important* history.

Below us were the famous stars on the Walk of Fame, though there were many fewer celebrities than I had seen on my visits to Los Angeles. Lucas had done some research on the era before we time traveled and told me that the first person to get a star was Joanne Woodward, an actress who I had never actually heard of. I tried to keep an eye out for her name.

Soon enough, we arrived at Miceli's. It was a quaint, warm restaurant with dozens of people eating inside. I noticed a few of the people inside give me a dark glance, which I hoped was towards my black clothes, but since some of their stares settled on my face, I figured out it was something else more unique about me in the 1960's, exactly what I had been worried about. I had hoped by 1967, people would be more accepting or at least accustomed to seeing Chinese people, especially in California. Then again, it was still the '60's and I probably could stop giving the people here so much credit. I peered over at Huilang, her brows were crinkled just like mine.

We were seated at a table by the window, so we could still look out onto the city. We ordered our food and it came out quickly, allowing us to get an early start on our lunch.

"Where are we going?" Lucas asked through a bite of pasta.

"That Pandora's Box place," Alden answered. "I already told you guys, it's iconic. The hipsters of their time protested at that club. It would be like nowhere else we've ever seen."

"So, what exactly happened there?" Pandora questioned.

"A bunch of teenagers were angry that adults said their club was causing traffic problems and had some sort of 'youth rebellion' about it. That riot didn't really work out too well for anybody involved since..." Alden moved his head closer to the table, asking us to lean in closer, too. "Well, it's going to be closed in August. Those teenagers can't even go there anymore, you need to be twenty-one. But, I'd like to take a look.

"Sorry to interject, but I don't think that's the best choice for you guys," Huilang stated.

Alden smiled at her. "I promise, I just want to see it for a minute... but do you guys also want to do anything else?"

"Roller skating would be fun," I inputted.

Lucas smiled at me. "I like your uh... roller skating. But, I will fall."

I patted his arm from across the table. "Trust me, so will I."

After the five of us finished eating, we headed over to the nearest skating rink. We rented skates and tried our best to keep up with everyone else in the rink. But just like he predicted, Lucas fell constantly, earning hypocritical laughter since we had too crashed onto our faces enough. Inside the rink, the song *I'm a Believer* was ringing through the skaters' ears. It sounded a bit off to me, like the tone of the voices was just too mellow for the lyrics. I remember hearing the song for the first time in *Shrek*, so I was wondering why it had come out so long before. But I'm pretty sure it had been recorded a second time for the movie.

When we had finished skating for about an hour, we found our way to the Sunset Strip, the infamous location of Pandora's Box and the riots that happened here not long ago. The nightclub was brightly painted, the pink walls covered in orange stripes. Some teens older than us were dressed in rags of clothing, ripped dresses and long pants, mismatched shoes and flattened hair. There was a strong scent of drugs, some of it cigarette smoke that I could recognize, and much more than I could not put a finger on. I was very *glad* I could not identify much of it.

Knowing that this small, dilapidated nightclub would be destroyed just months from now, I felt like I was looking at a zombie. This place was dead, its history unknown to nearly everyone alive in the time I knew. It was barely a memory. It was just concrete waiting to be smashed to pieces, a body dying of a terminal sickness. The smell of death even arose from the living who stayed by the nightclub, their flesh beginning to rot as they still breathed. Pandora's Box had lost the very thing the mythological story told of holding—hope.

Huilang shook her head and went to reach for Pandora's arm. "We shouldn't be here, we have to go. There's plenty to see, but this is not it."

"Just… just a minute," Alden pleaded again, getting an aggravated nod from Huilang.

"This is the saddest thing I have ever seen," Pandora stated. "And I've been to the Alloys."

"Yes, I want to go to Pandora's house, no Pandora's Box," Lucas added, whispering so Huilang could not hear.

Pandora smiled at him when he said that, patting his back. "See, he has the right idea. Let's get out of here before one of those guys over there tries to offer us some illegal 1967 drugs."

Along with Pandora and Lucas, I began to leave the premises. I was still speechless, feeling like there was nothing I could do to save this place, even if I wanted to.

But Alden didn't budge. He stood still, watching the short building with its chipping red roof. He was scanning each person beside it, waiting until nightfall to get in. His eyes were stern.

"So, this is history," Alden said. "It's drugged teenagers and broken-down cars and graffiti before this place even closes down. There were riots here, with celebrities, and it was written down in books."

"Alden!" I screamed. "Remember, be quiet."

He shook his head. "I always thought history was the most incredible thing imaginable, legendary and powerful and, well, bigger than this."

Seeing that he was not going to lower his voice any time soon, I walked over to Alden. "Dude, why are you being so loud? This was a nightclub in the 60's, what were you expecting? Don't you know that history's sometimes ugly?"

Alden wiped his eyes, which I noticed had tears budding in them. "I know it can be ugly, but not like this. Everything gets ugly, but in ways that people can't turn away from, like the blast of a bomb. This is just... this is basically nothing."

"I know, but it's not a big deal, Alden."

"Yes, yes it is, Keira! I've never seen anything like this. I have met presidents and emperors and Greek philosophers. They would never look twice at this nightclub, they might be disgusted by it. Why has this managed to go down in history when it wasn't anything at all?" he cried.

"Alden, history can be like that."

"My parents never let me know that, they only took me to the greatest places and times they could imagine. They told me that things that got read in history books would always catch my eye. They told me that I should become part of history just because of that. I guess they lied." And there was the bombshell. This had nothing to do with Pandora's Box, but the same exact thing that was always bothering him. He had constructed what he wanted the nightclub to look like as he planned the trip in his room at night, the room with the golden painted walls he had always known. History had been built for him by his parents to fit an aesthetic which they had been keeping a hold of. It was just like everything else, like whom he could like or what sports he could play. Pandora's Box was the ugly duckling that for Alden never found out it was a swan.

I took a hold of his arm, pulling him away from the building. "Come on, the Pandora we actually care about is getting impatient. Let's just visit her house and head home. Maybe we can grab some Clock Cookies at *Dolce's*, alright?"

Alden dried his cheeks. "Thanks. Sorry, I don't know why I started crying, it was just...weird."

I shook my head. "No, we both know why and it's okay. Now let's get going."

When we returned to Pandora and Lucas, neither of them said a word, which I could tell Alden appreciated. I leaned close to Pandora and asked her exactly how she was going to get away with her plan, still ignoring what had just happened with Alden. She said we would all, with Huilang, go up to see the houses in Beverly Hills and for a few minutes, leave her at a different house as we went to check out Pandora's, but come right back after. She would barely know we were gone. I had to admit, I already felt a little guilty, but the plan seemed pretty simple and exciting at the same time. It wasn't like we were leaving Huilang stranded in the middle of nowhere, she would just be a quick walk away.

We walked a bit further onto a main, cleaner road to pick up a taxi and take us to Beverly Hills. The driver cocked an eyebrow when we told him our destination. I guess our current location, where we showed signs of hanging around, did not fit the Beverly Hills' look.

The drive took quite a while, especially with all the twists and mountains we had to climb up. As we drove, I got a glimpse of the Hollywood sign, standing as proudly as it still would fifty years later. Fancy cars passed us as we drove upward, some of them surely carrying celebrities. Part of me wanted to hop out of the cab and take pictures, but then I remembered I did not bring a camera accurate to the time.

At last, we arrived at a house that was two blocks away from Pandora's (technically) future home. We all got out of the taxi, admiring the incredible royal blue roof and white columns before the home.

"Wow, I definitely like this more than the last place you all wanted to see," Huilang grumbled, obviously a little annoyed with the last place we had dragged her to. That only made the pit in my stomach heavier. I wanted to see what Pandora was up to, but I was so nervous.

"Do you want to walk around, look at some others?" Pandora asked.

Everyone agreed, three of us understanding what she truly meant and one of us left out of it. We followed the houses, blending in with a handful of other tourists. After about ten minutes, when Huilang had begun taking pictures and chatting with other tourists, we began to slowly lag behind until we were right out of view. Since we had begun walking in the direction of Pandora's house, it was only about four minutes until we got there.

It was a towering marble house with a massive pool in the back. I could see a chandelier hanging behind the front door due to the gold lined windows. It was perfectly shaped, like of a sculpture. It definitely looked like the home of a movie star.

Pandora pulled her keys out of her dress pocket as we neared the door. She was smirking. But Lucas quickly stopped her from moving further. "People in the house?" he warned.

Pandora nodded, acknowledging her mistake. She began to knock on the door continuously and then rang the doorbell, both bringing not a single answer. She then checked the driveway to see no cars. After, she winked at us. "I think I'm clear."

After she slid the key into the doorknob, Alden put his face into his hands. "Pandora, this is *trespassing!*"

"No, it's not trespassing. I live here, just... fifty years from now," she said. Then, all of a sudden, the door pushed open. Somehow, even after all these years, Pandora really still had the right key. What were the chances?

We entered the mansion. I still felt guilty about it. I know we legally had what was needed to be inside, but legally in a whole other century.

The home was gorgeous, not too different from Alden's, in fact. There was fine art and designer furniture. The kitchen was filled with gourmet food that was difficult to ignore.

"I want to go see what my room was like," Pandora screamed, locating a winding staircase. "And then, just after that, we'll go right back to Huilang. She'll barely know we were gone." Cautiously, the three of us followed, still worried that the actual family that owned this house would walk in any second. I didn't even want to *imagine* what dealing with the police would be like when you technically do not even exist yet. My house in Ithaca wasn't built until the 1980's, what if they asked me my home address? I would be thrown in juvie or whatever jail kids went to because all they would find was an empty lot. I really just wanted to leave.

We climbed up until the third floor where Pandora told us her room was, in the center of the hallway. We raced down, all four of us now just wanting to see the room and leave without being seen. Pandora found a blue painted door and turned the knob.

"I repainted it yellow," she told us before peering in.

Finally, the door was wide open. To be honest, it was the most anti-climatic event of the day. Even Pandora's Box was more exciting. The room just had a simple wooden shelf and bed covered in white sheets. It was not nearly as glamorous as the rest of the home and was probably just used for storage.

"Well," Pandora sighed. "At least I know that I have better style than whoever is living here now. Come on guys, let's get out of here before we get caught."

Alden, Lucas and I happily agreed, tiptoeing back down the steps. It still seemed quiet, until we heard a rustle on the first floor. It sounded like heavy steps and brushing against furniture. The four of us halted.

"People," Lucas whispered. "And we are in their house."

"I didn't hear the door open," I said, hoping to calm everyone down. "It might be outside."

Pandora bit her lip. "That's still not good if anybody is

close." She looked down at the bottom stair. "I'll go check, I'm the one who brought us here anyway."

Before we could protest and demand we go with her, Pandora was already heading down. She had her head ducked as she disappeared into the first floor, as if she thought that would conceal her at all. Unfortunately, at this point, if the family was inside, we didn't have a chance of escaping, at least without revealing our identities as Gradiens.

Like a burst of light from her blonde hair, Pandora came racing back towards the stairs. Her eyes were wide open and her arms were vibrating from how much she shook. I had never seen anyone look so mortally terrified.

"Not a person!" she screamed, obviously tearing at her vocal cords. "*Definitely* not a person."

CHAPTER 19

"WHAT DO YOU MEAN IT'S NOT A person?" I bellowed back.

Alden was holding his face. "Pandora, is it, is it, it can't be..."

"Watch Dog?" Lucas yelled in addition.

Pandora could barely nod as an answer. I couldn't blame her. The impossible had just happened and she was there to witness it first. Oh, who am I kidding, the impossible was *happening*!

"Well, what do we do?" Pandora breathed, her words barely forming. I still wondered what the Watch Dog looked like, if it could even be described.

Alden began looking into his pockets. "Here, I'll call the time travel Safety Building and report our location so they can send some Preservers."

Alden was cut off by the crash of glass against the

marble floor. That stunning chandelier we had seen before had just fallen, dangerous shards instead of beauty. We could hear the footsteps nearing as Alden fumbled with his multi, trying to get the machine out of compact mode so it could be used. But all of us knew he was taking too long.

Just as we crept further up the stairs in hiding, we could hear the Watch Dog moving in closer. I could still not see the creature of time, but I could hear sharp zaps through the air, like a million shocks all at once. That must have been its growl.

"Why is it following us? We're not going to take the Time Case," I asked, my teeth chattering.

"Well, Time Cases that they protect power off of used energy in order to delete time. Naturally, they just grow as time goes on but sometimes, probably most of the time, they want more fuel. Living things have energy which they can absorb if they kill us and while Idums are helpful, Gradiens have even more," Alden informed us.

"We are food?" Lucas pointed.

Alden shook his head. "No, we're batteries."

Lucas sighed, obviously trying to find a way to make the situation more tolerable. "A little better."

Fortunately, Alden was able to dial the code of the time travel Safety Building. Unfortunately, that was exactly when the Watch Dog bolted towards the stairs, frightening us all so much that Alden dropped his multi, allowing it to fall an entire flight.

However alarming and horrific you imagined the Watch Dog to look, it was a thousand times worse. When I used to think of monsters, I saw massive fangs and claws, matted fur or scales, blood stains left wherever it walked. That was not at all what this monstrosity looked like. The

Watch Dog was like if an entire movie screen had TV fuzz and it burst out into reality. Also, it had condensed under its own weight into a moving creature, with something close to a head, body and an odd number of limbs, that changed each time I looked. It was as tall as the ceiling, expanding across half the entire dining room. Its face was constantly blurring, though there were two sunken areas in the center of its skull that I assumed were the eyes. There were still bolts of lightning burning from the Watch Dog, mainly at the center of the body. That must have been the Time Case.

"I'll go first," I offered. "It's probably looking for me because of how much energy I have, because of my era. I must be the attraction."

"No, we're only in this house because of me," Pandora asserted. "I'll take the first strike."

Alden stepped up, no longer staring down at his multi which he dropped. "I've known I was a Gradien the longest, so I probably have the best knowledge of what to do."

Then, Lucas stomped down on the ground. "¡Estamos aquí! We are here, four people in this house. Four people with the Watch Dog. We all fight, no first, no second. Muy bien?" Lucas called.

In unison, the three of us nodded. I had not seen Lucas take much initiative yet, and him instructing us on what to do was definitely a surprise. But we probably would be going nowhere without him making us stick together.

"Ok, let's go," Pandora said. "Lucas, can we have the votans?"

He pulled off his backpack, handing us each our respective weapon. "We hit the chest, I think."

And that was our battle cry. *We hit the chest, I think.*

Considering our lack of confidence, inexperience and the likelihood that we would probably be dead in a few minutes, it really sounded perfect. From that, we began to aim for the chest.

All of us assumed we just would lunge at the creature and impale it with the votans, which would somehow inject enough positive energy to completely cancel out any strength of the Watch Dog. It was a lot easier said than done.

Pandora launched onto the ground, rolling under the Watch Dog. In tune with her, Alden slammed his votan into the Watch Dog's fifth leg-like appendage, yet it only brought about more of that electric howl. I could tell Alden was trying to distract the Watch Dog in order to give Pandora a better aim towards its Time Case, but instead, it was just angry. The Watch Dog slammed two of its feet onto the ground, nearly crushing my friend lying there. It would have squashed her if she hadn't rolled away immediately.

Pandora got up and ran against the far wall, obviously wanting to distance herself from the Watch Dog as much as possible. Taking her place, I too ducked under the Watch Dog, noticing as the energy raced above me. The worst part about the creature was that it could move without advancing an inch. Since it was purely composed of energy, which is not matter like we know it. It played by different rules that any other living thing—if it could even be counted as living. Its particles raced on top of each other, giving it new numbers of legs and changing its size by just a bit with every given second. It was impossible to track where you were trying to hit unless you held your eyes open constantly, which I for sure couldn't do. At least there was no skin to stab, so my stomach was twisting a little less than I expected. Don't get me wrong, though—I was still feeling incredibly sick.

Lucas, who was attempting to block the eyesight of the Watch Dog by stabbing into its eyes and hanging from a ledge in the wall, screamed at me to keep stabbing its underside. He did not seem to be having much success in blinding the creature (again, I didn't even know if it could be blinded) as it just swung its head at Lucas more. I was trying to listen to his instructions and move towards the chest of the Watch Dog, but new legs kept forming and blocking me and disappearing right when I backed away.

Pandora returned from the wall and threw her votan, which I noticed was somewhat thinner than mine, at the Watch Dog's behind. Feeling the impact, it reared back into a designer table, which was now just left in chunks. I had no idea how the family who lived here was ever going to figure out what destroyed their home.

Picking up her votan after it fell from the creature, Pandora ran to the front and aimed to hit it square in the chest. But the Watch Dog noticed her immediately and swung one of its legs against her side, pushing her into the banister. She fell immediately, a gash appearing along her left arm.

"Don't-don't touch it," Pandora groaned, clutching her arm. "Somehow, the Watch Dog is sharp, it's like a knife or something…" her voice began to fade as she further inspected her wound.

Seeing that we were down a person, at least for a moment, I moved from under the Watch Dog and began to run in circles around it. I thought maybe it would distract the Watch Dog and move its attention away from its closest prey, Pandora. The thing was, as soon as I was seen, the Watch Dog had a new hunt. As I headed in the opposite direction of the Watch Dog, it began to gallop after me around the house. I can tell you that I had never, *ever,* been that scared in my entire life. My head was pounding, I was sweating enough to soak my clothes and my heart felt as if it was one beat away from shooting out of my chest. My PE teacher back in Ithaca would tell you that I was a horrible runner. My speed right here would verify that.

The best I could do to escape the Watch Dog as it chased me was duck under assorted pieces of furniture before the creature crushed them and made me choose a new destination. I kept running and running, going into large rooms and leaving with quick turns, which each only bought me few seconds each time, but any extra time, however little, was what I needed.

As soon as I returned to the main room where my friends stood, Pandora was amazingly back up, standing between Alden and Lucas all with their votans ready.

"¡Otra vez!" Lucas screamed at me.

"You have to tire it out, Keira," Alden told me. "Then, we will hit when you come back in."

Seeing as I had no other option than being bait, becoming Shaggy *and* Scooby all in one person, I continued to run. Surprisingly, I was able to go faster even though I was getting more and more tired. I guess that's just what fear does to you. I kept along the same routine of going into rooms and leaving as quickly as possible, switching up my order the third time I ran around. By the fourth, I expected my friends to have prepared as well as possible to aim right for the Watch Dog's chest, yet they still stood unmoved.

"Keira, just one more time! We'll meet you on the other end of the house!" Pandora screamed.

"I hate *all* of you," I panted back, somehow still getting the Watch Dog to chase me. I really hoped that in the future, I would stop being objectified for my energy, if that was what was happening to me.

Taking a deep breath, I took a stab at the face of the Watch Dog, earning a growl in my direction. The Watch Dog kicked one leg at me, scraping the back of my shin as I just barely leaped in front. There was a small, stinging, bloody scratch, but I had no choice but to continue running.

I decided to pick a new track this time around, flying up a staircase other than the one we had originally used, which I hoped would take the Watch Dog off my path. For a second, I was sure I had made the right decision. I was alone on the second floor, only hearing creaking downstairs from my friends and of course, the Watch Dog. But things were a little *too* quiet. There were barely any footsteps or voices, let alone fast movements and screams. It was the sound of waiting, and in ways, I wanted to hear shrieks just to know that things were happening.

All of a sudden, the footsteps grew. I assumed my friends had started chasing the Watch Dog in my place, until I heard them getting closer. I looked down the stairs but they were clear, no one in my sight. Then I felt a spark.

Behind me, panting and scratching at the ground, was the Watch Dog. It had not climbed the stairs or jumped, but just appeared. I remembered then that this was not any part of our reality. The Watch Dog was closer to a ghost than an animal, passing through walls was likely the easiest of tasks. But even though it could pass through walls, thankfully, it never figured out to chase me that way.

I screamed for my friends, but they could not hear me because of the distance and the growl of the Watch Dog. It was slow for the first time, creeping towards me, one step at a time. I realized that maybe I could trick it, moving slowly when it expected me to be fast. But it was the Watch Dog that tricked me. Just as I decreased my pace, it sped up. The Watch Dog shot towards me, giving me not even a nanosecond to devise a plan. All I could do was raise my votan above my head and hope I survived.

Suddenly, a bright light exploded in the hallway, later leaving it pitch black. The light returned, illuminating the hall to make it appear like I was the only one there. On the ground before me was a small glimmering speck, which over a couple minutes finally dimmed to nothing. I had hit the chest. I had destroyed the Time Case.

"Guys!" I announced, after having stood alone for a few minutes. "Can you come up here?"

At last, I heard assurance that they were alive again. Stomps rang around the house from their quickness to get to me and soon enough, I could see them coming up the stairs. From where I stood, it seemed that Pandora's arm had begun to heal, as the blood appeared to be dry and was lighter at this point. I hoped I was right.

"Where'd the Watch Dog go, Keira?" Pandora asked. "We haven't been able to find it anywhere."

I grasped my votan tighter. "I...I killed it."

"What?" Lucas screamed, running to me. "What did you see? Was it cool?"

I stood still for another moment before answering. "It just bolted right towards me and I got scared, so I held up my votan and hit it in the right spot, I guess. There was just a flash of light then darkness, no sound at all. It was pretty cool," I answered, stifling a laugh. "Then, what I assume was the Time Case was slightly burning on the ground for a few minutes before just going dim."

"You've been just standing up here for a few minutes without calling for us?" Alden shouted. "We thought you were hurt or worse!"

Pandora pat his arm. "She saved all of our lives, Alden. I don't think there should be any fighting about this."

He frowned. "I wasn't trying to fight, I was just worried. I'm sorry, Keira."

Before I could tell him that there was no need to apologize, Pandora came over and hugged me. Lucas joined in next, with Alden as the tallest all wrapping us in. I had never had a group hug before and honestly, this seemed like the best moment for my first one.

As we all pulled away from each other, wiping tears at the realization that we had survived, we began to collect ourselves, as well.

"Alden, you will call time travel Safety, yes?" Lucas asked.

He nodded. "Yeah, just a second." He pulled his multi from his pocket, which I guessed he had retrieved, not having bothered to return it to compact mode.

As soon as he pressed the button for the department, a small ding sounded. Then, I heard the hum of a voice on the other side.

"Yes, I'd like to report a surprise Watch Dog encounter," Alden said.

There was more mumbling on the phone.

"The year is 1967, it is about 3:30 in the afternoon, and we are in Beverly Hills, California."

Again, a sound on the other side of the line.

Now, Alden held his multi below his chin, looking

straight at me as he did so. When he lifted the object back up to his ear, his stare did not leave my eyes. "No, the situation has been handled."

CHAPTER 20

WHEN WE GOT BACK TO LANA ILU,
we were instructed to go directly to the time
travel Safety Building and spill the entire story. We were
not to leave out a single detail. Alden had told me that
the man on the other end of the phone had been incredibly frantic, the opposite of what a crisis manager should
sound like. He was breathing heavily, stumbling upon his
words, trying to understand why such a thing had happened. It had been centuries, apparently, since there was
a surprise Watch Dog appearance, and the trackers had
been greatly improved since then. What had just happened was mind-boggling, nonsensical. It seemed like
everywhere I went in Lana Ilu, I attracted a craze.

"They asked to hear everything. Do we have to tell
them that we broke into a house? Oh my God, or that we
ditched our supervisor?" Pandora fretted on the walk over

to the building. First Aid had rushed to us as soon as we arrived back in the city, patching up any wounds that we had gotten. Now, all of our cuts were completely gone, including Pandora's injured arm.

"I thought it wasn't trespassing, *Pandora*," Alden mocked, obviously still bothered by the situation Pandora caused. "And it was your choice."

"Please, it was obviously following me or one of us in some way. It would've shown up absolutely anywhere in order to fight us, or you know, take us," I offered.

"I understand but..."

"People," Lucas announced. "House, no house. Year, no year. Lana Ilu only cares about the Watch Dog."

I nodded in agreement. "You're right. Let's just get there and tell them about what happened so I can go home and nap. That running tired me out." I glared at them, my eyes low. "You know, because I was galloping around a mansion over and over to buy all of you time just for me to..."

Alden reached for my arm. "Keira, don't do this. We owe you our lives and we, at least *I*, promise we'll never make you do that again. It just seemed like a good choice at the time."

"No, I know and I'm happy it's all done. I've got my story straight to tell whomever is at the building," I said.

Lucas crossed his arms. "You think this, the Watch Dog, is done?"

I shrugged. "Well yeah, it's been killed. We're safe home in Lana Ilu. Why wouldn't it be?"

"Um, Pandora and Alden say today was far from the first problem. They made changes. Do you believe these changes will work in the future? They did not today, tomorrow? I do not know," Lucas stumbled.

And that shook me to my core. Lucas was exactly right. There were no promises of our security. In fact, I had no idea why I thought that last glimmer of the Time Case was all I would see of them in my life. I had seen that in the Idum-world too often. The most horrifying events could begin to look normal. News channels in the United States showed clips saying *Largest Mass Shooting in American History*, one only a year after the other. But gun laws never changed. Record lows and record highs in temperature were recorded on the same day, but our cities only pumped out more gas the next. Hate crimes against transgender people occurred constantly, and our government thought the solution was to keep them from using the bathroom. I knew that hardships lost their scarcity quickly, and even in Lana Ilu where I trusted the Queen to help, there was only so much that could be done.

Soon enough we were at the time travel Safety Building, a pitch-black structure without a single way to see in. It looked like night as the sun rose. I was sure they had incredible air conditioning.

We were escorted inside by a group of Lana Ilu's police officers, guarding us from the reporters who had practically set up a blockade against the entrance door. There were cameras snapping, questions shouting in the air, and phones and tablets pushed towards our faces, though were all forced to keep on walking. Some of the reporters chased us, though, and from their speed, I think they could have done a better job with the Watch Dog than I had. I was tempted to scream that in their faces, to show them exactly what kind of mood I was in right now, but

I knew a sassy attitude would only work better for their newspapers. Their questions of *How did it happen?* and *Are you alright?* really seemed quite empty with their microphones. One of the reporters was even trying to file an entirely different story as she asked me if I had been seen with Prince Trevor lately because I had been invited as his date to the Royal Ball. It was just a pointless question since you needed to be at least a third generation to be eligible. Also, *privacy much?*

At last, we were brought to the much quieter top floor, the headquarters for situations just like ours. Since a surprise Watch Dog encounter had not occurred for hundreds of years, the entire office was busy preparing. There were also less than a dozen people taking up the floor. Considering what Lucas had said about this not being the end, I was positive they would be requesting more office space and some reassignments of workers from other departments.

The four of us were given levitating chairs to sit in (this city and its floating furniture!) as we faced a stern Safety Official, Agent Lee, clad in a heavily-ironed business suit.

"So, we understand you four were visiting Los Angeles in the year 1967 CE. Were you visiting anyone in particular or was this purely for spontaneous fun?" the woman asked us, a note taker by her side. She also repeated it in Spanish for Lucas, which I could tell she would be continuing afterward.

"This was just for fun, to show Lucas Acosta and Keira Sun here what time travel is like. They are pretty new to Lana Ilu so Pandora Dailey and I, Alden Fischer, wanted to take them somewhere relatively close to help them break it in," he explained.

"After telling us about the Zanaree and its Varem, er, Watch Dog and the Time Case, you gave us the address of a specific house. Why were you there if not to visit someone?" Agent Lee pushed.

I noticed Pandora begin to sweat. "Ma'am, I was going somewhere quite specific. My family lives in Beverly Hills, as I am an Idum-born from there, and I was curious as to what my old home looked like decades ago. The locks had not changed after all these years so I had the right keys. Afterward, we were inside."

"And how much time passed in this house before you encountered the Watch Dog? Also, who was the one to see it first?"

"Ten minutes," Lucas said. "And Pandora Dailey."

"Noted," Agent Lee said, even though she herself was not the one taking notes. "Where was your supervisor, Huilang Ma, at this time?"

Pandora peered down at her feet, knocking her heels together. "We, um, I asked us to leave her at a different house so we could try to get into my home. It was a horrible decision and it is not Huilang's fault and I just hope she is safe," she finished, her voice cracking.

Agent Lee nodded. "We were luckily able to contact her and she is back in Lana Ilu. You know that it is strictly against the rules to leave a supervisor on purpose, yes?"

Pandora's eyes were red. "Yes, I do know that. I'm so sorry, I never meant to endanger anybody."

"It would have happened either way, Pandora. It's ok," Alden coaxed, putting his hand on her shoulder.

"Considering the circumstances and it being the first

offense for all of you, we will let this one go, but never again. Anyways, you reported the Watch Dog as being very large. Could you give me a height estimate in feet?"

I ran through the memory. "I would say about ten feet, maybe a little less or a little more. It was definitely tall."

Agent Lee nodded. "Alright, so that would be fairly small. Probably recently born, maybe four hundred years at most."

Fairly small and *four hundred years*? It was hard to register those two being said in the same breath. Also, considering the trauma I went through just a while ago, positive I was going to die decades away from home, it was difficult to imagine the Watch Dog as small. I did not want to think about ever seeing a large one.

"And can you explain to me *exactly* how you killed the creature, step by step," Agent Lee added.

"So, I rolled under the thing to try and hit its chest where the Time Case is located," Pandora started. "Alden also began stabbing at its leg when I did that as a distraction, but it just made the Watch Dog angry."

From then on out, the four of us recalled every second of the fight. We talked about stabbing and kicking and rolling, some of which probably never happened, but it just seemed like it had. Lucas could have told me that he grew wings as we tried to kill the Watch Dog and I would have believed him. Every moment just blurred into another.

"And how come you did not call this building for a Preserver? We could have had two sent out in minutes and it would have taken the stress off you children greatly," Agent Lee chastised.

Alden sat straighter in his chair. "I actually did try, but I unfortunately dropped my multi and by then, well ma'am, I mean no disrespect but we did not exactly have a few minutes. We sort of just figured it out as we went, I guess."

"I understand, Mr. Fischer. Just from now on, if you are ever in this rare situation again, please do anything to call. Your safety as a citizen of this city, as a Gradien, and of course, as a human being are incredibly important. Find a way to contact us, however you can." Agent Lee took a deep breath. "Were all of you equally responsible for killing the Watch Dog and destroying the Time Case?"

I shook my head. "No... no, it was mainly me, Agent Lee. Because I was running from it so much and it was following me, the Watch Dog sort of fell into my hands. It appeared behind me when I went upstairs to escape it and just out of fear, I held up my votan and luckily stabbed the Time Case. I just saw it burst into light, then go dark and well, you get it." I placed my hands in my lap after my statement, suddenly feeling awkward. I felt like I had taken too much credit for something my friends had definitely helped in.

Then, Agent Lee put her hand out for a shake. I reached in, complying. "Thank you, Keira Sun. You are a hero and this city is forever grateful."

My face heated, not sure exactly how to accept her praise. Just before, I had wanted to smack all three of my friends across the face for turning me into bait, forcing me to do three-quarters of the job all on my own. But now, I wanted to hug them and never leave their sides. We had all been in that house together, and no heroic act of mine could change that.

A moment after, Pandora looked over my shoulder. "You can say *thank you*, Keira," she whispered.

I nodded. "Thank you, Agent Lee. I am just happy my friends and I are all alive. It doesn't matter who killed the Watch Dog, just that we all got back home safe."

Just as Agent Lee began to smile, the phones in the office abruptly went off, their rings tearing through the room. It was like the blare of a million fire trucks, rushing to save a house just beside my ear. Agents rushed to the phones, the fastest picking up one. Then, he closed his eyes.

"Toronto area, the year 3000 CE. Two sixteen year olds are just now hiding from a small Watch Dog. We need Preservers *now!*" the Agent demanded.

Theo and Holly, I thought. *Watch Dogs were everywhere.*

Just as everyone on the floor prayed that that call was the last of it, the phones rang again. And again.

And again.

CHAPTER 21

IWAS SO GLAD WHEN THE FOUR OF US were shuffled out of the time travel Safety Building after the scream of phones through the office. Preservers came running out of the elevators on each floor, clad in reflective gear and wearing votans strapped to their chests.

"Out, out, *out*!" They were shouting, zapping out of thin air at each second. Following our instance with the Watch Dog, four others had been reported in less than ten minutes. Alerts were being sent out to every multi in the city, saying that nobody was permitted to go to another time. The same was done to multis for those time traveling at the moment, hoping that they would return immediately. Unfortunately, like I had seen with myself, most people put their multis in compact mode and hid them away. Most alerts would not be heard because we tried to hide ourselves. I wondered how the government was going to handle this.

One of the guards drove Lucas, Pandora, Alden and me home, people waiting for us at every destination. Lucas and Pandora both had their friends from their sectors waiting with open arms. Alden's parents and older brother stood outside, but only Juliet had tears streaming down her face.

When I arrived back to my apartment, Mr. and Mrs. Handal were smiling right beside it. I noticed from afar that both of them had puffy faces and red eyes. They had been crying because of me. They really were like the parents I never had. I realized that if they knew about Theo and Holly in future Toronto—had they learned already, I wondered—it would be even worse.

"Keira!" Mr. Handal cried. "Oh, we are so glad that you are home safe."

Mrs. Handal came running to me. "And we are so very proud of you for killing the Watch Dog but *never, ever* do that again, alright? No more jeopardizing your life sweetheart, you almost gave me a heart attack."

"I didn't really have a choice..." I mumbled, still grinning at how much they cared for me. Mrs. Handal surrounded me in a hug—warmth that I really needed in this moment.

"Oh, I know. That doesn't mean I liked the choice. Now, do you want anything to eat? I made that vegetable dish you love so much," she huddled in closer to me. "And a cake that's all yours if you want it."

I beamed. "I'd love to have it tonight, Mrs. Handal. I really appreciate it so much, but I'm really just tired right now. I think I'm going to take a nap, but I'll be over tonight."

Mrs. Handal stroked my cheek. "Of course, dear. Get all the rest you need."

With that, I headed into my apartment and hopped into bed, wrapping the blankets around me. Hopefully I could swaddle the memory of the Watch Dog's growl out of my mind. I couldn't think of another way.

AFTER I WOKE up from my hour-long nap, I heard my doorbell ringing. I didn't especially want to talk to anyone, especially since I could barely see with all the sleep in my eyes, but I pulled myself out of bed towards the door. When I slid it open, I saw Theo and Holly, their eyes red as they were shaking. I noticed Theo's smile widen as he looked at me and Holly actually had tears falling from her eyes. I allowed the door to open and Holly immediately rushed to hug my shoulders.

"I'm okay, Holly," I assured her, knowing she was about to ask me how I was feeling since the Watch Dog.

She stroked my hair as she looked down at me. "I know, I can see that you're laughing and smiling and... I just want to make sure, Keira. You're kind of like the little sister I never had, so I'm going to get a little protective."

I nodded, blushing a bit at the term of endearment. I had a real older sister, definitely the best one in the world, but Holly didn't seem like too bad of a second one. She was my Gradien sister, there for the problems I could not turn to Willow for.

Theo wrapped me in a hug next, pulling me close as if he was terrified if he let go, I would be with that Watch

Dog again. I knew that they had gone through the same thing as me, yet they didn't seem to care about that. They just wanted to know I was safe.

"Keira... I can't image what that must have been like for you. Your first time doing this and you have to kill a *Watch Dog!* I guess it proves how awesome you are," Theo said.

"We were thinking about you until this second, I'm just so happy we have this family," Holly added.

She soon ducked her head, shutting her mismatched eyes. "Hey, sorry but my family's making me spend the night, actually the entire week with them. At least Great Uncle Wes is home from Tokyo, so I can spend time with him. That's probably the *only* upside of this Watch Dog crisis, that he has to stay here for a while."

"Isn't Uncle Wes always *drunk?*" Theo pointed.

Holly smirked. "He's always drinking, not *drunk.* His personality is more 'old man at a wine tasting in Tuscany,' not 'old man who just had his tenth beer on Wednesday night.' But anyway, they want you to come for dinner, Theo."

Theo's eyes bugged out of his head. "Your, your parents, Reginald and Lorelei Hawkridge want *me* to come to dinner. Is this as your boyfriend?"

"*Definitely* not as my boyfriend, my parents would hate to see that I'm already dating," Holly said, then almost ironically kissing Theo, who was very much indeed her boyfriend. "But nonetheless, you're in the big leagues now, Chevalier."

Theo blushed, but the grinding of his knuckles displayed that he was not too enthusiastic of having dinner with the notorious Hawkridge family when he was dating their only daughter—their *only* child—behind their backs. Just as the conversation was about to continue, each of our multis began to beep. Then, they all sprouted a holo-graphic image of Queen Prima simultaneously. She was dressed in a golden dress, perched at her bejeweled, towering throne. The three of us all focused our attention.

"My fellow Gradiens, my ever-timeless people," the Queen stated, shutting her eyes, "though I am certain all of you have heard of the recent Zanaree, or Watch Dog, appearances, I regret to inform you that their untracked presences have not declined, but rather spread both geographically and throughout the existence of time."

Theo, Holly, and I peered at one another, unsure of what Her Majesty would say next.

"Though it pains me to say, as the very action runs in our blood, I have been forced for the safety of every citizen...to place a ban on *all* time travel until further notice. This includes any ventures into the Idum-world, even modern time. Do not fear, our top Preservers have been sent out to protect all still trapped in years away from home and my most *trusted* researchers, including myself, will not stop until the problem is solved. Rest assured, no city under my reign will be a city in crisis."

CHAPTER 22

NONE OF US MOVED AN INCH AFTER the hologram shut off. As much as the Queen promised that the future of Lana Ilu was not bleak, the fact that we were forced to stay within the confines of the city did not support her case. Gradiens were born to associate with every second in time, past and future. Even though I had only time traveled twice, being forced to remain in the present seemed almost like a jail sentence. Worst of all, I couldn't see Willow, and as much as I appreciated Holly, she wasn't the big sister I needed for this.

"I, I don't know what to say," Holly croaked.

"Back in the U.S., the President tried to institute a stupid travel ban, too. I'll hand it to Queen Prima for creating one that actually makes sense," I said, trying my best to lighten the mood, though it admittedly wasn't very funny.

Theo shook his head. "Yeah, I know about that. But

anyway, I know that Queen Prima is making the right choice but... why does *this* have to be the right choice?"

"I thought you said not to ask about *whys*," I pushed towards Theo. He scowled back at me.

"I also added that *only time can tell*, Keira. It looks like we have a bit of a shortage of time at the moment."

"Hey!" Holly called out. "No arguing, even fake arguing right now. My parents just called me, they want us over soon. Theo, could you just go change into something nicer and a little less Watch Dog-beaten?" Holly then pointed at her own red dress as the height of the glamour he should be aiming for.

Theo nodded and waved goodbye to me as the two left my apartment. I was alone again, alone at the second Gradiens needed the most comfort. But I didn't want to speak to a Gradien right now. I wanted to speak to a very specific Idum.

I took out my phone, which still worked in Lana Ilu, and dialed Willow's number. In a matter of seconds, I heard my sister's voice on the other line.

"Keira!" Willow exclaimed. "I haven't talked to you in days! How are you?"

I debated about explaining the whole Watch Dog situation, knowing that she would be terrified to know I was in that much danger. Then again, I needed a reason for why I couldn't visit her for who knows how long. I couldn't just procrastinate.

"I'm... okay. A lot happened recently. Well, a lot actually today," I mumbled.

"Are you safe, are you alright?" Willow gasped. "Keira!"

"Willow, I said that I'm okay!"

I could practically hear her eyes roll over the phone.

"*Okay* has many meanings, Keira. It's all in the way you say it. Can you *please* tell me what happened?"

I suddenly wanted to avoid the entire story, pretend I could visit her any day and Lana Ilu was the same peaceful haven it was before. "Are you getting excited to go to Princeton?"

"What is it with you and avoiding the elephant in the room? I'm not answering until you tell me what happened to you! Keira, right now you are living in a time travel city in another dimension with all your other time travel friends time traveling! I'm going to get concerned occasionally," Willow scolded.

"Alright, alright... so I went time traveling for the first time today, other than when I saw you. It was to the 1960's in Los Angeles. Everything was really fun until... we saw this thing that we call a Watch Dog. Watch Dogs are these crazy creatures with all this negative energy that are just created, I don't really get how, and they protect these things called Time Cases that can delete time. I know, it doesn't make any sense. but just stick with me. Usually, they can be tracked so that the proper security people, we call them Preservers, can go and kill them without Gradien civilians who are time traveling being in danger. Well, that tracker is usually perfectly accurate... until today. We saw one and so did a ton of other people while they were traveling. I'm fine since I killed the one my friends and I saw... "

"You killed it? *You* killed it? Keira, YOU KILLED A TIME MONSTER AND YOU'RE ACTING LIKE IT IS *NOTHING*!" Willow hollered, my phone practically shaking from the volume of her voice.

"It was just a surprise and I really just killed it with luck. But... that's not the only thing I needed to tell you."

Willow sighed. "Keira, I love you, but what could you *possibly* have to add to that?"

I set down my phone on my dining table, just watching it collect dust for a moment. I didn't feel like telling any more to Willow, not that I did not want to talk to her and hear her voice, I always did, but I was worried it would change things. She always spoke to me in Lana Ilu with the belief that at any moment, we could see each other again. We acted like there was no divide, no wall between her being an Idum and me being a Gradien. Now I had to admit that we began building it weeks ago.

"Willow... I can't come back into the Idum-world to visit you," I told her.

"Wait, for how long? And why?"

"The Queen has not decided yet. Her team is still trying to figure out why the Watch Dogs are showing up. And we can't go out into the Idum-world because there could be Watch Dogs out there and Gradiens are their primary targets..."

"Primary????" Willow screeched. "Am I, an er, Idum, at risk? Are my friends? Are innocent little children?"

Her concern struck me. I wanted to tell Willow no. I wanted to tell her that she was perfectly safe and so was I and that she could pick up whatever she was doing before she answered the phone. I wanted to tell Willow that our two-year-old neighbor could sing her nursery rhymes as her parents rolled her around in a stroller without ever having to look appetizing to a Watch Dog. I wanted to tell her that even if she was in danger, we Gradiens would do everything in our ability to protect them.

I wanted to not lie to myself when I thought that.

"Willow, Watch Dogs look for energy, and while they *mostly* want Gradiens, Idums can be their fuel, too. It's rare, but it happens. Listen, tons of people in Lana Ilu are trying to fix our trackers. I'm sure we will do something to make sure you are safe."

Willow huffed. "I love you, Keira, but don't just look out for me or anyone else who's related to a Gradien. If we're in danger, we *all* need your help."

A tear rolled down my cheek. "I know, I will do what I can."

There was a long pause afterwards, perhaps the longest moment of silence ever between Willow and me. We could talk for hours without ever taking a breath before. Now, neither of us knew what to say.

"So, I'm getting really excited for Princeton."

WILLOW DECIDED TO leave the Watch Dog conversation behind, at least for today, relieving fifty tons of stress from my shoulders. She then began to ramble about Princeton, almost like a lullaby for my nerves. I *really* missed her.

After Willow hung up, I wanted to find something else to do. I wasn't tired any more, but I didn't want to ask my friends to go out. I decided to paint.

A few weeks after we had gotten to know each other, Lucas and I had went shopping for things to "fulfill" our hobbies. He bought a film camera and a vintage typewriter because he had always wanted to create movies, and I had helped him read some lines from scripts he had begun working on. He was absolutely obsessed with horror movies, and most of my lines were just me describing how much blood a monster had drank. Somehow, I was incredibly engaged. Lucas said that once he arrived upon a script he absolutely loved, he wanted to assemble friends from school to act in it. I couldn't wait to take on a role.

For me, I bought a couple dozen canvases as well as a set of watercolor and oil paints. I usually only went for watercolor, enjoying the way I could control just how much each shade would drip, but Lucas suggested I move out of my comfort zone. I picked up a cheap set of oil paints right before we checked out.

After my conversation with Willow, I began to long for the Idum-world, the Idum *life* for the first time since I arrived in Lana Ilu. I wanted to go to playgrounds where the scenery was not holographic. I wanted to have a crush without it being in every city's magazine. I wanted to travel and not have to fear seeing a crazy energy creature that wanted to absorb me!

I looked into my living room, scanning all the decor. I really wanted furniture that didn't always have to float.

So, I decided to paint the most mundane, Idum thing I could think of—my house. The small yellow house on Eastview Lane that I hated to look at each day and now could not get out of my mind. I opened my watercolors and began to dab a mix of mustard and daisy onto the canvas. I mixed and mixed, shaping it into a rectangle. I had been practicing shadowing in the months before learning that I was a Gradien, staying after school with my art teacher to learn the skills. It was still difficult for me to get the right ratio without going too dark, as I sometimes would even dab black paint in places where I was unsure. But, these paintings were just for me. There was nothing wrong with playing a guessing game.

Just as I was beginning to add details to the straight frame of the white entrance door, I heard my doorbell ring like it had so much today. I hoped it was Lucas, Pandora or Alden. Lucas I could laugh with about our Idum lives, maybe speak about his future movie career or mine as a painter. Pandora and I could tell riddle after riddle to each other, ending the night with chips and life stories. Alden could teach me about Lana Ilu and history and then we would forget being smart to trade stupid jokes. I really hoped it was one of them.

Instead of getting Daisy to answer the door, I rose up from my seat and did it myself. It was more of an Idum thing to do.

Shockingly, the pair of dark eyes facing me belonged not to Lucas but the Princess. She stood, arms crossed in an unconventionally casual outfit for a royal, a graphic olive tee-shirt with distressed jeans. Her curly locks were braided back into two buns.

"Princess Avarielle..." I breathed.

She raised her brows. "You don't have your apartment all hooked up to open the door for you?"

"No, I do, just felt like opening the door right now."

Avarielle knelt down, providing me with a dramatic curtsey. I was taken aback from the gesture, as due to our power dynamic (she the Princess and me... well, not), it should have been me taking the lower stance. "Well, thank you for your hospitality."

Without us talking any further, Avarielle sashayed into my apartment, scanning each and every room. She walked around the kitchen, my living room, the bathroom, but stayed away from where I slept. She still had a sense of privacy, I guess.

"Are you noticing that this whole place is half the size of your bedroom?" I observed.

Avarielle rolled her eyes. "Of course not, pay your Princess more respect... I'd say it's about a quarter of the size."

Just as I was about to retort, as much as I possibly could to my future monarch, Avarielle raised her hands in front of her face. She afterwards let out a chuckle after seeing me calm down.

"I'm joking, Keira! Just because I'm the Princess doesn't mean I'm stuck up. Your place looks nice."

I grinned, trying my best to show the Princess that I accepted that as true. After Avarielle had told me, someone she barely knew, that her grandmother was a liar, I had begun to wonder if she wasn't covering up her own untruthfulness. Then again, Avarielle had also explained every issue she saw with me and how she knew them in herself. She was an open book, but every other word was coded.

"Princess Avarielle, do you want anything to eat?" I questioned, beginning to walk over to my kitchen.

She shook her head. "I'm fine, I'm fine, I just want to talk. Can we go sit down?"

My shoulders tensed. Serious conversation with any of the Royals still absolutely terrified me. When I was in Queen Prima's study, I was so nervous about embarrassing myself in front of her that I actually scrutinized my breathing pattern, making sure one gasp was not heavy enough to ruffle a single paper on her desk. Her story about our similarities, despite the differences in eras, made my brain twist and sweat as I tried to understand every syllable. And don't even get me started on

Prince Trevor asking to leave a party with me to just go anywhere. If the Prince of Lana Ilu sincerely liked me in any real shape or form, I might have a heart attack.

And here was Princess Avarielle, wanting to sit and chat with me. I would feel calmer if George Washington had come back from the dead, looking exactly like a zombie, and walked straight into my home.

I allowed Princess Avarielle to take a seat at the table in my two-chair kitchen. I took the other, sitting straight across from her.

"So, Princess, what is it you wanted to talk about?"

Princess Avarielle peered down at the table, batting her eyes. I noticed her cheeks swell for a second as she took a deep breath, and she began to tap her fingers on the table. The thing about Princess Avarielle was that she was so obviously Royal that until I had these face-to-face moments with her, I forgot she was human. She was much taller than me and I never saw her back-slouch for a second. She was fifteen and could map all of time, was the face of every brand in Lana Ilu, and knew the name of each Gradien in the city. She was also incredibly beautiful, like mystifyingly beautiful, with clearer skin than I thought any fifteen-year-old could have, and straight white teeth that I knew I would never achieve, even after the magic of the braces I'd already had.

But she looked scared right now, jitters obvious in her every movement. In her everyday clothes and nearly curled-over position on one of my chairs, she might have looked like a girl I could pass by on the street. Not quite, but definitely closer than before.

"Keira, how, how did you do it?" Princess Avarielle asked, not making eye contact with me.

"Do what?"

"Oh, you know... kill the Watch Dog?"

Of course, she was here to ask that, I wanted to slap myself for not knowing it from the get-go. "Well, I held up my votan... "

Avarielle banged her forehead down on the table. "No, I know the *actions* you took, everyone does, but *how*? You never even time traveled before, but you were brave enough to kill it all on your own. I've lived in my city all my life, traveled more years than I could name, even seen some Watch Dogs in captivity before they were killed, but I've never actually fought one of those monsters. I don't know what to do with a Time Case or how to destroy it, I've only been taught as much as you. And if you're killing these things, I *know* I must learn how immediately."

I pulled on a strand of my hair. I never imagined that the Princess would come to me for some sort of advice. "Princess Avarielle, well, I was just scared. It was coming right at me and I didn't want to die. And I guess, mostly, I thought of my friends who still needed to be kept safe..."

"So, the trick to being brave is love? I suppose all those fairytales are right," Avarielle stammered.

"Well, I think it was more friendship."

Princess Avarielle rolled her eyes. "Keira, do you really think that the only kind of love is romantic? Friendship is a kind of love called *platonic* and it's love just like anything else. There's also family love, like... anyone who means the world to you in yours"

I nodded. "My older sister, Willow."

Princess Avarielle clicked her tongue. "Not your parents at all?"

I threw my head back, never exactly in the mood to

talk about them. "I mean, they're my parents so I have to love them, but they are... a lot. How about yours?"

"I'm lucky, my parents are pretty great. It's hard to have amazing royal parents that don't get obsessed with power. I mean, my Dad's technically first in line and my Mom's in charge of all Idum Relations, so you would expect everything would go to their heads, but... they always put being my parents first. I know they would give up anything for me."

"Does Prince Trevor feel the same way?" I asked, noting that the siblings didn't have much in common when it came to personality.

Princess Avarielle shrugged her shoulders. "I would *think* so, they're good people."

"I like Trevor, I'm sure he appreciates good people."

The Princess smirked, nodding as she grinned. "Well, he would love to hear that. Considering he literally talks about you constantly, it's all *Keira this* and *Keira that* at dinner, I can assume he likes you, too. You don't really fit our demographic to be his date but..." Avarielle laughed, "I'm sure my brother could bend the rules."

I felt my face heat up when the Princess said that. I just wanted to get back onto talking about the Watch Dog. Like I said, the Imamus got in your head. "So about killing the creature..."

Princess Avarielle snapped her fingers. "Yes, yes, that. Forget the whole love thing, I already knew that wanting to keep others safe makes you stronger. Just... the Queen is in absolute panic, Keira. My grandmother won't stop pacing and going into our research labs and then leaving and then going back and—it just won't stop. The city *is* in crisis. The last time, the *only* time we ever had an untracked Watch Dog sighting, time travel was banned for nearly a month. It's a million times worse now. We're going to need to start mandatory Watch Dog fighting classes for everyone, not just kids in school. We need to increase the strength of our weapons and build new ones in order to survive. With how insane everything is, Watch Dogs could start appearing in twos, which they never have before. We can't just keep people from time traveling. It's in our blood."

"Why aren't there any in Lana Ilu? Why are we safe here?" I questioned, grinding my teeth.

"I wish I knew. If I did, if any Gradiens did, we would be able to protect ourselves if we ever did have an attack. But the point of what I'm saying is... Keira, I don't know how to be the Princess in this situation. I'm always the girl that understands *every* aspect of Gradien life. Now, I'm just starting with the rest of the pack." Princess Avarielle's voice cracked. "How can I be their leader when I can't even lead myself?"

The room fell silent for nearly a minute. I had just thought of Avarielle as superhuman, the epitome of a monarch despite still just being the Princess. I had always thought she felt that way about herself, too. For the first time, I think she was doubting that.

"Nobody will blame you, Avarielle..."

"*Princess* Avarielle."

"*Princess* Avarielle, yes. Just so you know, as a lowly Gradien citizen, I can speak for the rest of the city when I say we're all in awe of you. I mean, I'm actually massively scared of you, much more than I am of any Watch Dog out there. And I'll admit, when you're in awe of someone, you can forget that they're human. Try to show Lana Ilu, like you never have before, that you're just like them. All leaders have to learn how to be good leaders. They even taught me that in elementary school. Just be a really good learner, with fighting Watch Dogs and everything that comes with it. From someone who has seen tons of leaders, like Presidents, who don't learn when things are going badly, I think all Gradiens will appreciate you as the Princess growing with them. You will be leading yourself, except just in a way everyone else has to. Maybe, just set an example in that. And it's okay if you're not the best Watch Dog killer in the history of the world. I just got lucky."

She wiped a tear that stained her cheek. "Thanks, I can learn. I'm good at learning. And by the way, I *will* be the best Watch Dog killer in the history of the world. I need to prove myself too."

I rolled my eyes. "Of course, Princess. Now, why—why would you come to me with this? We aren't even friends and I know you have other people you're closer with."

"No, I did say the same things to others. Sonam, Juliet, other friends, even Alden because I thought he deserved to know how I was feeling. But, these are people, especially Sonam and Juliet, who I'm closer with than anyone else. They love me too much to give me the truth sometimes. I needed to talk to someone who wouldn't have to worry about ruining a friendship, not that I would have been upset at all by them telling me I couldn't handle it. I just needed honesty, and you focused on learning and making mistakes. It just helps to hear that. It's very... human."

"Kind of Idum?" I snorted.

Princess Avarielle chuckled. "Idums and Gradiens are both humans, you know. But yeah, as much as I love being a Gradien and the Gradien Princess, being an Idum from time to time wouldn't be so bad."

CHAPTER 23

TONIGHT WAS THE ROYAL BALL, always hosted on the first Saturday of September. The dates of both the Prince and Princess had been announced. Unfortunately for Alden, even though Avarielle had expressed that she was sure he would be picked, another boy was chosen. It was some boy named Julius Almark whom Alden and Pandora both described as super nice with better manners than the Royal Family could even hope for, but not exciting enough to die like his namesake. For Prince Trevor, Sade Oladipo was chosen, a fifteen-year-old girl who, despite being so young, was already one of Lana Ilu's main socialites. Since she went to the East School, Alden didn't know her very well, but Pandora had been invited to plenty of birthday parties with Sade. All Pandora said was that she was nice and 'definitely knew how to make an entrance,' whatever that meant in terms of character.

One of the key parts of the Royal Ball was that if you were attending, you had to dress nice *and* you had to dress relatively accurate to your era. Since Holly was not too far behind me, she gave me some tips on how to dress like a human who's almost a mermaid (because of the higher water levels thousands of years from now), but still human. She also added that there would be a lot of radioactivity by then, so I ended up buying an aquamarine dress with an odd, wide shoulder shape so I could look like some radioactive creature of sorts.

After combing my hair out so that it would flow a quarter as nicely as a mermaid, I headed over to the Handals' to wait there for Theo and Holly. Mr. and Mrs. Handal never missed a Royal Ball, so the two of them couldn't wait to see me all dressed up for it.

Mr. Handal greeted me at their home, dressed in a darker shade of green than me. "Keira, very accurate to your era!" he exclaimed upon seeing me. "Come in, Mrs. Handal wants to take pictures and Holly and Theo should be here soon."

Just like he said, Holly and Theo came zooming through the door right after, quite an accomplishment for Holly, considering her high heels. Holly's hair was done in retro curls, aging her up so much that I would have never guessed that she was only sixteen if I had not known her. Theo, on the other hand, despite being well over six feet tall, could be younger than his age with his goofy smile and unruly red hair. Gosh, I really loved those two.

"You like?" Theo asked, grinning as he showed off his

blue suit. Other than the color, it had little to do with our era, but I could tell he didn't really care.

I gave him a thumbs up. "Definitely!"

Holly twirled her teal, mermaid-cut gown because, of course, Ms. Fashion Icon had to wear a pun. Hearing that my true people were genetically more mermaids than well, Homo sapiens, had definitely taken me by surprise. Apparently, when water levels rose, humans developed partial gills, some scales and webbed limbs to adapt to both land and water environments. I had to admit, I was kind of jealous of whoever had my true energy.

Oh my God, my true energy, my brain shot out to me. It was rare that my own thinking got in the way of *my* train of thought, but sometimes we surprise ourselves. Ever since I arrived in Lana Ilu, I was pretty much just focused on the whole time traveler side of me. It seemed complicated enough on its own. Thinking about living in the wrong body was too much for my fourteen-year-old, very confused and even more exhausted, brain to comprehend. Technically, I wasn't supposed to be *me.* My mind was built by different parents than my arms and my legs were. It was different than adoption, where the body and mind come from two people and the life (and mind) are shaped by the true parents. Adoption is one life, just taking a slightly different, but beautiful path to finding a home. Being a Gradien was having four biological parents, or three or five or however they made it work so far into the future. I knew I had my Mom's eyes and my Dad's small chin, but what about my energy's Mom? Was she the artistic one? Was my energy's father socially awkward and messy? Was it even a *mother* and *father*? I'm sure by the year 200,000, two women or two men could birth a child together. I at least hoped so.

What I was thinking about most now was, would I have been happier? Was I really meant to be with another family, a different set of parents, or did time do its job? I thought about Willow and the people in Lana Ilu I had met because of the switch. Time *must* have known what it was doing.

Flashing me back into the now was Mrs. Handal's hand, shoving me into a photo between Theo and Holly.

"Keira, you space out all the time. I ordered us a levitator so get focused, sweetie!" Mrs. Handal exclaimed.

Not wanting to upset Mrs. Handal anymore, I situated myself between Holly and Theo against the white wall, all draping our arms around each other. Our row of ocean-toned outfits made a ripple in color, much like the water we were emulating.

"You should join us in the photo, Mrs. Handal! You look wonderful!" Holly cheered.

"Pshhh, you flatter me, dear. But truly, I just want photos of you three! Ali's all grown now and Malak's in the Idum-world, so you are like my children," Mrs. Handal beamed.

"So are you saying the three of us are like siblings, Mrs. Handal. As nice as that is, Holly and I *are* dating so..." Theo teased.

Mrs. Handal rolled her eyes. "Omar, why do we have this one? It's figurative, Theo."

"I know, he's quite a bother," her husband chimed in.

We all laughed, Theo obviously having to pretend that he didn't like being made fun of. When you were being mocked by people who really cared about you, it actually felt much better than compliments. I had never really gotten to experience that before outside of Willow, but I now make those jokes with my friends every day.

After we finished a round of photos, the five of us entered the levitator waiting outside. The block had two other levitators waiting, one for each of the two other families. The Medicis and the Rockfords were gathering into the floating machines, just as we were about to. Unlike them, we were not one family. We were the Handals, a Hawkridge, a Chevalier, and a Sun. Actually, I take that back. Our different names meant nothing. We really were becoming family.

The streets were absolutely filled with levitators, both rented and owned. Since the saucers didn't require a driver, they were incredibly popular during the Royal Ball when much of the city was actually busy attending the party or hosting their own get-togethers. Since nobody could time travel yet, even after months of research, Lana Ilu was busier than ever before. New stores had been opened out of pure boredom.

Other than levitators, many people rode in cars of hundreds of different years, horse-drawn carriages and chariots, as well as boats along Rond Lake, the only large body of water in Lana Ilu. I always thought it was a hilarious name, especially considering the lake was a perfect circle. I imagined that the original Imamus, or someone who knew modern English thousands of years ago, said to each other than the lake was round. Then, they all agreed that it was too boring to just call it *Round Lake*, so they took out the *u*. Actually, I'm sure its name has changed a million times over the years.

As we neared the glimmering castle, the number of

levitators grew more and more. People were descending from the saucers by the second, sending them back off into the warehouse where they were kept until the party ended. But the area was so crowded the levitators were nearly hitting each other, like futuristic bumper cars.

"There are over 200,000 people coming into the building right now, everyone," Mr. Handal started. "We need to get out of the levitator right now before we get a dozen others yelling at us."

Understanding, we quickly moved out as soon as the hood lifted, practically jumping onto the ground. Once I landed on the paved walkway to the Palace of Time, I was surrounded by what seemed like every year, every *culture* imaginable. There were people dressed in traditional Japanese kimonos and stylized jet packs fit into suit jackets. Some women wore Aztec-patterned skirts while others were in smoldering gowns, earthy and raw. To my left was a man in a powdered wig and to my right was another in a holographic top hat. Lana Ilu fashion was literally for the ages.

The outer gardens of the Palace rung with orchestral music, blaring as if a parade were being held for the Queen. But in this case, the people were the parade. As the Handals, Holly, and Theo went ahead, I remembered that I had planned with my friends to meet at the entrance, so I waited outside once we got close.

"Are you not joining us?" Mr. Handal questioned.

I shook my head. "I'm going to wait outside for my friends, but I'll see you all here at the end of the night to go back home."

"Ok, we'll see you at 10, Keira! Now come on, Theo, we have friends to meet up with!" Holly called, already running into the Palace, edging by several dozen other guests.

Theo nudged my shoulder. "If Holly's going to be moving that fast, I'm going to have to dance with Kabir Sharma. He's definitely more my dancing level," he joked.

I grinned at him. "Have fun, whether it's with Holly, Kabir, or both."

He snapped his fingers and gave me a thumbs up, something which I noticed was Theo's signature move. I could tell from that that he was excited about tonight.

Within a few minutes, Lucas had arrived. He wore a light clay-colored suit covering an icy blue, button-down shirt paired with a palm-tree-patterned tie. I could tell he was trying to mold his sector into an outfit, the neutral tone from the architecture and his shirt and tie inspired by the range of plants of many different temperatures.

"Nice job on your look!" I told him. "Your era's so cool, with all the mixing of areas of the world, plants from one place ending up in another."

Lucas shrugged. "But, because climate change... not very cool."

I stifled a laugh, reaching in to hug him. I loved Lucas so much, even in just the little things he said. He really was my first friend, no matter how I looked at my Idum life. Of course, he was not the first person to talk to me. My "friends" in Ithaca always had plenty to say. Lucas was just... the first person who didn't make me feel guilty for making him listen, because he loved to listen. His listening from the moment I really entered Lana Ilu was how I knew that I had found the place I was meant to be.

"You're so great, Lucas." I stopped for a moment, trying to remember some of the Spanish I had been learning. "Tú eres... fabuloso?"

Lucas grinned. "Muy bien. Todavía no es perfecto,

pero lo aprecio mucho. You are... fabulous... too. Also, you have a very pretty dress. Is it water?"

"Yeah, supposed to be like it. I got the color right."

A moment later, Pandora appeared next to Lucas and me. She wore a simple white-sheath dress and a statement necklace. She had been wearing her hair up in a bun a lot lately, so it was just now that I was realizing how long it had gotten, falling nearly to her hips.

"Do I look okay, guys? I always feel weird about dressing in Egyptian clothing since it's not *my* culture so I tried to do something pretty chill, you know, ambiguous. It's just a regular white dress and necklace, kind of inspired but not really."

"You look amazing," I said, giving her a hug. "The dress fits you really nicely!"

Pandora beamed. "So does yours, and it's so unique! Also, loving the tie action, Lucas."

"Thank you, but I feel I look like... you know, old man on vacation on an island," he fretted.

Pandora smirked. "You kind of do, but in a great way. Like an old man on vacation in an island *after* he went shopping in a big, fancy city or whatever. So *very* stylish."

Lucas blushed as Pandora moved forward to mess with his hair, earning an annoyed growl from my friend.

"Hours, Pandora. *Hours* for hair!" Lucas yelled, quickly trying to move the curled-up locks back into place. "I make your hair bad!"

Lucas jumped forward, pushing Pandora's wavy hair in every direction. Pandora huffed, doing it again to Lucas, leaving me laughing in the background. I really loved my friends so, so, *so* much.

As the two were continuing to... restyle each other's

hair, Alden entered with his family. His parents were dressed elegantly, Mr. Fischer in a dapper suit from the 1910's and Ms. Fischer in a golden lined Greek chiton. Orville matched his father, though Alden had told me his time was further into the future, and in the Middle East, not the United States. Orville Fischer was an annoying case, a copycat, unoriginal, and unfortunately for anyone who didn't like him, disgustingly handsome. Juliet wore a stiff silver dress, its train running yards beyond her feet, with patches of a dozen other metals scattered in a disorderly pattern. She looked stuffy in it, crossing her arms, suggesting that she had wanted another option. But she looked beautiful anyway.

Finally, the last friend I was waiting for, Alden. He wore a brown suit with a puffy white shirt, almost like a pirate's. His hair had been combed down for an exact middle part. It was not the best look for him, even though, or maybe especially because, we all agreed how good his hair was.

"So, can you escape your family for the night?" I asked.

Alden groaned. "I didn't get chosen as the date, so I think they would like for me to escape them." He rolled his eyes. "I'm going to be the Fischer Family Embarrassment until about ten o'clock, and then for a while after."

"You're not going to blame Avarielle, right?" Pandora said.

"Of course not. She doesn't get much of a choice anyway and it's not her fault *at all* that my parents are obsessed with the marriage. If the Prince and Princess did get to choose, I'm sure Keira would not be standing here at the Ball with *us*," Alden replied, peering over at me.

I stuck my tongue out but knew he was right. It was

really weird to think about, but Avarielle had confirmed months ago that if the third-generation rule didn't exist, I would be on Trevor's arm tonight.

Pushing the thought aside, the four of us entered the palace, walking with hundreds of others into the main ballroom. After the first time I had been here with Prince Trevor, I was sure the number of shimmering chandeliers had grown. Art had changed on the walls, with updated portraits of each member of the Royal Family. I noticed that near the five major thrones was a smaller one to the left. I knew that though Queen Prima's father had died and her mother was spending her last days in the Idum-world, her uncle was still alive. The throne must have been set for him.

At last, I saw the Golden Grandfather Clock once again, far to my left. Dozens of Gradiens were bowing down to it, praying like people would do in a place of worship. Then I remembered that for many Gradiens, even if they practiced an Idum religion, that clock was like God to them. It was the center of everything, the center of time, built in a way so nobody would forget it. The Golden Grandfather Clock was the heart of the Gradien people.

"For Chanukah once," Alden said, leaning closer to me, "when I was really young, my parents got me a replica of that, a real working clock. Then, since I think I was only two or three, I dropped it. I'm sure my parents still think about that each year they come to the Royal Ball."

"Their fault for buying a two-year-old a fancy clock," I laughed, imagining a chubby little Alden already thinking of ways to rebel.

"I would ask you to tell them that, but I'm afraid you're still on the Penelope and Ulrich Fischer watch list.

Believe it or not, they blamed you. They said, and I quote, 'that Keira Sun girl has become more than a nuisance, making our son lose focus and blah blah blah,'" Alden mocked, exaggerating every syllable.

"They really said *blah blah blah*? I find that highly unlikely," I pointed out.

Alden flung his head back. "I think from that, I can tell you *and* my parents that the only reason I would ever lose focus due to you is that you are really annoying Keira, and I am now forced to deal with the stupid decision I made to become friends with you."

"Right back at you, Alden. But anyway, I can't believe your parents would speak about me that way when I'm so young."

"I told them it was weird since we're only fourteen, but to them, if I'm old enough to get invited as Avarielle's date, or you as Trevor's, we get sucked into this kind of thing."

"They do that in the Idum world, too, maturing kids when they're still young. I hoped for better from Lana Ilu."

Alden shrugged, shaking his head. "Life lesson, Keira. Don't think better of anywhere, Idum *or* Gradien. As much as I love Lana Ilu, it's all the same."

"Hey Lucas!" Alden yelled, attracting my other friend's attention. "My parents, they like you, yeah?"

Lucas beamed. "Yes, yes! They say I am nice and um, interesting because I like movies. I saw your Dad in your sector, I with Ken Kimura. He asked me to eat dinner with your family other time! I uh, talked... no, *said* yes."

Pandora leaned into the group. "Oh, your parents never want me coming back. I had dinner there once, and they told me I had an 'uncomfortably sarcastic attitude not befitting their young son.'"

I laughed, adoring Pandora's sarcasm myself. Then again, I don't think I had really anything in common with Alden's parents, so where was the surprise?

Alden lowered his brows. "Well, at least I've got one really close friend that my parents can stand. Any anyway, Lucas is better than all of us combined so he really deserves to be the favorite."

Lucas rolled his eyes. "Better than you? It is easy!"

"Oh, keep talking like that and we'll take it back, Mr. Lucas Acosta," I commanded.

Just a second later, a horn blew from the front of the front of the ballroom. Nearly two hundred thousand heads turned to face it, Queen Prima sitting in her throne besides the blaring sound. She raised her hand and immediately, the musician beside her lowered his instrument, a long, winding animal horn. To her right were Princess Bahati and her daughter, Princess Avarielle. To her direct left were her son, Prince Oladayo and *his* son, Prince Trevor.

"My fellow Gradiens, my ever-timeless people," the Queen proclaimed, earning a round of applause from the entire ballroom. She wore a golden dress, jeweled and fitted perfectly, appearing like she had spent months with the tailor.

"I don't understand," I whispered to Pandora. "I thought you were supposed to dress like your era and Queen Prima shares that with like, *really* early people. Did cavemen or whatever have better fashion than we thought?"

Pandora laughed. "No, no, they dressed pretty simply. Basically, Queen Prima doesn't want to show up wearing pelts to the most important event of the year, so instead of going with her era's culture, she chooses her own biological ancestry, which is totally different. I believe she's wearing an outfit made of pieces called the iro and buba, which are from I think Nigeria. And of course, it's made of *pure* gold."

"How does she stand and walk in it? It must be so heavy?" I asked.

"She's Queen Prima Imamu of Lana Ilu. There's *nothing* she can't do."

At that, I looked back to her Majesty again.

CHAPTER 24

"AS ALWAYS, IT IS MY *GREATEST* honor to commence the Royal Ball, a night that celebrates our unity as a people, as a city and as a family more than any other I can name. For those of you who have attended a previous Royal Ball, which I know is a large majority, you expect that I will announce my favorite spots for time travel in the next year, places which have inspired some *wonderful* adventures and vacations, and promise that there is only peace in our future." Queen Prima took a deep breath, the gulp in her throat echoing around the massive room. "I wish more than anything that I could continue with that tradition this year... yet we all know, I cannot. I would have to lie to my people, an act I could never bring upon myself or a single citizen of my beloved Lana Ilu."

Queen Prima shook her head, her curly black and grey

locks bouncing. "This is not a speech of a guarantee for peace. This is a speech of a guarantee for work towards it."

The room fell silent. No more cheering. No more laughing, no more talking. Our Queen was speaking, and all we could do was listen.

"To start, I will be referring to Zanarees as Watch Dogs and Varem as Time Cases for my speech, to add as calm and casual a tone as I possibly can, considering the situation. As you all know, our city has fallen under difficult times before. I do not mean the one instance of an untracked Watch Dog. That was unfortunate and strange, but as far as we can tell now, it was nothing more. Lana Ilu, like any Idum location, has dealt with its poor leaders. My father himself was incapable, pulling money from our Idum-born minors to finance the Palace further. He never traveled outside the city even once—for reasons still unknown. We are incredibly lucky that the appearances of Watch Dogs did not occur under his reign, or I fear we would have fallen into disaster.

After him, just a few years into my rule, we encountered a different obstacle, one rare for our usually peaceful city—a terrorist. A hateful, egotistical, power-hungry terrorist. This was a man, barely a man, who attempted murder, destruction, a coup, all in the name of taking over this city to overpower the Idum people. He called himself a Suprem and he called Idums Simplexes, even referring to some of our own people as such, despite it being a disgusting slur that I hesitated to share at this moment. He tortured my now late husband with threatening letters, calling him a weak man for continuing with our marriage and for allowing me to care for our son, a son who is here today as the heir to the throne. He wanted to push us into a life threatening, an *existence* threatening, war for Gradiens against the Idums. But he is in the most protected jail in any universe now. We survived Waldron Hawkridge. We can survive this."

And then the cheering began again. There were screams of joy, of excitement, of hope. Lucas, Pandora and Alden all reached to me, forming a group hug like we had done after I had killed the Watch Dog. I wanted to enjoy it and to feel grateful for having survived, but as Lucas had said months ago, there was no end. The Queen was mainly trying to raise morale and she still had to tackle the Watch Dog situation. I couldn't feel so safe yet.

Worst of all, I thought of Holly. She was a Hawkridge like her great uncle but perfectly innocent. She hated talking about her family history, especially because none of it was her fault, none of it in her control as she had not even been born yet, but she still had to carry the weight. I hoped that nobody mentioned this speech to her after the Ball. Holly didn't need to worry about an evil ancestor she never met. She had her Uncle Wes to fill in Waldron's place.

"Now, everyone," Queen Prima announced, quieting the room, "I cannot let you all dance without completing my speech, and that means addressing the Watch Dogs. After months of extensive research, my team and I believe we have identified a possible cause of the appearances. The first Time Case, created with the blast of the Big Bang, has been hidden since its birth. Like any other Time Case, it grows as the years go on, becoming more powerful and gaining a higher capability to delete large amounts of time. The power of the first Time Case is beyond our knowledge. Its negative energy could remove all of existence if gotten into the wrong hands, or even just confused hands. With that strength, I presume that it could be diluting the energy of other Time Cases, clouding their presence on our trackers. We are not sure how this can be fixed—if our trackers can be strengthened any more than they have been. But my team is searching throughout all of time, every location on Earth and even just beyond the atmosphere for this Time Case. I truly believe that with our diligence, Lana Ilu will not have to wait long for its discovery. Until then, I have decided to implement Watch Dog combatting classes this December, taught by previous Preservers, in both the schools and for all adults. We are developing these as we speak. They will be *mandatory*. In addition, we have begun to build stronger weapons, which should aid in our survival, to be used on Watch Dogs only. My fellow Gradiens, my ever-timeless people, if these plans succeed, we should all be time traveling again soon after!"

Screams broke out around the ballroom. Many cried "May our Queen be immortal!" People were crying and Pandora grabbed my face as she jumped. She kissed my forehead, overjoyed, and I couldn't help but join in. I had to stop being so horribly pessimistic. Bad things would always happen, and if they kept me from living my life, they were winning more than if I smiled through each day. I couldn't wait for those few months to be up.

Immediately, the dancing began. Music was played of every year and every culture, bringing everything from salsas to the jitterbug to ballet and more. I was not much of a dancer myself, so I stayed more in the department of the Macarena and talking to kids I knew. On the other hand, Pandora and Lucas were really giving it their all, moving exactly to the music. I couldn't help but laugh as they slipped and fell once, but they just got up and started swirling and jiving again. Neither of them were especially good dancers, or moderately okay dancers to be honest, but the amount of fun the two were having could have given them first place in a world competition.

"You don't dance?" Alden asked, leaning up against the wall.

"Nah, I always felt too awkward to go to any of the middle school dances, you know, the worst things in creation, so I just know the Macarena. My sister Willow's not bad at dancing, but I never asked her to teach me."

"I had to learn when I was younger, in preparation for this Ball if I ever got chosen. My teacher says that I do a *perfect* waltz," Alden chimed.

I laughed, having to cover my mouth. "You have a dance teacher? How didn't I know that?"

Alden scratched the back of his neck. "I try to keep it hidden; it's very embarrassing sometimes. Lucas doesn't know and he's at my house all the time. Heck, I didn't even tell Pandora!"

"Well, you'll have to show me," I joked.

Suddenly, I saw Alden extend his hand towards me. His eyebrows were raised, awaiting my answer.

"I know you are kidding, but I might as well. This is Lana Ilu's Royal Ball, not a middle school dance. We're not really allowed to be standing on the side."

My face warmed, as I had never been asked to dance before, not even in the one dance I went to in fifth grade where everyone was dancing with someone to look cool. Then again, this was Alden, one of my best friends, who was probably just trying to join in on the party. There was nothing to feel weird about.

"You're sure your parents won't behead me?" I asked, my hand hovering above his.

He shrugged. "Avarielle's not my date, so what's the concern? Come on, we should dance while Lucas and Pandora are still doing whatever crazy move they just made up. I honestly have no idea what they're doing. It just looks like they're avoiding falling for the most part."

"Well, let's start," I responded, finally taking Alden's hand. We walked to a slightly cleared out area of the dance floor, even though it was truly crowded to every edge. Then, Alden placed one of his hands on my back and began instructing me what to do.

"My right foot is going to move forward, so at that moment, you left foot needs to move back so we don't step on each other," Alden told me. "You got it?"

I looked straight into his eyes and nodded. "Got it."

The thing was, I hadn't "got it." Every time he moved forward, I was too slow and my foot immediately got crushed. I was shaking and my palms were sweating, making it difficult for Alden to not slip away.

"You have to move your foot backward, Keira!" Alden said, starting to get a bit annoyed.

"I'm trying!" I yelled back.

We continued, and for a few steps, I began to understand the flow. We moved in a careful circle, not wanting to make too large a radius as to not bump into anyone else. We were very close, awkwardly close to the point where I could feel him breathe, so I was unsure if to stay right there or not. Then, I quickly took a half step back, creating just the tiniest more distance. I could tell Alden noticed my change as he too stepped slightly away, pulling us farther apart. I didn't want to stop dancing with him at all, I just didn't know, at least with Alden's parents likely having some sort of bird's eye view on me, if it felt right to stand so close. Also, I'm pretty sure his face might melt off if we danced any closer, considering he was starting to look like rhubarb.

Just as we were approaching our third smooth circle, Alden surprisingly stepped incorrectly, making us both stumble and completely lose focus.

"Alden, I thought you said you did a perfect waltz!"

He huffed. "Well, I usually have a perfect partner, my *teacher*, to dance with!"

"I *am* the perfect partner, Alden, you just don't know it yet!" I countered, not being able to keep myself from smiling.

When Alden was about to respond, I felt a hand tap my shoulder. Slowly, I turned around to see Princess Bahati and Prince Oladayo standing behind me. To a certain point, I had gotten used to seeing their children, but the parents? Not so much.

"Keira, I realized earlier that over the months, I never got an opportunity to properly thank you for killing that Watch Dog." Prince Oladayo said, dressed in a modern purple suit. He was a handsome man, with great resemblance to his son, though the father smiled much wider. I could see what Avarielle had said about him not becoming proud from his power, as his smile was gentle, wide, welcoming. He felt almost like... a universal father. "So, we are here to resolve that issue."

Princess Bahati now stepped forward, wearing a gown whose patterns changed every second with a holographic effect. The Imamu women all look so incredibly royal, the men as well of course, but in a different way. The women always sat like the chair was a throne and walked as if there was a red carpet beneath their feet. Princess Bahati looked almost exactly like her daughter, though her skin was darker, nearly the shade of the night sky. I could see why Prince Trevor and Princess Avarielle were so good-looking.

"Keira, you were and I imagine still are incredibly brave. Please know that the Royal Family *adores* you," Princess Bahati charmed.

"Yes, especially our son!" Prince Oladayo added, chuckling. "Only my mother makes the decisions about who is chosen as the date. The *third-generation* rule still very much exists. In fact, my wife, Bahati here, is only a third generation herself and I had to beg my mother to allow me to be with her."

I noticed Princess Bahati blush. "My husband loves that story, he thinks it makes him seem *so* romantic..."

"It *does* make me seem romantic, but continue."

"As I was saying, we should not bother you with any of these stories. I'm sure, Keira, that the Lana Ilu tabloids have written enough articles about you with my son," Princess Bahati said.

I nodded. "Yes, they definitely have, Princess. I've just gotten used to it at this point."

"Well, of course you have! From the moment you got here, someone pegged your name as *The Girl from the End of Time*. I think you've handled being such a young media darling quite well, Keira," said Prince Oladayo.

"Thank you, I appreciate it."

Princess Bahati began to turn, waving goodbye with her manicured fingers. "We will leave you alone for now, but please, we have an open Palace. Speak with us whenever you want."

Oh great, I thought. *Now I really am involved with the Imamus. That's stressful.*

Wanting a bit of a break, I told my friends that I was going to walk around the ballroom for a while, maybe just speak to some other people. I wanted to find Theo and Holly, especially the latter to make sure she was okay after the Queen's speech about Waldron Hawkridge. Finally, after winding through thousands of people, I spotted Theo's red hair.

When I got to them, they were not dancing directly together, but more in a group with a dozen other friends. I was curious why, as they had been looking forward to acting like a couple tonight, until I realized that directly behind Holly stood her grandfather. Wilfred Hawkridge was a brooding man, with thick eyebrows and deep wrinkles. He was watching the people at the Ball carefully, scanning around the room. He looked to be close to seven feet tall, making my neck feel as if it were breaking when I tried to see his face.

Suddenly, I felt Theo pull my arm. "Hey!" he yelled, trying to be heard over the loud music. "You having fun?"

"Yeah!" I screamed back, noticing that the speakers definitely worked better here. "Have you been dancing a lot?"

Theo put his hands on his knees. "So much, yeah! I'm exhausted but none of my friends or Holly are so I gotta keep dancing!"

I laughed. "Good luck!"

I then moved over to Holly, who was doing some sort of modern dance with a few other girls. She looked pretty into the music, so I knew I would have to be loud to get her attention.

"Hi!" I announced, reaching for her shoulder.

"What the he... oh, hi, Keira!" Holly responded.

"You're a really good dancer, Holly! And hey, I just wanted to make sure you're feeling good and everything."

"Thanks! And oh, because of the speech? Yeah, I'm fine!"

"Good!" I said, now not really knowing what to say.

"Keira, I'm sorry, but I'll see you later tonight, okay?"

Realizing that I was being shoved out, just in a very nice way, I backed off. I had lived near Holly for long enough that I was beginning to forget she had a life, a very popular and social life, outside of our little sector. Just as I was leaving, I bumped into that seven-foot-tall man I had seen before.

"Sorry, I didn't..."

"Keira Sun!" Wilfred Hawkridge bellowed. "I'm glad we've finally met."

I peered up at him, honestly terrified to say a word. I felt like he could crush me. "Yes... me too..."

"You have a lot of relations to our family, you know. You share a sector with my granddaughter... amongst *other* connections," Mr. Hawkridge heaved, obviously referencing his younger brother, Waldron. I didn't even think about how he felt after the speech partly "dedicated" to his evil brother. Wilfred Hawkridge had probably lived through it the most.

"Yes, I like Holly a lot," I responded, thinking it was a perfectly mellow thing to say.

Wilfred Hawkridge did not look like he acknowledged my comment at all. "You know, a jail guard coined *The Girl from the End of Time*. A little odd, right?"

"Definitely," I said, before running away. I didn't know how to end the conversation, so for the first time, as I usually tried to be polite, I just evacuated the premises.

I hoped to run into someone I felt more comfortable around next, so I began to walk closer to the thrones hoping to find Juliet or Sonam with the Prince and Princess. Luckily, I did.

"Juliet!" I yelled, getting her to turn around. "I just learned that Alden takes dance classes! How could you not give me such hilarious information?"

Juliet smirked. "Oh, I think it's funnier that you found out yourself. He show you his waltzing abilities?"

"Yeah, and then he messed up and we nearly fell!"

Juliet laughed. "Alden gets a big head, so don't listen to him too much about his talents. If he ever tells you that he's a good singer, run for cover, okay?"

"Alright, I will!"

I then felt a hand take mine and twirl me, looking to see Sonam Sharma. "Hey Keira, I haven't seen you much! Do you dance?"

I shook my head. "No, not much, sorry."

"Oh, well I take that as *I still need to learn*." She began twirling me more and I couldn't keep myself from laughing as we both got dizzy.

Pulling away, I patted Sonam's shoulder. "I'll work on my skills for next year!"

I then began to walk more, looking to return to my friends until I saw Prince Trevor and Princess Avarielle. They were not dancing with their dates, but speaking in a hushed tone to one another. I realized now that I had never seen them together, as they were usually pretty independent. He was wearing a relatively modern, pure black tuxedo, making me think that as his year was 3000, the people of that time reverted back to the fashion of today. Princess Avarielle on the other hand was wearing

a flowing, long-sleeved purple gown, with a round head-
band inspired by her era.

Even though I was walking in the opposite direction
of the siblings, I could hear one of them following me. I
looked back, noticing Prince Trevor just a step behind.

"Keira!" he called. "Wait up!"

I turned around, standing until he caught up to me.

"Are you excited for school to start again?" he asked.
"You know, real school for you with teachers and such?"

I smiled. "Definitely, the Magistones can get pretty
boring."

"I wish we went to the same school, but I'll see you in
town anyway," Prince Trevor said.

My face warmed. "Yeah, we can meet up at *Dolce's*
after school."

"Oh, like how we met? Yeah, I like that. Also, I think
you'd be a great one to talk to about the new Watch Dog
fighting classes. You really know how to get it done,"
Trevor offered, looking down at me.

"We've been through this over the summer, Trevor. It
was just luck."

He shook his head. "Trust me, when something
amazing happens, it's never just luck."

A second later, a girl tapped his shoulder, asking him
to come back and dance. I could tell right away that this
was his date, Sade, the girl he was probably *supposed* to be
talking to.

Trevor shrugged his shoulders. "I have to go, but keep
in touch, okay?"

I nodded. From the way Trevor spoke, and his obvious
dedication to try to get me to *speak*, I could tell that Sade
was probably not going to be his date next year. It felt a

little weird being so obviously crushed on by the Prince, but for a girl who was ignored her entire life, I'll admit that it was definitely an ego booster. And to be fair, there was plenty to like about Prince Trevor.

Before I left to return to my friends, I tried to get a word in with Princess Avarielle, who looked to be deep in thought in the middle of the dance floor.

"So, is she right? That they're looking for the first Time Case and it's going to be found soon?" I questioned, standing directly next to the Princess.

"Yes, that they're looking for it, not that it's going to be found soon. That thing has been hidden for billions of years. It's going to take some very creative looking," Princess Avarielle responded.

"Is it like Lana Ilu's a whole new city now? Has everything changed in the Palace?"

Avarielle ducked her head, seemingly decoding the tiles in the floor. "Keira, we are a city that exists knowing how all of time has and will happen. We don't usually get surprised."

And the conversation ended there. We tended to talk like that, matter of fact until there was nothing left to say. Then, it just stopped. I knew that Avarielle had plenty of fun in talking with her friends. I had seen it before. But with us, everything was said and done. I liked it that way. It was reliable and she was probably the smartest person the city had to offer. There were definitely worse people to talk to, far worse.

To spend the rest of the Royal Ball, I headed back over to my friends. Pandora and Lucas were still dancing as Alden watching with a toothy grin. Behind them, I could see the Golden Grandfather Clock watching over